EXIT STRATEGY

Looming above Zach Ramsey's hometown of Blaine are the smokestacks of the truck assembly plant, the greasy lifeblood of this Detroit suburb. Surrounded by drunks, broken marriages, and factory rats living in fear of the pink slip, Zach is getting the hell out of town after graduation. But first, he's going to enjoy the summer before senior year.

Getting smashed with his best friend Tank and falling in love for the first time, Zach's having a blast until he uncovers dark secrets that shake his faith in everyone—including Tank, a wrestler whose violent mood swings betray a shocking habit.

As he gets pulled deeper into an ugly scandal, Zach is faced with the toughest decision of his life—one that will prove just what kind of adult he's destined to be.

EXIT STRATEGY

EXIT STRATEGY

Ryan Potter

flux™
Woodbury, Minnesota

First Edition
First Printing, 2010

Cover design by Lisa Novak
Cover photo © 2009 iStockphoto/David Edwards

Flux, an imprint of Llewellyn Publications

Library of Congress Cataloging-in-Publication Data
Potter, Ryan.
    Exit strategy / Ryan Potter.—1st ed.
        p. cm.
    Summary: Seventeen-year-old Zach, his best friend (and state wrestling champion) Tank, and Tank's twin sister Sarah, an Ivy League-bound scholar, are desperate to leave their depressing hometown of Blaine, Michigan, after next year's graduation, but plans go awry when Zach uncovers a steroid scandal and falls in love with Sarah.
    ISBN 978-0-7387-1573-5
    [1. Friendship—Fiction. 2. Steroids—Fiction. 3. Michigan—Fiction.] I. Title.
    PZ7.P8563Ex 2010
    [Fic]—dc22
                                            2009027697

Flux
Llewellyn Publications
A Division of Llewellyn Worldwide, Ltd.
2143 Wooddale Drive, Dept. 978-0-7387-1573-5
Woodbury, MN 55125-2989, U.S.A.
www.fluxnow.com

Printed in the United States of America

Acknowledgments

Many people have helped make this dream come true.

First, I need to thank Michelle Andelman for taking a chance and saying yes. You never gave up on me, and for that I'll always be grateful. Also, I owe a huge thanks to Jen Rofe for taking the reins and handling the transition so flawlessly. I appreciate your efforts more than you know.

I am indebted to the incredible team at Flux, especially former editor Andrew Karre, who went to bat for me at a time when I thought Zach's story might never get told. Additionally, I'd like to thank current editor Brian Farrey. Your numerous suggestions have made this book what it is. Also, thanks to Sandy Sullivan, whose attention to detail is simply amazing. I also need to thank Lisa Novak for designing such a wonderful cover. It was as if you were reading my mind.

Finally, I owe everything to my wife, Lisa.
She knows why.

For anybody who knows there's more out there.

SEPTEMBER

1

If I have any advice after everything that's happened it's this: never fall for your best friend's twin sister, especially when her brother is an overprotective psycho who also happens to be a three-time state champion wrestler. Such a concoction is nothing but a recipe for pain, trust me on that. I know this because I recently committed the blunder identified above, yet somehow—and this is the part I'm still trying to figure out—I'm alive to talk about it. It's a miracle, really, that I'm breathing on my own at this moment and not hooked up to some freaky medical contraption.

Anyway, it's true to say that my story, the story of seventeen-year-old Zach Ramsey, is a tale loaded with all the drama, action, love, and betrayal that have been in my life the past few months. I mean, I've witnessed some really insane stuff lately, which, of course, is the reason I'm writing this sentence right now. And I've never written anything in my life outside of schoolwork.

Think about it. Who writes a book when they're seventeen? Nobody I know. Nobody in Blaine, Michigan, anyway.

This story has no hero. In fact, if you're into the hero thing at all you might as well put this book down and move on to something else, maybe visit the fantasy section of your local library or something. Personally, I think I'm about the farthest thing from a hero as one can get.

As for a happy ending, well... sorry, but there isn't one of those, either. I guess that's because everything here actually happened, and one thing we all know is that life can suck pretty badly sometimes. Happy endings sell a lot of books and movie tickets, but I didn't write this to *escape* reality. I wrote it to *deal* with reality. *My* reality.

One last thing: you know that old saying about nobody being perfect? Well, I'll be the first to defend that statement. I've done some questionable things over the past three months. Regardless, I actually do have a strong sense of right and wrong. It might take some digging to find sometimes, but it's there, especially when it comes to adults and how they should behave.

So, I'm not perfect. I freely admit that.

And my best friend, the psycho wrestler... Oh, man, he is definitely not perfect.

As for his twin sister, the girl I currently love and always will, she's actually pretty close to perfect, but not quite.

Here's the thing: the three of us, we're only seventeen.

Seventeen! I'd say that gives us a good excuse for messing up every now and then.

But what about all of the adults behaving badly in Blaine? You're about to meet them. What's their excuse? I mean, I always thought part of life involved growing up at some point, getting your act together, and trying to live more responsibly than you did when you were...oh, I don't know...say...seventeen? But that's not the way it is, at least not in Blaine. I know that now. I wish I didn't, but I do.

So I'll end this beginning with a confession followed by a question.

The confession: given everything I've been through, if I had the chance to go back and play this thing through a second time, I might have thought twice before accepting that first fifty dollars from Huey Dawkins.

The big question: who are you supposed to look up to when it seems like every adult you know is more screwed up than yourself?

I'm still struggling with that one.

JUNE

2

Let's rewind three months.

Eleventh grade is finally over and I can't wait to be a senior in the fall, because being a senior means constant partying and the beginning of my BEP (Blaine Escape Plan), right? I mean, the end of my life in this depressed *Twilight Zone* of a town is within sight. College is my ticket out of this dump, the key to my BEP. I say bring it on as quickly as possible, because the last thing I want to be in life is a Blaine factory rat enslaved by a doomed American car company.

Speaking of constant partying, I have this older brother named Justin. He could write a bestselling how-to book on partying. My brother used to be my idol. Right now he's twenty and comes home drunk every night. His one-year educational "break" after high school quickly turned into two. He says he's having the time of his life, but I have a feeling he parties so hard because he's freaked about entering the real world and has no idea what to do with his life. Justin isn't exactly the brightest bulb in the light store, but he's not stupid, either. He hasn't made it out of Blaine yet, but lately he's shown signs of progress. I'm pulling for him and watching him closely. With Justin, it's all about baby steps.

It wasn't like that a few years ago, however. Justin was an all-state football player bound for a full-ride athletic scholarship, but he quit the team after his junior year. The whole town was shocked, especially yours truly. I couldn't believe it. Talk about pissing away your future. To this day he doesn't like to talk about why he quit. He was really miserable for a couple of years, but he finally saw the light and came up with a revised BEP a few months ago. He starts community college in the fall and has an interest in business. Then he plans on heading to Eastern Michigan University over in Ypsilanti to finish his degree. There. That's his BEP. Yeah, it might not be the most ambitious plan in the world, but it's something, right? And something is better than nothing, which is exactly what most people in Blaine have. Nothing.

Nothing.

Anyway, we live in this small, blue-collar subdivision lined with tiny old bungalows, mature maples, and uneven sidewalks. For the adults, it's a safe, tight-knit world, the kind of place where everybody knows, or tries to know, what everybody else is up to. For guys like me, it's like being a piece of shrapnel inside of a ticking bomb. I just want the thing to explode and propel me as far away as possible.

My best friend Tank Foster lives five houses down. His parents are divorced. Tank never sees his mom. Nobody ever sees Tank's mom. She's a drug addict and lives somewhere in Detroit. I guess you could say she made it out of Blaine for all the wrong reasons. As for Tank's father, Dale, he's some kind of undercover cop. I admire Big Dale Foster because he's the only adult male in the neighborhood who doesn't work at the Michigan Avenue truck assembly plant that towers over our neighborhood like a giant prison guard tower. The man is hardly ever home, so we have the house to ourselves often. Nice.

Sarah, Tank's fraternal twin, she's seven minutes older, but their proximity in age doesn't carry over into genetics. Physically and socially, she and Tank are total opposites. Tank's incredibly strong and kind of psycho, always looking for fights and other insane ways to act out his violent urges. Despite his social popularity, however, he's stupid and gets bad grades. I let him cheat off of me constantly, and I know he would have failed a grade or two without my services. Regardless, Tank's grades aren't a vital part of his BEP. But his body is. He's been getting letters of interest from the most elite wrestling colleges in the country since he was a freshman. Barring some catastrophic physical injury as a senior, Tank Foster will definitely make it out of Blaine.

As for Sarah, now, she's a genius, a bookworm with thick glasses and a set of braces that look like a roll of aluminum foil when she smiles. She has long, scraggly dark hair and wears these sundresses that remind me of wrinkly old ladies in Florida. Tank and I taunt her every chance we get, often breaking her to the point of tears. She spends most of her time avoiding us, but when it comes to her and guys, Tank's obsessively overprotective of her and she knows it. He's always telling me how happy he is that his twin sister is an ugly geek, because he fears he might kill any guy who asks her out.

Sarah Foster.

As of mid-June, she's the last girl I expect to fall in love with.

So, on June 15th, the day after school lets out for summer, Tank and I walk the two blocks to Huey's Party Store after lunch, a routine we've followed since middle school.

We're about halfway there, talking about *Maxim* models, when I say, "Hey, I was channel surfing last night and saw Captain Rick on CNN."

"Cool," Tank says, squinting from the sun and wiping sweat from his brow. "Is he on that mission he was talking to us about?"

"Yeah," I say, noticing Tank's bulging biceps and stump-like thighs. "That's the thing. I mean, the guy's in *space* right now." I point toward the blue sky. "One month ago he's giving a talk in our school gym, and now he's orbiting the planet." I shake my head, amazed. "So I'm watching him give this interview from the shuttle and I'm thinking, man, now there's a guy who got the hell out of Blaine."

Tank laughs. "I'd say Captain Rick holds the record for the greatest distance between a human being and Blaine, Michigan."

"I can't wait to pull a Captain Rick."

"Same here, man." Tank pats me on the shoulder. "One more year, Zach. One more year."

Huey's Party Store is an ugly green building across the street from the assembly plant. On hot days like this, I look forward to the blast of air-conditioning that always hits me when I enter. Inside, a massive floor-to-ceiling beverage cooler occupies half of the the rear wall. There's an open doorway in the middle that leads to a small back room, where the stock boys hang out and load the cooler through its rear-entry door. The cooler is this sort of blue-collar, beer-drinking holy site. Everybody in Blaine knows about Huey's prized possession and respects him for maintaining the coldest beverages in the state. That's the rumor, anyway. I like to think of Huey's as the nucleus of Blaine. Without the store, the city dries up and dies, guaranteed.

We say hello to Huey, who has his elbows on the counter, reading the paper with one of those old school no-filter cigarettes wedged between his lips. His eyes are bloodshot, but his dark, thick hair and deep tan give him a healthy glow.

I'm following Tank to the Gatorade section of the cooler when Huey calls me over. As usual, classic rock plays loudly through two ceiling speakers.

"Hey, Zach, come here a second," he says.

I stop and turn and walk toward him, thinking about how in the six years I've been coming here he's never said anything to me outside of a standard greeting. Tank is close behind me, so I turn toward him and shrug. He shrugs back.

When I reach the counter, Huey's reading the sports section, studying the horse numbers from the Northville track. A cloud of smoke forms in front of his face every time he exhales, but he seems used to it, doesn't even bother waving it away.

Without looking up, he coughs and says, "I asked for Zach, Tank, not you." I turn toward Tank again, who rolls his eyes and heads back toward the cooler.

"What is it, Huey?" I ask.

He folds the paper and glances to his left and right. Then he stares at Tank for what seems like a full minute. "The kid's old man is some kind of cop, right?" he whispers. Smoke streams out of his mouth and nostrils when he speaks.

"Tank's dad?" I whisper back.

"Yeah, Tank's dad."

"He's a cop, but he's never home." I look behind me. Tank has his back turned, scanning the Gatorade and energy drinks. I turn toward Huey. "It's some kind of undercover work, but that's all I know, and I think that's all Tank knows."

"What's he look like?"

"Depends on the day. He changes a lot. You know, because of all the undercover stuff."

"But, in general," Huey says, still whispering, keeping an eye on Tank through a pair of large, circular security mirrors mounted in the upper corners of the back wall. "What's the guy look like?"

"I haven't seen him in a few months, but he's got a lot of muscles, kind of like Tank but even bigger. Last time I saw him he had one of those nasty black mustaches that curls up at both ends, but he shaves it off every now and then. Does that with his hair, too. I mean, it's usually long and black, like the weedheads at school. But sometimes he's totally bald."

Huey nods and rubs his eyebrows with his right hand as if he has a headache. He takes another look at Tank through the mirrors.

"What about tattoos?" he asks, lighting a new cigarette from the still-burning end of his previous one and stubbing out the old one in a red plastic ashtray. "He have any tattoos?"

"Yeah." I point to my right forearm. "A big green dragon, right here."

"Son of a..." He trails off and shakes his head. Then he reaches beneath the counter, raises a can of beer to his lips, and takes a huge gulp before putting it back.

I turn. Tank's browsing the protein bars, an unopened can of something in one hand. He catches me looking at him. I turn away.

"Listen," Huey says. "Do me a favor and keep an eye out for Tank's old man, okay? If you see him, let me know what he's looking like. Peek around the house a little if you can. See if you can learn anything more about what he does, where he works. Stuff like that."

I squint. "You want me to spy on my best friend's dad?"

"Call it what you want, James Bond."

He reaches into his front pocket and pulls out a thick wad of cash, peels off a fifty, and slides it across the counter toward me. Then he raises his eyebrows and points at the bill, my signal to take it. I grab it and shove it deep into my front pocket.

"There's a lot more where that came from, but you have to earn it." Huey shifts his gaze toward Tank. "He's gonna ask what we talked about. You tell him it was personal stuff about your family, got it?" I nod. "Think you can handle this?" I nod again, totally into the idea of earning easy money.

A crashing sound comes from the back room, like shattering glass—a lot of it.

"Aw, Christ!" Huey shouts. "What's going on back there, Brandon?"

Brandon Watkins, a tall, thin dude with red hair and white skin peppered with freckles, comes running out of the back room, a pained look on his face. Brandon is Justin's age, attends Michigan State, and works for Huey during the summer.

"Sorry, Huey. A whole stack of bottles fell. I need some help."

Huey says, "Well, idiot, if you stack them right, things like that don't happen." Poor Brandon disappears into the back room. Huey checks his watch. "Man," he says, "the noon shift lets out in ten minutes." I realize he's talking to himself. "Better clean it now," he mumbles.

He finishes what's left of his beer, winks at me, and makes his way out from behind the long front counter that runs the length of the store. He tells us to wait for him at the register if we decide to buy anything, says he'll be back in a minute or two to get ready for the rush. Then he hustles into the back room.

"You want one of these?" Tank calls, showing me a shiny and colorful can of the latest energy drink.

"Yeah, I'll try one." I turn and face the cooler. "Grab me a Slim Jim, too."

Watching Tank grab the drink and Slim Jim, I tease the fifty halfway out of my pocket and gaze at it for a moment before shoving it back down.

"What was Dawkins whispering about?" he asks, laying our items on the counter.

"Nothing, really, just some stuff about all the layoffs at the plant. He told me not to worry about the gossip, said my parents' jobs are safe."

"That guy's never liked me." Tank stares at the fully stocked liquor and cigarette shelves behind the counter. "He always gives me dirty looks."

"Huey likes everybody, Tank." I turn and gaze out the windows at the assembly plant. The noon shift is letting out, dozens of filthy men in blue exiting.

"He likes everybody except me. He's a prick when I'm around."

We hear Huey and Brandon cleaning up the mess in the back room, Huey swearing, Brandon apologizing. Outside, the workers march forward, an army of tired faces and sweaty bodies. Most of them smoke cigarettes. Some talk on their cells. The older ones carry metal lunch pails that gleam in the sunlight.

Tank looks back toward the stockroom for a moment, then gives me a look and a crooked smile before hopping over the counter with the agility of an Olympic gymnast. He grabs a pint of Jim Beam and a pack of Marlboros, the red ones, tucks them both in the front of his waist and pulls his shirt loosely over them. Then he jumps back over to my side, completing the crime in less than ten seconds, too fast for me to utter a single word. He gives a playful elbow to my bicep and smiles.

"What's that all about?" I ask.

"Huey Dawkins is a prick." Tank says it calmly. "The guy deserves it," he adds, again with no emotion in his voice.

Seconds later, the sounds from the back room stop. Huey comes out with a fresh beer and rings up our items. Tank and I pay with loose change, and I'm careful to keep the fifty out of sight. Huey's spirits lift as he watches the workers approach the entrance. He lights a cigarette and tells us to have a nice day, giving me a nod as Tank walks toward the door.

The autoworkers stream in as we leave, most of them complaining about unfair Japanese trade practices, future layoff notices, and all the white-collar executives who have murdered the American automotive companies.

Passing them, I recognize the familiar smells of metal, grease, and smoke that I associate with Mom and Dad's arrival home every evening.

3

A few days after Tank's theft, I have this heated argument with Dad about why I have to continue playing football, a sport I hate. We're in the kitchen and Mom's making dinner, her famous meatloaf and mashed potatoes. She's yelling at us to stop, which we finally do. Then Dad grabs two cans of beer from the fridge and storms out the front door.

I'm on my way to my bedroom when Mom pulls me aside and sits me down at the kitchen table. She sits across from me. I'm readying myself for another lecture, but when I look at her I see tears in her eyes. Now, Mom's a tough woman and she rarely lets me see her cry, so watching her like this gives me a lump in my throat.

She wraps her hands around mine and squeezes. I'm still shaking from the fight.

"You have to stop asking to quit, Zach."

"Why? I'm horrible and I hate it. I hate the practices. I hate the games. I hate it all."

We stare at each other for a few moments. Rays of late-afternoon sunlight slice through the side window and strike her face. She looks old. This is the first time I've ever thought that.

She looks away, clears her throat. "I know it's not your favorite thing, but you have to stop asking to quit. I'm asking you to stick with it for one more year. Do you understand that? You need to play football as a senior, and you need to like it."

"Why? He let Justin quit after his junior year. Why not me?"

"Because part of him dies every time you complain about it." She stares over my shoulder, looks at the front door, then back at me. "You're his last hope, Zach. The only thing he has left. You know how much he loves football, how he always talks about his high school playing days. He made a mistake with Justin and he knows it, letting him quit like that. Your father, he always said he'd never force his boys to do anything they didn't want to do." She pauses. "But with football, he figured you two would just naturally love it, like it's in the family blood or something."

"Justin didn't hate *football*, Mom. He hated Coach Horton. He was on his way to a full-ride, but then, boom! He quit out of nowhere and still refuses to talk about it."

"Yeah, good ol' Coach Horton," she says, letting go of

my hands as she glances at the oven. "That man's a piece of work, I'll admit that." The smells of meat and onions fill the kitchen.

"What would happen if I did quit?"

"That's not an issue, because you won't. You need to do this for your dad, okay?" I realize she's not asking anymore, she's telling. "Stick with it for him, for me, and for you." She forces a smile. "Look, that's all I'm saying about it." She stands and walks to the oven.

"Does he actually think I can get a scholarship? I mean, I suck pretty bad. I'm the worst player on the field. Everybody knows it. Justin has all the athletic genes in this family, not me."

"I think your dad says things like that to keep you motivated."

"Mom, he's not exactly joyful at the games. He's a psycho up there."

"You know what I mean," she says. And then, with a serious look: "Look at it this way, Zach. If you do this, and you will, you're going to help him...and me." She looks around the small kitchen and gazes out the window above the sink into our tiny backyard, staring at the assembly plant and its towering smokestacks in the distance. "He doesn't have much. Nobody in Blaine does. I mean, yeah, it'd be nice if we lived in Blaine Heights, but we don't." She pauses, still looking out the window, as if imagining the wealthy lifestyle she's never known. Then she grabs a dishtowel, dries her hands, and turns to open the oven.

I stare at the empty chair across from me. Arguing further would be pointless. But deep down I still totally hate the fact that they let Justin, an all-state athlete, quit and not me. The last thing I want is to spend the first four months of my senior year as a football prisoner, and that's exactly what the football program at Blaine Memorial High School is, a prison that sucks away your life much like the assembly plant sucks away my parents' lives.

The front door opens and Dad comes in for dinner. We eat in silence, the only sounds those of silverware scraping plates and lips smacking food. I glance at Mom and Dad often. They don't look at each other or smile during the entire meal. Typical behavior, especially lately.

But, hey, at least the meatloaf and potatoes taste wonderful.

4

Okay, it goes like this: I'm jealous of Tank because his dad gave him the entire basement as his bedroom, complete with his own sixty-inch TV, a sweet cell phone, and the latest laptop. It's the total hookup. See, Mr. Foster is so proud of Tank's wrestling achievements that he gives him stuff whenever he wins a tournament. Well, Tank wins a lot of tournaments. My dad can barely afford basic cable. We have one box and one ancient TV, both of which are in the living room, where Dad drinks beer and smokes cigarettes from five to midnight every evening.

So this is totally embarrassing and all that, but usually the only way I can watch cable is to go to Tank's.

And this is even more totally embarrassing, but the only computer in our house is in Justin's room, but Justin's never home and he always keeps his room locked when he's out.

Translation: the only way I can surf on a regular basis is to go to Tank's.

So I walk to his house four days after the silent dinner with Mom and Dad, hoping to snoop around a bit to see if I can dig up anything on Big Dale. It's a hot and muggy evening. I'm dripping sweat by the time I reach his porch, kind of excited about the prospect of doing my first real professional spy work.

Since Sarah and Mr. Foster are never around, I'm used to walking in without knocking, something Tank insists I do because he hates coming up from the basement to let me in. This always makes me nervous because … well, you know, his dad's a cop and all that and has plenty of guns and stuff lying around, so I always make a point of peeking through the glass triangle at the top of the white front door before turning the knob.

But tonight the house isn't empty. Strange. I can see Tank's dad and sister eating dinner in the kitchen, right there at the old brown Formica table, a big bucket of Kentucky Fried Chicken resting in the middle. Tank's dad is sitting at the far end, facing me, and Sarah is at the opposite end, her back to me.

One thing about the Fosters: they live off of fast food, which is another reason I'm so jealous of Tank. I mean, I can totally smell the Colonel's special recipe out here on the porch. And one time—and I so swear this is true—Mr. Foster served Taco Bell in place of turkey on Thanksgiving.

So I'm about to knock, but I pull my hand back at the last moment and decide to do a little surveillance on Mr. Foster, a man I haven't seen in nearly three months. I also realize that once I do enter the house, I might be able to make my first play on him. If all goes according to plan, I'll get him to reveal some information that will earn me another fifty bucks from Huey.

Dale Foster wears a white tank top that sticks to his bulging muscles like a second skin. He has a deep tan and sports straight black hair, slicked back and shoulder length. His mustache is thick, but the twisted-up corners are missing, a fact that pisses me off a little because ... well, let's face it: you don't exactly see mustaches like that very often.

Despite his intimidating physical appearance, Mr. Foster is smiling and laughing, listening to Sarah talk about something, probably bragging about her grades again. As he reaches into the bucket for a chicken leg, I catch a brief glimpse of the green dragon tattoo on his right forearm, but I see something else, too: a gun. There it is, tucked along the left side of his ribcage, a big black rubber handle sticking out of a black leather holster. I wonder if he's ever killed anybody. Tank said his dad served in the first Gulf War but never talks about it.

Yeah, I decide, the guy's definitely killed people, probably lots.

I'm debating whether to leave when, for some reason, I look at the back of Sarah's head. There's something different about it, but I can't figure out what.

After a few moments it hits me. She's gotten a haircut, a big one, at least eight inches taken off. And her hair isn't dirty and matted anymore. It's smooth and shiny, a thick, luxurious-looking tumble of dark hair ending just above her shoulders. Her sense of fashion has changed, too. She's all Abercrombied-out now.

Wow.

Now I'm staring at the white tank-top straps resting on her tan and otherwise bare shoulders. She's actually wearing an in-style shirt! Looking at her legs, I notice a pair of denim short shorts that make me feel funny inside.

Then this thought: Is this *really* Sarah Foster? No, it can't be. It has to be some other girl. Maybe it's one of Sarah's friends? No, wait, maybe it's Tank's mom. Maybe she's cleaned up and they're trying to work things out. Yes, that's it!

No, that's not it.

Because the more I study this mysterious female, the more I realize she *is* Sarah. I mean, the way the back of her head bounces slightly from side to side as she talks. The way she gestures with her right hand, extending it out and rotating her wrist wildly, totally engrossed with whatever story she's telling. These are signature Sarah Foster moves.

Then other thoughts, troubling ones: Why am I staring at her if I know it's just geeky Sarah? After all, this is a girl I've picked on for years, Tank's nerdy twin who's so easy to make cry. Yet now I can identify her—even after her pre-senior year makeover or whatever—without seeing her face. It's her, but it's not her. But, of course, it is Sarah. Sarah Foster. So what's happening? Why is my stomach flipping around like this? Why do I recognize her simply from her head and arm movements?

I take a deep breath and swallow, aware of my Adam's apple bobbing. I suddenly feel like a total perv, standing here drooling over my best friend's sister's copper shoulders and legs.

I'm about to run home, but when I look up for one last glance, I see Dale Foster's scary eyes staring at me through the glass triangle. He gives me one of those cop looks, like he's always expecting danger, and I half-expect him to reach for his gun, but he doesn't. He just looks at me and cocks his head to the right. I try to play it off the best I can, waving my hand in front of the window and ringing the doorbell, but I'm pretty sure he's just busted me checking out his daughter.

He says something to Sarah.

She stands and turns.

And I fall in love.

She sees me through the glass triangle and rolls her eyes. I look down at her hips, swaying gently in those short shorts, and notice that she has curves. This catches me totally off guard and makes me nervous, makes me realize I'll never tease her again. How did this happen so quickly? How does a girl go from geek to goddess overnight... without plastic surgery?

She opens the door, holds it for me.

"Hey, Zach," she says. I nod, unable to speak, which must look funny because she simply turns and walks back to the table, leaving behind a lavender-scented breeze.

At this point I realize her smile has changed, too. It's so big and so ... *white*. The braces—they're gone! The Sarah Foster aluminum railroad has been dismantled and replaced with a smooth ivory highway.

"Tank's in the basement," she says, looking at her dad now.

I step into the kitchen. Dale Foster stares at me and gives me the once-over like I'm some wanted suspect. He gives me a nod. "So what's new, Zach?"

"Not much." I steal a glance at his gun. He notices, brings his left arm down over the holster. I look for a badge or some other form of ID clipped to his belt, but I can't see behind the table.

I glance at Sarah. She's looking at me out of the corner of her eye. She looks away, but there's a moment there, a little eye flirting that releases butterflies throughout my stomach. I shift my gaze back to Mr. Foster, who proceeds to shift his gaze between his daughter and me.

"Haven't seen you in a while," he says. "Your mom and dad doing okay?"

"Fine," I say. "They're still slaves to that stupid factory."

He raises his eyebrows. "You think you're better than them, the people who work there?"

"No, not better. I didn't say that. I just have different goals is all, like getting out of Blaine one day. Don't take this the wrong way or anything, but everybody around here always seems so depressed, like they can't believe they're stuck working in a truck plant. Me, my goal is to cross Michigan Avenue one day and settle down in Blaine Heights, because this place, well, it pretty much sucks. I'm gonna pull a Captain Rick and blast the hell out of here."

He stares at me, expressionless, for what seems like a minute. Then a slight smile crosses his face. "That's good, Zach. It's good you have goals. Goals are important." He looks at Sarah. She smiles and looks down at her plate. "Tell Zach the goal we were just talking about."

"No, Dad, please," she says, embarrassed.

"Come on, Sarah," he says and laughs. She shakes her head. "Fine," he says. "I'll tell him." To me: "Sarah has a goal of getting into Harvard." He pauses. "How about that?" He holds up a folded piece of paper resting near the KFC bucket and smiles. "And with these test scores, she'll get in *anywhere*."

"Well, if anyone can get into Harvard, it's Sarah," I say.

She looks at me as if in shock. As far as I know, this is the first compliment I've ever given her. Another thing: I've never noticed how big and green her eyes are before, and there's a reason for that, I finally realize. She's not wearing glasses! Those thick lenses and ridiculous frames are history. Thank God.

"Thanks, Zach," she says and looks down again.

"So, are you sticking with football for senior year?" Mr. Foster asks.

"It's summer. I'm trying not to think about football." I pause. "Hey, you know Coach Horton, right?"

He laughs. "Yeah, I know Hank Horton. He's all right, I guess, but don't believe everything the guy says."

"Oh, I don't," I say. "Trust me. I mean, people worship the guy, but there's always been something about him that creeps me out. He's a great football coach, but...I don't know." I shrug. "Never mind."

"Well," Mr. Foster says, "I can tell you that he doesn't exactly practice what he preaches."

I'm not sure what to make of that comment, so I say, "My dad thinks Horton's a god."

"Looks can be deceiving."

An awkward silence.

"Well, it was nice seeing you, Mr. Foster." I turn toward the living room, where the basement stairs lead to Tank's underground palace.

"Hey, Zach, wait a second," he says. I stop and turn. "Anybody ever tell you you'd make a good cop?" I shake my head. "You're a quick thinker and you call things like you see them." He shrugs and looks down at his gun. "I deal with a lot of dishonest people in my line of work. You seem like an honest guy. I hope you stay that way."

"Thanks," I say, deciding now is a perfect time to make the play I was thinking about on the porch. "By the way, Huey Dawkins was asking about you the other day."

"He was?"

And he says it in the totally coolest cop way, all calm about it like it's no big deal. But there *is* a noticeable change in his body language. He's not holding my gaze anymore, just studying the bucket of chicken like it's a textbook.

Sarah looks at me and shrugs.

"What did he say?" Mr. Foster asks calmly.

"Not much. Just wanted to know how you were doing. I think he was drunk."

"Huey's always drunk."

I laugh and decide to press on with the lies. "Oh, and he said he thought your dragon tattoo was cool."

"He said that?"

"Yeah."

"Interesting," he says, looking at me again. "Thanks, Zach. You want some chicken?"

"No, thanks. I just ate."

"Let Tank know it's in the fridge." He stands. "Sarah, I have to make a call. Be ready to leave when I come out." He reaches for his cell and disappears down the hallway leading to his bedroom.

Sarah and I stare at each other.

"Sarah, you look really … great."

She smiles and is about to say something, but then she looks over my shoulder for a moment and quickly turns away.

From behind me I hear my best friend's voice: "The hell you talking to the geek for? Get down here, Zach."

I turn and follow Tank down the steps. Halfway down I realize something. I'm basically a double agent now. Dale Foster likes me, and I like him. I respect him for not working in the plant, respect him for not being a drunk, and admire his efforts to be a good dad, especially with Tank's mom out on the streets. I want to know more about the man, but not for Huey Dawkins's benefit anymore—for mine. Of course, if I can earn some more fifties in the process I'll gladly take them.

The big question now is whether to let Tank in on the secret.

Then there's the second secret: I'm totally hot for his twin sister. But there's no way I'll tell him about that.

At least not yet, anyway.

Man, what a way to start the summer.

5

Tank's pissed.

He sits down on this old, cheap blue sofa, nothing on but a pair of shorts, and starts doing bicep curls with thirty-pound dumbbells. Then he quickly drops the dumbbells and presses the mute button on the remote. He's watching a *Cribs* repeat. The ultra-thin sixty-inch screen looks bigger than my bedroom.

He points at the ceiling. "So, you obviously noticed her, right?"

"Yeah. She looks ... different."

"And it's all his fault." He's still pointing at the ceiling.

"Who, your dad's?"

"Exactly." He stands and gives one of the dumbbells a light kick with his bare foot. "I don't know what's gotten into him, Zach. All of a sudden it's like he decides he *wants* to be a dad. You know, like he knows he messed up with me, so now he's trying to make it up with Sarah before it's too late." He paces back and forth, entering one of his "psycho" moods now. Never a good thing.

"Tank, you've got it made." I wave my arm around the basement. "He buys you anything you want."

"That's the problem. That's his way of trying to make up for things. But I see right through it. The guy's an idiot if he thinks spoiling us makes him a good dad. We're smarter than that. You know that, and so does Sarah."

"He was really cool to me just now."

"There, you see? He's trying it with you, too. He's trying to win over my friends now." Tank puts his face in his hands and grunts. "I can't believe what he's done to her, buying her all that...that stuff. He's coming home more often and even brings more food home now...which I guess is the only good part about it."

"Speaking of food, there's chicken in the fridge. KFC."

"Screw the KFC," Tank yells. "Don't you see what's about to happen? Jesus, man, it's only a matter of time before guys come around. We're seniors now, Zach. *Sarah's* a senior. With a brain. And now she has this trendy new look or whatever, and..." He rakes his hands across his head, frustrated. "God! I can't take it. I know what's coming, and I just can't take it." He pauses, looks at me. "All guys are the same, especially seniors. I mean, take you and me. What topic dominates our conversations?"

"Uh...partying?"

He gives me a look. "And?"

I say nothing.

"Say it, Zach."

"Say what?"

"You know what. Say it!"

"Fine," I say, throwing my hands in the air. "Sex."

"Exactly," he says. "Which means dudes our age will now start thinking about Sarah that way." He points toward my chest. "And I can't have that, my friend. No, sir. That is something I just can't have."

"Well," I say, unable to look him in the eyes. "She does look good, Tank."

"Shut up! What, do you like her now or something?"

"No, no," I lie, "not like that. I'm just stating a fact. She looks good, okay?"

"Jesus. I can't deal with this. Sarah's brilliant. She's going places, places I'll never see. I don't want some idiot guy stepping in and blocking her path."

"That's very noble of you."

"Noble?" He cocks his head. "Don't use big words. What's that mean?"

"Honorable," I say. "Noble means honorable. Forget it. I meant it as a compliment."

He turns off the TV and starts to dress. "The way I see it," he says, digging through his top dresser drawer and sliding on a pair of jeans, "I'm responsible for Sarah until she's eighteen, which means she's under my control for one more year."

He finishes dressing and hustles over to a paneled

wooden door to the right of the stairs. The door leads to a basement crawlspace. It's Tank's favorite hiding spot, so I'm not surprised to hear him open and close the squeaky door quickly, walking back toward me with his hands behind his back and an all-knowing smile on his face.

"Hey, Zach, look."

I look.

He brandishes the Jim Beam and the Marlboros as if they're weapons. He shoves them into the waist of his jeans and pulls his T-shirt loosely over them, just like he did in the store the day he stole them. Then he flashes a mischievous grin.

"It's summer, and it's the weekend. Let's party."

"Sweet," I say.

We hear the front door slam upstairs, Mr. Foster and Sarah off to who knows where.

"He's dropping her off at the mall," Tank says. "Great, more clothes. Just what she needs. I bet dudes check her out in the stores." He pauses. "And I bet she's starting to like it." He looks around the basement. "Damn. I don't have a lighter. Do you?"

"Nope."

"It's cool," he says, taking a deep breath. "I'll get one from my dad's room. Let's go. I need tobacco and alcohol in my system to deal with this crisis."

"What crisis?"

"Sarah, idiot."

"Oh."

I follow him upstairs and wait in the kitchen. Although Mr. Foster keeps his bedroom door locked, he uses a combination lock that Tank has somehow learned the numbers to. When I hear him pop the lock and open the door, I walk over to where Sarah was sitting and stare at the empty seat. Then I lean over and smell the back of the chair. Her lavender scent fills my nostrils again. I close my eyes and savor the aroma. I've had my share of girlfriends, but I realize this is the first time I've ever truly appreciated the smell of a girl. It does things to me, makes me feel all powerless or whatever.

Stepping back into the living room, I take a quick look around for anything that might reveal more information about Tank's dad. Problem is I don't find anything. The room is oddly bare, as usual—a sofa, coffee table, leather recliner, and new home entertainment system taking up most of the space. I don't even see any drawers I can rummage through. As for pictures, the only one I spot is an old, framed family photo up in the top right corner of a mostly bookless bookcase.

Somebody has pushed the photo far back into the corner, as if they don't want to see it. Moving closer, I discover the dusty picture is from back in the day, at least twelve years old, back when Tank's mom was clean, sober, and beautiful. Staring up at it, a strange wave of sadness flows through me. Big Dale and his wife look so young and proud, huge smiles plastered across their faces. Tank and Sarah can't be older than five, sitting between their parents, looking safe and content. I'm not surprised somebody has shoved this happy memory into the top corner. It has to be hard to look at.

I'm stepping forward, with plans for reaching up for the frame, when my foot strikes something loose but bulky on the floor beside the recliner. Looking down, I see it's Tank's wrestling bag. I stare at it and poke my foot against the canvas a few times, feeling and hearing all kinds of things moving around inside.

I hear Tank rifling through drawers in his dad's bedroom, and I think about just how good of a wrestler he is, light years beyond the competition. In the past three years, Tank Foster hasn't come close to losing a match. He's the total package on the mat, dominating his opponents both physically and mentally in ways that even the most experienced college scouts admit they've never seen before. I can't remember how many weight classes he's moved up since freshman year, but he's put on at least sixty pounds of pure muscle since then.

I guess, deep down, I've always known Tank's on the juice. I mean, dudes my age don't turn into muscle-bound freaks without a little assistance. Of course, sometimes you don't need to know the whole truth about your friends, but the little spy mode or whatever I'm currently in has boosted my curiosity to new levels … convincing me that maybe I do need to know for certain if Tank's cheating or not.

Crouching for a closer look, I unzip the bag and probe around inside, finding the usual stuff: headgear, wrestling shoes, smelly singlets and socks, athletic tape, and athlete's foot spray. Down at the bottom, however, I see two empty amber-colored pill bottles with white safety caps. Inspecting the white labels, I'm not surprised to see the following printed on each: Dianabol (D-Bol).

I know what this stuff is. Dianabol is one of the most common oral steroids available. Anybody can buy it online. So yeah, I'm a little disappointed with the fact that he's cheating to get ahead, and part of me is wondering how much more of this junk he might have stashed away in the crawlspace, but on the other hand, he's just keeping up with the competition, because anybody who doesn't think certain elite high school athletes pop steroids is living in denial.

So big deal, right? It's really none of my business, is it? No, of course not.

So I simply shove the bottles back down to the bottom of the bag and tell myself this little discovery never occurred. It's his body, not mine.

I hear Tank close and lock Big Dale's door, so I hustle back to the kitchen. Tank rounds the corner and raises a yellow Bic lighter and a glossy magazine above his head as if they're wrestling trophies.

"Dude, check this out," he says, handing me the publication and walking into the living room. "My dad left it on his dresser," he says over his shoulder.

I flip through the pages of a magazine entitled *Michigan Cherries*, amazed at some of the physical positions the women have managed to twist themselves into. Funny thing is I don't find any of it hot. I mean, yeah, the *models* are hot and all that, but I get the sense from the looks on their faces that they're more concerned about getting paid than turning their readers on. I also find myself somewhat let down that Dale is into this type of thing. I mean, on one hand I'm cool with it. The guy is single, after all. It's not like he's married and cheating with magazines. On the other hand ... well, it sort of puts a crack in that aura of cool respectability he struck me with earlier.

"Dude, were you looking through my bag?" Tank says.

I close the magazine and look up. My heart's pounding and my throat feels like it's full of dry sand. Tank's staring at me, wrestling bag dangling from his left hand.

I forgot to zip it, I say to myself. I forgot to zip the damn bag!

"What?" I say squinting and stepping into the living room.

"My wrestling bag," he says, giving me a harder look now. "Did you go through it?"

"No," I lie. "I was in the kitchen the whole time. Why would I go through your wrestling bag?"

Silence, Tank studying me for what seems like an hour.

Finally, he zips the bag and tosses it back beside the recliner. "Whatever."

Changing the subject, I raise the magazine and say, "Who still looks at magazines when all the good stuff's free online?"

Tank shakes his head. "I know my dad. He's paranoid

about technology. The guy doesn't even like checking his email or using his cell. Must be a cop thing." He looks back toward the bedroom. "Man, I bet he has a ton of other stuff hidden in there."

"Maybe." I look down and shake my head.

"What's wrong with you?"

"I'm not sure," I say. "I just think there might be certain things we don't need to know about people."

"Whatever, man. Personally, I think it's funny as hell."

He turns and decides to grab his bag, and I'm about to hand him the magazine when I see a phone number—729-8274—scrawled in tiny blue print along the bottom margin of a cigarette ad on the back cover. My first instinct is to mention it to Tank, but I don't, telling myself to do whatever it takes to remember the order of those seven digits—729-8274.

"What are you thinking about?" Tank asks, turning back toward me, wrestling bag slung over his shoulder.

"Nothing." I hand him the magazine, cover side up. "I was just wondering if other states have magazines like this. You know, like *Georgia Peaches* and *Hawaii Coconuts* or whatever."

"Oh my God," Tank says, grabbing the magazine and laughing all the way to Big Dale's bedroom. "Or *Florida Oranges*," he yells from the hallway.

"There you go," I say.

When I hear him open the door, I take out my cell, punch in 729-8274, and save it as an unknown contact.

6

It's dark when we leave Tank's, close to ten o'clock. I have to be home at midnight, giving us two hours to party. Walking along the sidewalk, we're nearing the end of the street when Tank says, "How about the school field?"

"Works for me."

Tank says, "God, I wish we had our own cars like all the pretty boys over in the Heights."

"We could always walk over there and steal one for the night."

Tank stops, gives me a look. "Zach, don't tempt me like that. Seriously."

We cut through an asphalt path that opens onto a large field behind our old elementary school. Decaying bungalows line the other three sides of the field. Sometimes people party out here on weekends, and tonight is no exception. As soon as we step onto the grass, I hear my brother's unmistakable laugh off to my right.

He and three friends, two of them girls, are no more than ten feet away, standing close to the chain-link fence that separates the homes from the school property. Tall privacy hedges run along the other side of the fence, making it impossible for any homeowners to see Justin and his crew through their back windows.

It's dark, but I notice four tiny orange cigarette embers bobbing up and down. I want to turn around, but it's too late.

"Hey, Zach," Justin calls. "Come here, man."

The girls laugh. So does the other guy. I don't recognize the girls' voices, but I know the guy's. It's Victor Hodge, an all-state baseball player who throws a one-hundred-mile-per-hour fastball. He's currently attending the University of Michigan on a full-ride athletic scholarship. He's one of the lucky ones. His BEP is fully funded, the ultimate Captain Rick. I'm not surprised to see him smoking. It seems like everybody in Blaine smokes.

Tank and I walk over.

"Hey, Justin," I say, finding it strange to see him here. Until recently, my brother worked full-time as a stock boy for Huey, a job that allowed him to save enough money to buy a decent used car. Personally, an elementary school field is the *last* place I'd be if I had my own car.

Now I recognize the two girls. One is tall, the other short. They used to drop Justin off from school every now and then back when they were seniors. Regardless, I don't know their names. They're hot, though. Not nearly as hot as Sarah, but hot enough.

"So, what's going on?" I ask. Tank stands behind me. I look down, notice a twelve-pack of Bud on the ground between Justin and Victor.

The girls keep reading and sending texts, faces glued in idiocy to their chrome phones.

"Not much," Justin answers, sensing the awkwardness. "Just coming from a graduation party, getting ready to go to another. Figured we'd stop here for old times' sake."

"No offense or anything," I say, "but you're twenty years old. Why go back and revisit the high school graduation circuit?"

"Why *not*?" Justin says, slurring his words a bit. "Everything's free and we know a lot of people."

I shrug and look away.

Justin eyes Tank and extends his hand toward my best friend. "What's up, Tank?"

"Not much," Tank says, shaking Justin's hand.

"What's up, Foster?" Victor Hodge adds and offers his hand, which Tank also shakes. "Heard you're bumping up to 189 this year."

"That's the plan," Tank says.

Victor nods and studies Tank's body like it's a side of beef. "Man, it looks like you're already there."

"Gettin' close," Tank says.

The short girl puffs her cigarette, looks at me and says, "Oh my God. Your brother turned into a total hottie, Justin." She's so drunk she's swaying.

"So is his friend," the tall girl says. She seems even drunker and is having trouble with her balance too.

"They're seniors in September," Justin says.

"Oh my God, you guys are gonna love next year," Tall Girl says.

"Yeah," Short Girl says, "it's the best. It goes by so fast, though."

Victor Hodge nods. "She's right. Getting old kind of sucks." He shuffles his feet and looks down.

"Tell me about it," Justin says. "I'm actually thinking about taking one more year off." He says this more to his friends than me. Regardless, my stomach seems to drop to my knees. "I mean, why not kick back and catch my breath until I'm twenty-one, you know?" His friends nod their approval.

"I thought you were going to Wayne County in the fall," I say. "That's your plan, right?"

He shrugs. "Well ... yeah, probably. I'm just keeping my options open. Besides, it won't matter if I take another year off. I'll just enroll the next fall."

"You've already taken two years off. Why wait any longer?" I shoot him a look. "It just prolongs the end."

"The end of *what*?"

"Of *this*," I say, holding my arms out wide and looking around.

"Mind your own business, Zach," Justin says. "Jesus, you sound like a counselor." He pauses. "The hell you guys doing out here, anyway?"

"Just getting ready to party," I say, realizing he's changed the subject on purpose.

Victor finally acknowledges my presence. "You playing football next year, Zach?"

"I don't know," I say. "I'm not sure I can take another year of Coach Horton's act."

The girls look at each other and scrunch their noses. Then Tall Girl looks at me and goes, "Oh my God. Horton's a total perv. He used to stare at me every time I walked past him."

"Me, too," Short Girl slurs. "He's such a creeper."

"I've heard he's done a lot more with some female students than just stare at them," Victor says.

"Shut up, guys," Justin snaps. "Drop the Horton thing already."

There's an uncomfortable silence.

"You guys want a beer?" Victor asks, reaching down into the twelve-pack and offering us two cans.

Tank and I gladly accept.

"Thanks," I say, popping the top. Warm beer fizz sprays the top of my hand. "How'd you get it?"

"The beer?" Victor says. "Brandon Watkins gets it for—"

Justin elbows Victor. "Don't worry about how we get it, Zach." He picks up the twelve-pack. "We have to go."

The girls each grab one of Justin's arms for support. Victor shrugs. The four of them walk toward the path.

When they're gone, Tank and I slam our warm beers, toss the cans, and continue through the field.

"I'm so pissed at Justin."

"Why?" Tank asks. "Because he's with girls and you're not?"

"No. Because he told me he was starting college in the fall. It's his only way out of here."

Tank laughs. "Man, relax. You sound like an old lady. Let your brother live his life."

"Whatever." I pause. "Those girls are hammered, by the way."

"Which means your brother's a lucky man. Drunk girls are the best. They do things they normally wouldn't and never remember in the morning." He smiles. "And that's exactly how I like it."

"Sounds perverted."

"My dad says all guys are perverts, but most of us are sane enough to know the difference between fantasy and reality."

We walk in silence. I decide the time is right to make a play on my best friend.

"I know I've never really asked you this, but what kind of cop is your dad, anyway?"

"What do you mean?"

"You know, like, what city does he work for?"

"I don't know," Tank says, eyeing the school.

"He's never told you?"

"I've never asked."

We reach the asphalt basketball court, where Tank mimics a last-second, game-winning three-point shot and does a funny little celebration dance. He laughs and gives

me a high five, as if I'm a teammate in his imaginary sce
nario.

We head toward our fifth grade classroom. "So who pays him?" I ask.

"What?"

"Your dad," I say. "Who pays him?"

"I have no clue."

"You ever seen one of his checks?"

"No," Tank says, giving me a look. "What's it to you?"

"Just wondering," I say, cupping my hands around my face and peering through the dirty classroom windows. Tank does the same. "Dude, I bet your dad's a big-time cop. I mean, he never wears a uniform or drives a cruiser, does he?"

"No," Tank says. "Man, this room looks exactly the same as it did when we were in it."

"I was just thinking the same thing."

We study the classroom in silence.

Then Tank says, "I know my dad has a lot of power."

"How do you know that?" I turn away from the windows.

"Well, my mom gets arrested a lot, but she never gets charged with anything. He takes care of stuff like that. Sometimes I hear him on the phone, giving orders about what to do with her or where to take her."

We walk back to the basketball court and stare out over the field. The humid air is thick and heavy, like an invisible blanket. Beads of sweat cover my forehead.

"So, can I ask when you last saw her?"

Tank takes a deep breath. "It's been about eight years. I think we were nine or something." He shuffles his feet, shoves his hands in his front pockets. "I'm playing tag on the front lawn with Sarah and the babysitter, when this loud car comes by and stops in the middle of the street. So the three of us look over and see this lady in the driver's seat, and she's staring at us with a smile on her face. But you could tell she wasn't happy. It was a sad smile, if that makes any sense. She looked horrible, actually, all skin and bones." He pauses. "Anyway, Sarah and me, we knew it was Mom right away, so we waved, and that must have really hit her hard, because she started crying. Then she waved back and drove away. The babysitter asked us who the person was, and we just looked at her like it was no big deal and told her it was our mom. She freaked and dragged us inside. Then she called my dad. I guess he took over from there."

"You still think about her a lot, huh?"

"Well, yeah, idiot. She's my mom."

"Sorry," I say. "I think my parents are fighting now, too."

"About what?"

"I don't know, but something's going on. It's like the exact opposite of your situation, though."

"What do you mean?"

"I think it's my dad who has the problems," I explain.

"Hey, if they divorce maybe we can get your dad together with my mom."

"Oh my God, if they got married we'd be related." Tank laughs but quickly falls silent. "Actually, I think my dad has a secret girlfriend right now."

"Maybe that's why he's in such a good mood lately."

"I guess," he says. "Sometimes I listen outside his door when he's on the phone. I can't make out every word, but I know he's seeing somebody."

"You're cool with it, right?"

"Yeah, I guess I'm cool with it, but what's up with the secrecy?" He wipes sweat from his brow.

I swallow hard, and I'm suddenly feeling so guilty that I consider telling him about Huey paying me to find dirt on Big Dale, but instead I go, "I'm sure he only keeps things from you for a reason. Being a cop and all, he has to see some sick stuff and deal with some sick people. And with the girlfriend thing…I don't know, maybe he's just not ready to tell you."

"Whatever," Tank says. "That's why Sarah amazes me so much. She handles it all so well. If I was a stranger who'd just met her, I'd never guess she comes from a screwed-up family." Looking me in the eyes, he adds, "I guess that's why I'm so overprotective of her. I don't want her to end up like my mom."

"Yeah," I say. "I can understand that."

We gaze skyward for a few moments and notice bats darting around. I find myself feeling guilty for being hot for Sarah. I mean, yeah, she *is* hot, no doubt about that, but she's Tank's sister. Hello? I'm already spying on his dad behind his back, so it's probably wise to draw the line there. So, as much as it pains me to do so, I decide not to pursue my feelings for Sarah. As of right now, Sarah Foster is taboo.

"This place is depressing," Tank finally says. He taps the Jim Beam and Marlboros under his shirt. "Let's go party at the railroad tracks."

"Genius," I say. "I can't even remember the last time I was there."

We head back through the dark field, the humid air pressing down on us like a heavy weight.

7

When Justin was in middle school or whatever, he and some friends dug an underground fort into the top of a steep slope that borders the railroad tracks. The tracks run behind the bungalows across the street from our house and overgrown brush covers the slope, making it a sweet hiding place. When Justin and his crew outgrew the place, Tank and I took it over.

The fort's a good thirty feet from the rails. It's basically a cellar, complete with a wooden entrance door made out of two-by-fours concealed with brush. The underground space is about four feet deep, so you have to kneel or squat or sit on one of the plastic milk crates Justin stole from Huey's during his four-year stretch as a stock boy. Although maximum capacity is four persons, there's barely enough room for two to sit comfortably. When the trains come roaring past at full speed, our bodies shake from the vibrations and we have to yell to hear each other. Loose dirt falls from the ceiling often, which is why one of the rules is never to look up when a train passes. Regardless, I'm confident the place is one of the coolest forts in the world.

The only bad thing is that it's a sweatbox during warm weather, so when Tank and I arrive from the elementary school field we decide it's too hot and dark to go inside. Instead, we clear a space in the brush and sit, staring at the railroad tracks and the low-rent apartment complex located just beyond the large brick wall on the far side of the rails.

"These mosquitoes suck," I say, slapping them away left and right. "We need to get central air for the fort."

"Now that would be the ultimate," Tank says. He leans back, removes the pint of Jim Beam from his jeans, and lays it off to the side.

Next he tips the Marlboro box upside down and packs the smokes, rapping the top of the pack hard against the palm of his left hand several times. Then he peels off the upper portion of the clear plastic wrapper and flicks it into the weeds. Opening the top, he pulls out the silver foil and slides out two cigarettes, popping both between his lips.

He flicks the lighter. An orange and blue flame dances above his thumb. He touches the flame to the cigarettes and closes his eyes. The ends of the smokes turn orange and brighten to a blazing red. Smoke flows out of his nostrils as he hands me a cigarette.

I draw hard on the Marlboro, sucking in smoke and enjoying the slight buzz that always greets me during the first few hits.

"Man, I love smoking," I say. "Why does it have to be so bad for you?"

"No big deal." Tank's cigarette dangles from the corner of his mouth as he twists the cap of the Jim Beam and breaks the seal. "Just quit when you're in your thirties and you'll be fine."

"I like how you think." I exhale a cloud of smoke into the night.

"So, what's the game tonight?" Tank asks, removing the cap from the bottle and smelling the Jim Beam as if he's some sort of professional bourbon taster.

"I don't care. You decide."

"Excellent," he says. "Here it is. Famous hot celebrities. If either of us disagrees with the other person's choice, then the person who made the bad call drinks. No pauses allowed. You have to give a name instantly. Delay means drink."

"Dead or alive?"

"What?"

"The celebrities," I say. "Can we choose dead ones?"

He thinks about that for a moment. "Yeah, I don't care."

"Deal. I like it. You first."

Tank hits his cigarette. "Scarlett Johansson."

"Great opener," I say. "Linds—"

"Drink," he says, cutting me off and passing me the bottle.

"Why?"

"That was a two-word delay. Thanks for the compliment, though." He laughs. "Drink, fool."

I hoist the bottle, raise it to my mouth, and take a healthy swallow—which is followed by a long wheezing sound. My eyes water from the alcohol burn, and the bourbon feels like lava as it flows into my stomach.

I exhale deeply.

"There," I say. "Got the first one out of the way." I cough. "It's like the devil torched my throat."

"Give a name or drink again."

"Lindsay Lohan. Have you seen her lately? She's—"

"Shut up," Tank says. "No commentary. The Olsen twins."

"Beyoncé."

"Shakira."

"Emma Watson."

"Who's she?" he asks, squinting.

"The girl who plays Hermione. She's hot now."

"Oh," Tank says, thinking. "Yeah. She did get hot."

"Drink." I pass him the bottle.

Tank laughs. He takes a gulp and hardly makes a sound, just a smooth exhale followed by a hit on his cigarette.

"All *Maxim* models," he says.

"Miley Cyrus."

"Drink!" Tank hands me the bottle. "Oh my God. Drink twice!"

"Dude, she's totally hot!"

"Sorry, bro," he says. "She'll always be innocent little Hannah Montana to me."

"Fine."

I take two generous swigs and feel the bourbon reversing its course in my stomach, but I have no intentions of puking in front of my best friend. I swallow hard to keep the booze and bile down.

"Jimmy Fallon," Tank says, laughing.

"Drink." I roll my eyes and pass him the bottle. "I see where this is headed."

"So join in." Tank takes a mammoth drink.

"Okay," I say. "Oprah."

Tank laughs so hard that he spits a mouthful of Jim Beam all over himself. Still laughing, he offers me the bottle. I grab it and drink. It goes down easy this time. My throat, esophagus, and stomach seem numb to the sting and burn.

We stub out our cigarettes and share the rest of the bottle in silence, draining it quickly. Typical for us. Then we hear a train horn in the distance. Judging from the volume, the engine will pass in about five minutes.

"Another smoke?" Tank says.

"Yeah."

He puts two between his lips, lights them both and hands me one.

"Buzzed?" he asks. "If not, we could always go to Huey's and wait for a buyer."

"Or you could steal some more," I say, taking the cigarette and drawing hard on it.

"True." He holds up the empty pint, admiring it. "I think I'll toss this in the fort."

"That's cool, like a keepsake or whatever."

Tank stands up to open the door to the fort, but once he gets to his feet he stumbles and has to grab my right shoulder to avoid falling. Letting go of me, he takes a few meandering steps, like he's lost and has amnesia. He finally makes it to the fort door and drops to his knees. He pulls on the door but can't seem to open it. Determined, he keeps yanking on it, but the door won't budge.

"Zach, get over here and help me with this. It probably hasn't been opened in years."

The train horn grows louder, only two crossing gates away now. A drunken tingling sensation starts in my head and quickly spreads throughout my body.

I stand and walk toward him. On the way over, the alcohol makes me say the following: "Tank, I think I'm in love with your sister."

Tank doesn't reply at first. He's just kneeling there beside the fort, looking up at me with glazed eyes. Then he says, "I'll pretend I didn't hear that. And if you ever hit on her, I swear to God I'll rip your balls off." He pulls on the door with both hands, giving it everything he has. There's a cracking, metallic sound, followed by a quick snap. Tank has torn the door from its hinges. He's holding it like it's a shield, a surprised look on his face. He studies it and lays it aside.

"Guess I opened it," he says, looking up at me with a smile and a shrug.

That makes me laugh, and I'm about to plop myself down beside him, but just as soon as I take a step forward, my back foot slips and I fall into the weeds. Unable to control my body, I roll down the steep slope, grasping in vain for something to hold on to. Twigs and pebbles scrape against my arms and feel like a thousand bee stings.

I end up on my back, staring at a starless sky, chest rising and falling quickly. The train horn blows again, loud enough to shake my body. I hear Tank yelling from the top of the slope, saying something about wanting to break more stuff. I turn my head to the left and realize I'm lying in the raised bed of gray rocks that border the railroad tracks. The smells of tar and steel are overwhelming. I sit up and rub my eyes. The rails are barely three feet away from me.

I turn and look toward the crossing gates.

The train has just passed through and is about a football field away, closing quickly. The bright light of the approaching locomotive blinds me.

"Tank," I yell. "I could use some help here."

He doesn't hear me.

I scramble to my feet and somehow manage to get back to the brush before falling down again. I hear wild laughter behind me. Turning, I see Tank charging down the slope like some psycho murderer in a horror film. I figure he'll stop when he reaches me, but that's not what happens. Instead, he sprints right past me. I watch in horror as he steps onto the railroad tracks and starts waving his arms at the locomotive. I scream for him to get away, but the deafening roar of the train drowns out my voice.

The engineer must see Tank, because the train's horn emits a series of short, desperate blasts. But Tank stays put, doing some wild dance on the rails, playing some twisted game of chicken. I start yelling all this stupid crap about steroids making him crazy, but I know he can't hear me above the thunderous roar of the train and horn.

Finally, with the locomotive barely fifty feet away, Tank scampers off the tracks, dives toward the brush, and crawls over to me. My stomach drops as the train speeds past.

"You're crazy enough sober," I yell. "But you're insane when you're drunk."

"Don't worry about it. I'm always under control." He pats me on the shoulder.

"Whatever."

"I'm serious about what I said up there, Zach. Don't even think that way about her."

"I know," I say. "Don't worry. I was just kidding."

I steal glances at his bulging arms, chest, shoulders, and legs. Then I think about what I just witnessed—a seventeen-year-old challenging a freight train—and decide I might need to know more about where Tank's getting the juice from.

8

We sit there and watch the freight cars flicker past, our bodies trembling from the vibrations. When the caboose rolls by, Tank stands and walks toward the rails. He gathers several rocks in his arms, carries them over, drops them in front of me, and sits down.

"What are these for?" I ask.

"It's a new game. I call it 'Hit the Windshield.'"

He grabs a rock and cocks his arm. The rock sails in a high arc and crashes against the tall brick wall bordering the low-rent apartment complex on the other side of the tracks.

"What are you doing, Tank?"

"It's simple. Can you see the cars parked on the other side of the wall?"

"No."

"That's the game." He reaches for another rock. "Whoever breaks a windshield first wins." He launches the second rock. This one travels over the wall and lands with a dull thud, another miss.

"What if you hit somebody?"

"Do you hear anybody?"

I listen. "No … not right now."

"So if we hear somebody we'll stop." He hands me a rock. "Try one."

Okay, so Tank Foster is a psycho who has nearly fifty pounds on me and happens to be my best friend. If I tell him to stop, he won't think twice about backhanding me across the bridge of my nose or putting me into some torturous, medieval wrestling hold. And the fact that he's buzzed doesn't help the situation. It only makes him more unpredictable than usual.

So what I do is play along and toss the rock, but I underthrow it on purpose and it lands in front of the brick wall.

Tank shakes his head in disappointment.

"Check this one out." He fires another shot. The rock clears the wall and lands with a loud bang. Glass doesn't break, but he's obviously hit a car.

"There's a nice dent." He laughs.

"Tank, I don't know about—"

"Shut up. Just a few more."

And there's nothing I can do to stop him. He tosses rock after rock over the wall in all possible directions. Most of them end up hitting automobiles.

Satisfied, he finally stands. "Okay, let's bolt."

I force myself to my feet, still buzzed but able to maintain decent balance. As we make our way up the slope and past the fort, we hear the echo of a sliding door opening from the apartments.

An angry male voice: "The hell you think you're doing over there? You can kill somebody like that."

We stop and turn. A man is standing on his second-floor balcony, looking in our direction. Then we see a police cruiser pulling into the apartment entrance off to our far left, near the crossing gates. The siren isn't on, but the blue lights on the roof flash wildly.

"Run," Tank says. "Fast."

I follow him through the familiar backyards leading to our street, and I'm glad I know the route because my legs feel like putty. We run up the street, avoiding sidewalks and staying close to the homes, not stopping until we're back on the asphalt path leading to the elementary school. My throat burns and my heart pounds through my skin. My thighs are twitching, too, like I have one of those palsy things. All I can taste is Jim Beam and cigarettes.

"That was close," Tank says.

"I'm going home." I turn and walk toward the street. "That was stupid."

"Yeah, let's call it a night." He catches up to me and puts his arm around my shoulder. "Man, we're crazy, aren't we?"

"You're crazy." I pull my shoulder away, irritated.

Tank laughs.

When we reach the end of the path, a police cruiser pulls up and blocks our exit. The spotlight that shines on us seems ten times brighter than the one from the train locomotive.

Tank and I shield our eyes and turn away.

An officer's amplified voice tells us not to move.

We don't.

I mean, not even Tank's that stupid.

The two cops are large, muscular men who remind me of Marines. One is black, the other white. They walk up and ask us what we're doing. Tank's cocky about it and tells them we're enjoying an evening stroll. The officers look at each other. The white one asks if we've been drinking. Tank tells him it's none of his business. The officers look at each other again. The black cop asks if we've been throwing rocks at the apartments. Tank's about to get smart for the third time, but I don't let him.

"Yes," I say, "we threw the rocks. It was stupid but we did it."

"Shut up, Zach. My dad can get us out of this."

"And who's your dad, big guy?" White Cop asks.

"He's got more power than you. Let's put it that way."

The cop looks down, shuffles his feet, and shakes his head. His body language makes it clear that Tank has totally crossed the line.

Black Cop says to me, "You know how many cars you damaged?" I shrug.

"Seven," he says. "A couple of them brand-new."

"Sorry."

"You're apologizing to the wrong guy."

White Cop says, "How old are you two?" I tell him. "What are your names?" I give them. They look at each other when I mention Tank. "Where'd you get the alcohol?" White Cop asks.

How does he even *know* about that? I figure he must smell it on us.

So this is when I decide to lie, because although I'm quite pissed at Tank right now, he's still my best friend.

"We had a guy buy it for us. We waited in Huey's parking lot until we found somebody."

"Stay here," White Cop says.

They walk back to the cruiser and turn the spot back on us. The police radio crackles with static as they communicate with the dispatcher. A few neighbors watch from windows and porches. Great. This means all of Blaine will know by dawn, maybe sooner. In fact, somebody's probably already sending the email. And if any video of this ends up online, I'll be totally pissed.

"You better pray they let us go," Tank whispers. "Why'd you tell them all that?"

"Look, they know, okay? The guy on the balcony saw us plain as day. Besides, you're not exactly unknown in this city."

"Still … Jesus, Zach, we're totally screwed because of you."

"Big deal. You should be thanking me for not telling them you stole the Jim Beam." I pause. "Stop being a dick and they might give us a break."

"Screw you." He punches my shoulder hard enough to knock me off balance. "I'll take you down blindfolded with my arms tied behind my back."

"Whatever," I say, rubbing my aching shoulder. "You're missing the point."

The officers come back.

They tell us to turn around, face the fence, and order us to put our hands behind our backs. Wonderful.

The bastards make a real show of it, too, talking loudly so the neighbors hear every word. They pat us down and find the cigarettes. Then they walk us to the cruiser and put us in the back seat. I figure we're going to jail, but when they ask where we live, I know exactly what they have in mind.

They pull into Tank's driveway first, keeping the blue lights flashing and the siren off. Black Cop is in the driver's seat. He gets out and walks to Tank's front door.

While we're sitting there in the idling cruiser, an odd thing happens. Tank starts to cry, something I've never seen him do before. The tears come slowly at first, but when I ask him what's wrong, he just loses it and bawls all over himself. It's one of those snot-dripping cries, too, all uncontrollable and messy. And poor Tank can't use his hands because they're handcuffed behind his back, so he just keeps sniffling and snorting mucous back into his mouth and swallowing. It's totally gross, and I feel bad for him, but it's kind of funny at the same time. I mean, he's the idiot who snapped and got us in trouble. He *should* feel bad.

I look toward the front door. Dale Foster stands on the porch, wearing that same white tank top, thick arms folded across his barreled chest. He's nodding and listening to Black Cop, who has his back to us. Mr. Foster looks pissed, and when Tank sees his dad, he cries even harder.

"Easy, Tank," I say. "They could've taken us to jail. We're getting a deal here."

"Your friend's right," White Cop says without looking back. "And don't get snot all over my back seat."

"He's gonna kill me," Tank says. He takes a few deep breaths and starts crying again.

White Cop says to Tank, "Ain't a cop around here doesn't know Dale Foster. And you're right, pal, your dad's got a lot of power. Judging from what I've heard about him, he's probably gonna tear you apart in about five minutes." The cop laughs.

"Hey, come on," I say. "Is that necessary?"

"Shut up, skinny," he says. "You're next."

Black Cop comes back and opens Tank's door as White Cop gets out. Together, they escort Tank to his waiting father.

That's when I see Sarah looking out the living room window. The distance from the back seat to the window fogs her image, but even as a fuzzy blur she looks hot.

Shifting my gaze to the porch, I watch Dale Foster grab his son by the neck of his T-shirt with one hand and slap him hard across the face with the other. My chest tightens and I wince. Tank's head jerks to the right and his chin drops. His dad nods to the cops and they remove the handcuffs. Then Tank follows his dad into the house. Big Dale Foster slams the front door shut.

And at that moment, I lose all respect for Dale Foster. The sight of him hitting Tank is harsh enough, but the thought of him doing something like that to Sarah unleashes a rage inside of me that spreads like some high-speed virus.

The two cops smile at me as they walk back to the cruiser.

And when I look back toward the Foster living room, Sarah is nowhere in sight.

———

The cops follow the same pattern with me, keeping me in the back seat as one of them walks to the front door to explain things to my parents. I'm not nervous or crying. To my parents' credit, they don't believe in violence as a form of punishment, so I know the worst that can happen is a severe lecture.

But when I see Mom put her face in her hands ... well, that gets to me.

The cops escort me to the porch. Mom and Dad are silent as the officers unlock the handcuffs. Mom keeps looking to her left and right, embarrassed at the sight of neighbors gawking from porches. Dad just shakes his head and steps inside. Although the cuffs have been on less than twenty minutes, my wrists are raw and aching. I raise them in front of my face and see pressure lines where the metal has pushed and rubbed against my skin.

Mom and I watch the cruiser pull away, blue lights still flashing. The neighbors go inside, surely excited to fire off emails, make phone calls, and, God forbid, post YouTube clips.

We sit at the kitchen table. Justin is still out partying. Mom and Dad look at each other, probably wondering who should speak first. Mom nods to Dad, her signal that this is to begin as a father-to-son talk. He shrugs and lights a cigarette, stares at the tabletop for several moments to gather his thoughts. I feel Mom glaring at me from across the table, and I can't bring myself to look at her.

Finally, Dad says, "Look, Zach, I was no saint when I was your age." He's still looking down. "But I knew a stupid idea when I heard one." He looks at me. "Do you realize what you did was stupid?"

"Yes."

"Those cops saved you, buddy. What do you think Coach Horton would do if he found out about this?"

"I don't know," I say. "Probably kick me off the team."

Man, that would be *so* perfect.

"That's right, sport," Dad says. "He'd kick you off, and this family would be the laughingstock of Blaine. Jocks don't get in trouble, pal. We get a little crazy, but we sure as hell don't get caught." He leans forward, rests his forearms on the table. "You're the best football player in Blaine."

I can still feel a slight buzz, which is probably why I say, "Look, I have to tell you, Dad, I heard something bad about Coach Horton tonight." I'm about to go into the details, but then I feel Mom's foot driving into my shin and decide to hold back.

"Well, it's all lies, Zach," he says, wagging a finger at me now. "That man's done more good for this town than the rest of the population combined."

"Whatever."

He looks at Mom, then back at me. "Listen, Zach, do you understand what I'm telling you here? Everything I've said, has it registered?"

"Yes. You want me to play football even though deep down you know I suck and I hate it. Great parental advice, don't you think?"

Dad looks at Mom again. "Congratulations, Karen. Your son has become an official wiseass."

Mom says, "He's your son, too, Bill."

And I say, "Jesus, what's going on between you two, anyway?"

And Mom says, "You shut up and watch your mouth, Zach Ramsey."

Dad sucks down what's left of his beer and slams the empty can down hard on the table. "I'm tired of quitters." He draws hard on his cigarette. "This family's sinking."

"Oh, and I suppose none of it's your fault, is it?" Mom says.

After a long silence, Dad says, "I'm done with this for tonight."

"Wait," she says. "Who pays for the damage to the cars?"

Dad nods slowly, thinking. Then he rubs his chin and stares out the window into the backyard. "You're gonna pay for every cent, Zach, which means you need to get a summer job." He turns toward me. "I'm taking you to see Huey Dawkins tomorrow. He needs another stock boy now that Justin is gone. You'll get a little taste of what it's like to work for a living. Maybe that'll fix your newfound attitude problem."

He gets up and leaves the room.

I realize I could act all pissed off and say the last thing I want to do is work during the summer before my senior year, but I'm actually cool with the idea. I mean, I'm already doing "work" for Huey, so we have that relationship going for us, and Justin always said being a stock boy at Huey's Party Store was the best job in the city. He never explained why or anything, but he said it enough for me to believe him.

"I'm sorry," I say to Mom moments after Dad has left the kitchen. "Can I go to my room now?" She nods. "Thanks." I stand and walk away, grateful to get off so easy.

"Just one more thing," she says. I stop and turn. "If you ever come home in a police car again I'll make sure you spend the night in jail."

"Fair enough." Then I pause. "Why did you kick me? Why'd you stop me from talking about Coach Horton?"

She folds her hands in her lap and looks down, thinking. "I'd rather not talk about it right now."

Figuring it has something to do with Justin quitting, I go to my room and pass out on my mattress, still fully clothed.

A few hours later I awaken to a spinning ceiling, and I barely make it to the toilet to puke. After a few good hurls of burning, chunky, yellowish gunk, Mom walks in and gives me a wet towel. Then she closes the door and leaves me alone.

The next morning I can still taste the sour vomit. Sitting up in bed, I massage my aching temples with my fingers and stare at the faded wood floor until my vision clears. Troubling questions race through my head. Is it possible that Big Dale, with his massive physique and willingness to slap around his own son in front of other cops, is on the juice as well? The more I think about it, the more it makes sense. This guy has always been a physical specimen, equipped with the kind of muscles you see on bodybuilders. And last night there he was, totally 'roid-raging or whatever, belting his kid on the front porch for the whole street to see.

But I suppose the most disturbing question of all is this: If Big Dale is on the juice, is there a chance he's supplying his own son with the stuff? Is it a case of an unethical father giving his jock son an unfair edge on the competition? The thought makes me feel sick to my stomach, but it's out there now and I have to pursue it. And regardless of the outcome, one thing's for sure: I saw and heard enough last night to know that Big Dale Foster might be nothing more than another failed Blaine father, a species that runs rampant in this town.

So I make a mental note to tell Huey every piece of dirt I've learned about Big Dale. This so-called big-time cop has to go down, and I decide I'll do everything in my power to make sure it happens. At the same time, however, I decide I need to dig for more information about the steroid thing, which means poking around more into the lives of Dale *and* Tank. And if I can do all of this while still earning cash from Huey...well, that sounds like a sweet deal to me.

Looking at my cell, I suddenly remember punching in that phone number from the back of Big Dale's magazine: 729-8274.

Tiptoeing out of my bedroom, I enter the living room and find Justin snoring away on the sofa. Like me, he's wearing the same clothes from the night before. Passing him, the odors of stale beer and cigarettes gag me. I study him for a few moments and think back to what he said last night, that stupid comment about taking another year off. If he takes that route, he might as well stay drunk forever.

Anyway, he stinks so bad that I have to cover my mouth on the way to the kitchen, where I quickly use our landline to dial the mysterious number. On the second ring I glance at the microwave clock and realize it's barely seven o'clock, Saturday morning. I'm about to hang up, but somebody picks up after the third ring. My stomach feels like it's dropped a mile, and just as I'm ready to say something, I hear a female voice deliver the following recorded message: "Hello, you've reached Helen Dawkins. Unfortunately, I can't take your call right now. Please leave a message and I'll get back to you as soon as possible. Have a great day."

I hang up without saying a word, my heart thumping wildly against my ribs.

I know Helen Dawkins. She's Huey's wife. When Justin was a stock boy, he was always complaining about how mean she was to everybody when she came into the store. He said she was the only bad part about the job.

So, if this is the same Helen Dawkins, why does Tank's dad have her number written on the back cover of an adult magazine?

Man, no wonder Huey is so interested in Tank's dad.

9

Turns out Huey is more than happy to hire me, almost desperate. He needs a stock boy badly. In addition to Justin's recent departure, Brandon Watkins apparently found a better summer gig. He put in his two weeks' notice on the same day Tank stole the pint and cigarettes.

Huey puts me on the three-to-eleven shift, Monday through Saturday, and pays me five bucks an hour cash under the table, every cent of which goes to paying half the insurance deductibles on the damaged cars. After those are paid, Dad says the money is mine to do as I please with. Mom says otherwise and makes me open a savings account.

Anyway, Tank's dad agrees to pay the other half of the owners' deductibles, but he refuses to make Tank get a job, saying wrestling is his son's full-time occupation. However, he *does* decide to ground Tank, sentencing him to the basement and taking away his cell phone and laptop, meaning I'll have to come up with some creative tactics if I want to communicate with him during his home imprisonment.

Thanks to Brandon Watkins, I learn the job quickly. Huey places him in charge of training me, saying Brandon and my brother are the two best stock boys he's ever had, meaning I have some big shoes to fill or whatever. Brandon tells me to watch out for Huey, especially when he comes in drunk toward closing to check up on things. He says Huey's a happy drunk but sometimes flips out over little things, like small amounts of broken glass. But Brandon says as long as I keep the floor clean and the cooler stocked, there's little chance of the boss freaking.

First day on the job, Brandon takes me straight to the back room, a narrow, rectangular space where the nasty job of sorting and bagging returnable containers occurs. I notice a small bathroom immediately to the left, but the remainder of the back room is behind the massive walk-in cooler, making it impossible to see from the main floor. Seven waist-high wooden rectangular bins, each lined with a thick red garbage bag, span the back wall.

"These are the returnable bins," Brandon says. "Every hour or so, go out on the floor and check the two shopping carts for bottles and cans. They're usually full."

"Man, that's a lot of empties."

"Yeah, well, most states have a five-cent deposit law, but for some stupid reason I'll never figure out, the great state of Michigan offers a dime per empty, meaning most people around here make a point of returning their bottles and cans." He pauses. "And it also means plenty of extra dirty work for us." He looks toward the entrance. "Follow me. I'll show you what I mean."

We walk out to the middle of the store, where the two carts are overflowing with empties. Huey's behind the counter filling out a liquor order. He looks at us, grunts, and resumes his paperwork.

Gazing at the carts, I realize Huey's patrons prefer beer as their beverage of choice, because I don't see any soda containers in there. Some of the empties are stored in paper bags, others in garbage bags or their original cardboard cases. But most are crammed into the carts as loose singles, a collection of aluminum and glass of varying colors and designs that, when viewed as a whole, remind me of a jig-saw puzzle devoted to breweries around the globe.

"Wow," I say to Brandon. "It's like some abstract piece of art or something."

"Look underneath."

He rolls the carts back toward the cooler. A large pool of clear liquid has accumulated beneath the carts, the back-wash of who knows how many men, women, and children.

"Dude, that's just gross," I say.

"It's amazing how many people don't rinse out their empties. If I do one thing consistently for the rest of my life, it'll be to rinse out every can and bottle I ever return for a deposit." He scrunches his nose. "Can you smell it?"

"Sour beer?"

He nods. "You have to mop it up every time you take the carts back." He points toward the bathroom. "There's a mop and bucket in the john." He nods toward one of the carts. "They usually leak more as you roll them back, so be sure to mop the whole path, okay?" I nod. "I'll take the carts," he says. "Meet me at the bins when you finish mopping." He grabs the push-handle of the first cart and steers it toward the back room.

I'm heading back to grab the mop and bucket when Huey calls me over.

"I've been waiting to talk to you," I whisper. "I have some info."

Huey's eyes sparkle. He smiles and pulls the wad of cash from his front pocket. Laying a crisp fifty on the counter, he says, "Lay it on me, Ramsey. What do you know?"

I snag the money and quickly update him on Dale Foster's current physical appearance—the long straight hair, the mustache minus the handlebars, the larger-than-ever muscles—and his obvious high-ranking law enforcement status, as evidenced by his dealings with his ex-wife and the two cops from last night.

But all Huey does is shake his head in frustration. "I already know most of what you're telling me. Anything else? If not, hand back the fifty."

"I watched him hit Tank." I swallow hard, nervous. "It was a hard slap. The guy beats his kids, Huey."

"The girl, too?"

"Well, he didn't hit her, but I'm guessing if he hits his—"

"No," he says, shaking his head. "You can't assume that. But you saw him slap Tank, huh?"

"Hard, and right in front of his idiot cop buddies, too."

"Okay. That's something. I might be able to use that. What else?"

"Dale Foster likes *Michigan Cherries.*"

Squinting, Huey takes a hit on his cigarette. "So the guy likes fruit, big deal."

Realizing my error, I say, "No, no, no. I'm talking about the magazine. You know, *Michigan Cherries.*"

"Okay, so the guy's into the low-class stuff." He looks off to his left, eyeing his store's high-class adult magazine section. "Personally, I only offer the best, which explains why I don't carry *Michigan Cherries.*" He flicks ash onto the brown tiled floor. "Ramsey, do you have *anything* else?"

"Yeah. I found a phone number on the back of the magazine."

"What number?"

"I think it's your wife's number: 729-8274."

His eyes bulge like softballs.

My heart rate skyrockets. "And if he has your wife's phone number...well, I'm thinking maybe...you know..." I trail off, too embarrassed to speculate any further.

He doesn't say anything at first, but it's creepy how his face gets all red and this look of wild-animal-like rage fills his eyes. I take a few steps backward. He mutters something under his breath like "I can't believe she's..." but his words meander off into a series of mumbles.

"You okay, Huey?"

My voice must bring him back to reality, because he immediately clears his throat and takes a deep breath, during which his face resumes its normal color.

"Yeah, I'm fine. Thanks for the info. Nice job. Keep digging." He offers me another fifty.

"Gladly." I step forward and take the money, the easiest hundred bucks I've ever made. "Take this guy down, Huey. He's scum."

"Don't worry about it. Just keep doing your job." I nod and turn around. And then he goes, "Hey, Ramsey?" I stop and turn. He says, "I'm glad you're my new stock boy. The timing couldn't be better."

"Thanks, Huey."

Fetching the mop and bucket, I think about what Huey said under his breath ("I can't believe she's … "). And then I remember Tank saying he's pretty sure his dad is seeing somebody. So, of course, my theory that Dale Foster's new woman is Huey's wife seems to be on target, which means I can add dating another man's wife to my "Reasons Why Dale Foster Must Go Down" list.

I also realize what a beautiful situation I'm presently in. My new boss is paying me cash on the side to get information on a guy I need information on myself. From now on, as I dig for Huey I'll pursue my own interests as well, the most important of which is trying to figure out where Tank gets his juice from and whether Big Dale plays any role in that.

Something else is eating away at me as well. It involves my brother. Justin has always been mysterious and downright weird when it comes to why he quit playing football. All he ever says is that he had some personal issues with Coach Horton. Well, the top players on our team are huge dudes who are obviously popping more than multivitamins. So, knowing that Tank's juicing, is there any chance that steroids had something to do with why Justin ditched football, the only sport he loves? Justin was phenomenal on the playing field, but he was always one of the smallest guys out there, especially toward the end of his junior year. Did another player, or players (or adult/adults), try to get him to use the stuff? I mean, it's all just wild speculation, but I've always had this feeling that something other than a disagreement with Coach Horton figured into why he left the team.

Anyway, after cleaning up the sticky beer pond, I meet Brandon at the returnable bins.

Both shopping carts are still full.

He gestures toward the seven wooden bins. "This next part's easy. All you do is start picking out cans and tossing them into the correct bin. See the signs?"

There's a piece of cardboard taped to the wall behind each bin, listing the brands you can place inside. Brandon picks up two Budweiser cans from the top of a cart.

"Like these Bud cans," he continues. "They go in the first bin, along with all the other Anheuser-Busch stuff." He tosses them in and they clang lightly against others already inside. "You'll be a little slow at first, but you'll have them memorized after a few days. I can empty a full cart in less than five minutes." He says it with pride. "If you're not sure where one goes, just look at the signs."

"Cool."

"Look." He plucks out a case of empty Miller cans. "Some people are nice and clean about it, like the guy who brought these back. I bet he lives in Blaine Heights." He holds up the case. "If it's a full case, or you look in the bag and they're all the same kind, just dump them all in. Miller goes in the second bin." He turns the case upside down over the bin and shakes it. The cans spill out like candy from a busted piñata. "Break down all the cardboard and use the first empty cart for garbage. Put all the bags in there, too." He flattens the empty case and drops it on the floor.

"Seems easy enough."

"There's one little trick, though." Brandon reaches into the cart and digs around for a few seconds before pulling out a brown bottle and holding it up to my face. "What do you notice?"

"It's not empty. There's a half-inch of beer at the bottom."

"And?"

I look closer.

"Gross. There's a cigarette butt floating in there."

"There you go," he says. "People are slobs, man, especially the Blaine people. Blaine Heights folks are always neat and tidy about everything, even returnables. That's the only good thing about those rich bastards." He pauses. "One time I found a condom in a bottle."

"No way."

"Totally serious, dude."

"Was it used?"

"What, you think I pulled it out to check?"

"No, guess not," I say. "Do we have to rinse the dirty ones?"

"Nope. So the trick is to always keep the loose ones upright when you take them out. You minimize the mess that way." He steps away from the bins. "You finish this cart. I'll start on the other."

True to his claim, Brandon empties his cart in less than five minutes. It takes me nearly twenty to finish mine.

As I work, I notice a large metal door behind the bins that looks like it hasn't been used in years. Spider webs adorn every corner of it. The door is thick and reminds me of an entrance to an old bank vault.

"Why's that door blocked?" I ask.

"It's been that way since I've worked here." He pauses, staring at the door. "But I think I know why."

"Why?"

"It opens to the back alley, right next to the Dumpster where our trash goes. I mean, yeah, it'd make our lives a lot easier if we could use it. You know, just open it and roll the carts ten feet, empty them and bring them back."

"Exactly." As I finish my cart, I realize warm beer has

spilled down my arms and stained my T-shirt in several spots. "So why's it blocked if it's there to help us?"

"Think about it. I bet somebody got caught stealing through there. It'd be so easy. Just have your buddy pull up at a certain time and hand him a case of beer or two out the back door." He reaches for the knob and turns it. "I've never seen this thing open once."

"So how do we take out trash?"

"You have to roll it through the entire store and out the front door."

"That sucks."

"Yeah. All because some idiot stock boy got lazy when he was stealing."

After emptying the carts, Brandon notices that the red plastic bag from the Anheuser-Busch bin is full. He points toward the top of the beverage cooler, where a four-foot gap separates the top of the cooler from the ceiling. The gap surprises me. On the main floor side there's a lattice, which makes it look like the cooler reaches the ceiling, but now I realize there's plenty of storage space on top.

"Okay," he says. "When a bag is full, you have to pull it out of the bin, wrap a twist-tie around the neck, and toss it on top of the cooler. It stays there until the distributor comes in for his weekly delivery. It gets pretty crowded up there." He points at the top of the cooler. "Look."

I look up and see at least a dozen full bags pushed together. They look like massive red balloons full of aluminum and glass.

Brandon says, "That brings us to the dirtiest part of this job, something you pray Huey won't make you do more than once or twice a year."

"What is it?"

"The bags. Some of them are up there a whole week and leak all over the place, kind of like the carts." He scrunches his nose. "The top of that cooler gets to be like a Slip 'N Slide full of pop and beer, all slimy and sticky. After a few months, the whole store reeks. Usually Huey's too drunk to notice, but if enough customers complain, he makes you get up there and clean it with rags." He shakes his head. "When it comes time to do it, be sure to wear old jeans and a sweatshirt you don't mind getting rid of. Your clothes get so wet and gooey that you'll have to throw them out when you're done. Hope you have a strong stomach, too. Every time I'm up there I gag from the smell. You never get used to it."

"Thanks for the warning."

"No problem." Brandon looks around, shrugs. "Well, that's all the important stuff. Just keep the cooler stocked, the shelves full, and the floors clean. If you can do that, this job's a breeze." He looks around as if somebody's watching us. Then he whispers, "It has a lot of perks, too. Biggest thing you need to know is that Huey's too hammered to keep an inventory." He smiles. "The man has no clue what's in the store at any given moment." His freckles seem to brighten as he talks. "The guy doesn't keep track of *anything*, Zach. You can steal him blind and he'll never know. Even *with* the back door sealed."

"Really?"

"Really." His face looks like a big radish now. "I mean, not cash or anything. Stock boys never get to work the register, but you can basically take whatever else you want." He points to the rear-entry door of the monstrous beverage cooler. I haven't been inside yet, but the storage area of the cooler takes up three-quarters of the back room.

"That's a goldmine right there, Ramsey. It has all the beer you could ever want. That door's the only way in and out. Nobody out front ever sees what you're up to, but you can see out to the main floor through the glass doors the customers use. You'll know when the time is right to make a heist." He pauses. "There's food inside, too, beef sticks and lunchmeat. Find a few customers you can trust, and you can make a little side money selling them beer. Don't tell more than a few people, though. You'll probably get busted if you do."

There's a silence.

Then I say, "I can see taking a pack of cigarettes or two, or even a bottle of whiskey, but how do I steal a case of beer?"

"It's simple. After you empty the returnable carts for the last time, just before closing, you take a cold case from the cooler—has to be cans, bottles make too much noise—and put it in the cart. Cover it with all the empty bags and broken down cardboard and put it all in the Dumpster."

"What if Huey or a cashier checks the cart when I take it out?"

"If you hide it right, they won't."

"Has anyone ever been caught?"

"Not that I know of. It's foolproof."

"Man, how come Justin never told me about any of this?"

"That's just how it is here with the stock boys. You don't get the knowledge unless you're one of us. I didn't know any of this stuff until the guy who trained me filled me in. Plus, knowing Justin, he doesn't want you to drink as much as he does." He pauses. "Your brother can pound some serious beer, Zach."

"It's a talent that runs in the family."

Brandon laughs. "He ever say anything to you about why he quit playing football?"

"No. You?"

"No." He shakes his head. "God, he was so good. It's really too bad he dropped it."

"Tell me about it," I say. "All I know is that it had something to do with Horton."

"Horton?"

"Yeah. Ever hear any rumors about him?"

"No. He comes in here sometimes. So do a lot of the assistant coaches. They're all cocky bastards, big bodies with pea-sized brains. Do they act that stupid during practices and games?"

"Pretty much," I say, laughing. And here I decide to make a play to see if Brandon Watkins knows anything about the juice in Blaine, either back when Justin played or right now. "I'm always on the bench," I say. "I'd get more playing time if I could put on weight."

He sizes up my scrawny frame and nods. "You're skinnier than me. I didn't think that was humanly possible."

"I need to get bigger," I say. "This is my last season. Any idea where I can get some help?"

"Help with what?"

"Getting bigger."

Silence.

"What, you mean like steroids or something?"

"Maybe." I shrug. "There. You said the magic word. Do you know anything?"

"Zach, look at me. Do I look like I take steroids?"

"I didn't mean it like that."

"Dude, I know what you meant."

"Good," I say. "So who do I talk to?"

"Man, I don't know anything about that shit!" He squints and then rolls his eyes. "Ask somebody on your team. Horton's players were using when Justin and I went there, and I *know* it's still going on. Some of the players who come through here are monsters." He pauses, studies me. "What? Don't tell me you never knew. Come on. You're on the damn team, Zach."

"It's not that," I say, shaking my head. "I know certain guys use, but I've never known exactly who to approach to get my own."

"Maybe you should start with somebody who uses." He studies me again, a look of disapproval on his face. "Justin would kill you if he knew you were looking to buy. He's totally against that shit." He takes a deep breath. "Anyway, like I said, I have no idea who deals. Ask a juiced-up jock, not me."

"Right," I say, convinced he knows nothing more than what he just revealed.

Brandon looks back out onto the empty main floor. Huey's left without saying anything to us, and I have this weird vision of him marching over to Tank's to shoot Dale Foster. Anyway, I see this twenty-something woman sitting on the cashier's stool behind the front counter. She's reading a paperback and listening to Pink Floyd, a dead giveaway that she's a total Blaine girl. She's really into the book, too, not even looking up as she reaches for her cigarette from the ashtray beneath the counter.

"Who's she?"

"Brenda," Brandon says. "That's another thing. The cashiers make all the difference. They come and go like clouds, man. Always women, too. Your brother and me, I bet we've worked with thirty women the past four years."

"Why so many?" I watch her as she takes a big swig of Diet Coke, followed by a drag on her cigarette. She still hasn't looked up from her novel. She looks nice enough, kind of hot, too, in a rough, blue-collar sort of way. "Does Huey fire them all?"

"No. They all quit. I don't think he's ever fired one."

"Why do they quit?"

"Lots of reasons. These women, most of them have kids but no husbands. This is a temporary thing for them until they find something better, which they usually do." He pauses. "But sometimes Huey hits on them when he comes in drunk. I've seen him do it, and so has your brother. It's totally gross, dude. The girls, they usually slap him and quit on the spot. One thing about Huey, he likes the ladies."

"What about his wife?"

"Helen? She's the meanest bitch in the world. She hardly ever comes in, but when she does, stay out of her way. All Helen Dawkins knows how to do is complain. Huey keeps a picture of her below the register. Check her out sometime. She's hot, but she's a terror." He laughs. "Man, I don't blame Huey for trying to score with all the cashiers."

"Do the cashiers steal?"

"Some do, yeah. You have to get to know them at first, get a feel for their attitude. That's why I said they make all the difference. Like Brenda out there. She won't pay for that Diet Coke, and I know she takes cigarettes, but that's about it. She won't steal alcohol or anything. Little details like that, they tell you a lot. So Brenda steals Coke and cigarettes and doesn't try to hide it, which tells you she's cool with you doing the same thing." We move back behind the cooler, out of Brenda's sight. "But the best thing to do, Zach, to be safe, is to keep it all to yourself. Don't say anything to the cashiers about what you take, no matter how cool they seem." He looks around and nods. "Cover your tracks and you'll be fine. It's like an unwritten stock boy code. You're gonna love it here. I know I have."

"Then why are you quitting?"

"It's time for a change. A guy I go to State with got me a job with his uncle's landscaping firm in Okemos. I just found out a few days ago. We're sharing an apartment up there. I'll be out of Blaine for the summer and working outside near campus. Finally." He pauses. "Once you go away to college it's hard to come home and stay with your parents all summer." He shrugs. "Well, at least for me it is. You'll see. Besides, Huey's been on me for everything lately. I don't take it personally or anything. I think he's just pissed because your brother quit and he knows what a pain it is to break in new blood." He gives me a puzzled look. "Does Justin even know you're working here?"

"I doubt it. My dad just decided last night."

"Well, tell Justin I'm quitting too."

"Why does he need to know?"

"Don't worry about why. He'll explain."

Suddenly, I remember Victor Hodge mentioning Brandon's name as their beer supplier last night. I also recall Justin elbowing Victor right after he said it.

"I get it. You steal beer for him, right?"

"Correction," Brandon says. "I *used* to steal beer for him. That's your job now." He smiles. "Man, it's amazing how things just seem to work themselves out around here."

He pats me on the shoulder and leaves.

———

Later that night, I tell Justin about Brandon's departure and my new position.

All he does is shake his head and say, "Well, welcome to the club."

We shake hands.

And it feels good, shaking Justin's hand like that.

JULY

10

Two shift changes occur at the truck assembly plant during my eight-hour shift at Huey's, one at five o'clock, the other at ten. These, along with the noon change that Huey handles on his own, constitute the bulk of his business.

I spend the first two hours of every shift with Huey, from three to five. He's usually drunk when I arrive, and it's a rare sight to see the man without a beer and a cigarette. I never see him pay for anything, either. Basically, he totally drinks and inhales his profits, and I find it amazing he's stayed in business all these years.

My job during these two hours is to sort empties and stock the cooler and grocery shelves for the five o'clock rush. I repeat this process in the evening to get ready for the ten o'clock invasion, spending the time between rushes and after the last rush doing the occasional garbage run, floor sweeping, and stocking of whatever.

After one week I'm able to complete the pre-rush stocking in less than twenty minutes, and I learn that only one thorough floor cleaning is necessary, a damp mop ten minutes before closing. So, by the end of my second week, I'm doing physical labor for no more than two hours per shift, which allows six hours of down time to do whatever I want. Which eventually leads to a lot of smoking, drinking, and stealing.

And Brandon Watkins was right about making some good side money selling beer. I know he said I shouldn't tell more than a few people, but I decide to go all Donald Trump and broaden the enterprise, coming up with this cool business idea that goes like this: between Tank's wrestling buddies, my football peers, and all the other guys in the neighborhood, I'm thinking I can eventually clear at least an extra fifty to hundred bucks a week.

I even have a name for the company: The Bootleggers of Blaine.

I do some practice runs during my first week, sneaking one case of beer out at a time. I follow Brandon's exact directions, burying the case deep within the trash-filled cart at the end of the shift and rolling it through the store like it's no big deal. I'm nervous as hell the first time or two, breaking the law right under Brenda's nose, but once I'm out that door and moving across the pot-hole-filled asphalt lot toward the Dumpster near the back alley ... well, I know I'm home free. From that point forward it's a breeze. I just toss the case into the Dumpster as if it's a normal piece of trash.

So when I have four cases sitting in there after four days, I know it's time to get some customers, because the truck that empties the Dumpster comes by once a week, and the last thing I need is for my supply to disappear.

Getting customers is so easy it makes me laugh.

One day I'm outside sweeping the lot when I see Tony Banks and Mike Foreman, two relatively cool guys I played middle school football with, sharing a cigarette in the back alley. (They quit playing sports after eighth grade, grew their hair out, started listening to metal, and quickly became legendary weedheads.)

I stop sweeping and walk up to them.

They nod and say, "What's up, Zach?"

And I say, "Not much. Can I hit that?"

And they laugh and go, "Yeah, it's cool, bro."

So I hit the smoke and say, "You guys drink beer?"

And Tony Banks looks at me and goes, "Who doesn't?"

And Foreman says, "Problem is it's impossible to get a buyer around here."

So I say, "Ten dollars a case. Interested?"

"Hell, yes," Banks says. "When and where?"

"Payment in advance. Always."

They look at each other for a few seconds and shrug. Then Mike Foreman teases a ten out of his pocket and hands it to me. Not wanting to reveal the true location of the product, I tell them to look *behind* the Dumpster at eleven-thirty.

"Cool, Ramsey," Foreman says. "Thanks, man."

"No problem," I say. "Feel free to spread the word."

We shake hands and I walk away.

When I look over my shoulder they're already texting people.

Two days later I'm forty bucks richer and have a growing client list. I even got a call from Victor Hodge, Mr. Fastball himself, requesting a case every Thursday night during the summer.

———

I get along well with Brenda the cashier. We become good friends, and despite the fact that I'm stealing the place blind right under her nose, I begin thinking of her as the big sister I never had. In between rushes we talk about everything: music, TV, movies, men, women, partying…you name it. She's cool because she always wears the same tight, faded denim Levis and a white tank top that shows off her monumental breasts. At first I'm convinced they're fake, but then I realize there's no way she could afford the surgery…well, unless she totally charged it or whatever.

Anyway, she's twenty-eight and divorced, raising two little daughters on her own. She seems to have gotten over the bitterness of the split, because she's always laughing and saying how stupid she was to have married so young.

One day she advises me never to marry my first love, especially if that person happens to be my high school sweetheart. I don't question her about it at the time, but it keeps bugging me, because despite the efforts I've made to forget about how hot I am for Tank's sister, Sarah Foster keeps popping into my head and dreams as if she's on a programmed loop, a never-ending rerun in the Zach Ramsey world. I soon become convinced that I'll marry her someday.

"That thing you mentioned last week about not marrying your first love," I say. "What if I told you I planned on doing just that?"

She's sitting on the stool behind the register, reading one of her romance paperbacks and smoking a cigarette. Brenda's a chain smoker. She closes her book, looks at me. She has this dark and totally feathered hair that makes me think of eight-track tapes and the Eagles and the 1970s and all that.

"Sounds like somebody's in love," she says in a raspy voice. "Hold old are you, anyway, Zach?"

"Seventeen."

"That's about what I thought. That's how old I was when I met Ron." She reaches down and turns off the classic rock. The store falls silent save the constant hum of the beverage cooler. She lays an open pack of Marlboro Lights on the counter. "Do you smoke?"

I don't say anything. Despite our many conversations and budding friendship, this is the first time she's actually offered me a cigarette. Actually, it's the first time *any* adult has offered me a cigarette.

"Reason I ask is because I started when I was seventeen," she adds. "But it's cool if you don't. I mean, you play football, so of course you don't." She laughs. "It was a stupid question."

She's reaching for the pack when I grab it and slide out a cigarette. "Yeah, I smoke. Started when I was twelve." I pop the Marlboro between my lips. "Got a light?"

"Started when you were twelve, huh?" She strikes a match and holds it up for me. "So who's the lucky girl?"

"Her name's Sarah. Sarah Foster."

"How long have you been together?"

"Uh ... I guess technically we're not."

"What's that supposed to mean?"

"It means ... I guess it just means we're not together right now."

"You broke up?"

"No."

"Zach, I'm confused."

"Okay, it's like this: I've loved her for a couple of weeks now, but I've known her for years."

"Does she love you?"

"Yeah. I'm totally certain of that."

"She's told you?"

"No, more like a look I got one night, when she was eating fried chicken with her dad."

"And this look," Brenda says, lighting a new cigarette off her previous one, "this fried-chicken gaze she gave you. That's all the evidence you have that she loves you?"

"It's there, Brenda. You know it when you see it."

"How often do you talk with her?"

"Well, we haven't said a word to each other since that night."

"Oh my God," she says and explodes into laughter.

"Hey, don't make fun of me." But I'm smiling when I say it, because I realize how completely insane this whole thing sounds, but at the same time it feels good to finally speak with somebody about it, especially a woman.

"I'm not making fun of you," she says, catching her breath. "Sorry." She pauses. "Okay, so what I'm wondering is why you haven't said anything to her. I mean, if you're gonna marry this girl, it'd be nice if you told her about it."

"I can't talk to her."

"What, she doesn't have a cell phone?"

"I don't know. It doesn't matter. I can't talk to her right now."

"Why not?"

I tell her about Tank, leaving out the steroid suspicion. Afterwards, she's silent for a few moments.

"Okay," she finally says. "Now it makes sense. You're in love with your best friend's twin sister, but your best friend is a nutcase who'll kill you if you make a move on her."

"Exactly."

"And the reason he'll kill you is because this girl's a female Einstein, and he doesn't want her to have any boyfriends until she's at least in college."

"There," I say, raising my hands in the air. "That's all of it." I lower my hands. "Well, almost all of it."

"What else?"

"The dad's a psycho cop and I think he beats them. Well, I *know* he beats Tank, anyway."

"Then that explains Tank's behavior."

"You mean the 'like father like son' kind of thing?"

"Yup."

"So, what do you think?" I ask. "You're the first person I've told."

Silence.

"Zach, I think you're screwed."

"Screwed?"

"Screwed."

"Why screwed?"

"Because," she says, "if you're too afraid to talk to her, then nothing's ever going to happen. Make your move or move on."

"Damn. You're tough, Brenda."

"I've learned to be blunt. Your dilemma comes down to this: if you're too afraid of getting killed by this Tank guy, then you don't deserve his sister. First thing you need to do is let her know how you feel."

"And don't say anything to Tank?"

"Not yet," she says, hopping off the stool and coming out from behind the counter.

I glance at a Budweiser clock on the wall above the front windows. The ten o'clock rush is ten minutes away.

"Why not?"

"Because if she turns you down, there's no reason Tank needs to know about any of it." She heads toward the restroom. "That'll save you from getting slaughtered."

"Yeah, but she *won't* turn me down. Like I said, she gave me a look, *the* look."

Brenda laughs again. "If that's the case, then you go to the next step," she says from the back of the store. "Which involves breaking the news to Tank." She enters the restroom and closes the door.

I look around the store. The coolers are full, the shelves stocked. Then I look at the cigarette compartments behind the register, also fully stocked. Above the cigarettes, liquor bottles line the aluminum shelves like disciplined soldiers awaiting orders. We're totally ready for the rush.

I notice Brenda has left her smokes lying on the counter, and I think about what Brandon said about Brenda stealing her cigarettes and Diet Coke. He was right. I've yet to see Brenda pay for anything.

I take the last puff of my cigarette and realize the ashtray is behind the counter, so I hop over, kneel down, and stub out the butt. I'm about to stand, but then I see Brenda's large black purse tucked in the back corner of the bottom shelf, just behind the extra paper bags.

I peer over the top of the counter. She's still in the bathroom, so I pull her purse toward me and open it. Three unopened packs of cigarettes lie inside.

Yeah, she definitely steals.

I also see Huey's framed picture of his wife, Helen, a few feet to the left of the paper bags. Staring at it, I realize Brandon was right. Helen Dawkins is incredibly hot for a woman her age. But what Brandon failed to say was that she's wearing a yellow bikini in the picture! If I'd known that I would've checked it out weeks ago. Anyway, she's lying on her side on a white sandy beach, leaning on her elbow and smiling at the camera. She's super tan and has one of those big teased-out heads of long blonde hair. As for her body, well, she's not *Maxim* material or anything, but you can tell she keeps in shape.

If this is Big Dale Foster's girlfriend, the man has chosen well.

Looking away from the picture, I reach behind me and shove two packs of Marlboro Reds and a pint of Jack Daniels down the front of my pants. Then I turn to replace Brenda's purse, but when I push it toward the back of the shelf, I feel something hard and heavy at the bottom. Originally, I'd pulled the purse out by its straps, missing the solid mystery object.

The toilet flushes.

Curious, I take one last look inside the purse and move the cigarettes and her cell phone off to the side.

A handgun lies at the bottom of her bag, a black one with a rubber grip.

The bathroom door opens.

Frantic, I move the cigarettes back over the gun, close the purse, and shove it back into the corner.

"Zach, where are you?"

Her brisk footsteps grow louder, closer.

"Right here," I say and stand, my heart thumping. "I was just putting out my cigarette."

Looking over my shoulder and out the window, she says, "Well, get back out *here*, because here they come."

Turning to look, I see the slaves in blue exiting the mechanical dungeon and heading toward us, more than ready to further blacken their lungs and poison their livers.

––––––––––

Something weird happens in the middle of the rush, something that makes me forget about Brenda's gun. I'm in the back of the noisy store, keeping an eye on the dwindling beer selection, eavesdropping on as many conversations as possible, when I overhear two guys with beards and beer guts talking about Blaine Memorial football, a popular topic in this city. I don't know them personally, but they obviously know my parents from the plant because they always refer to me as "Bill and Karen's youngest," a nickname I could do without.

Their ID tags inform me that their names are Tom Stevens and Jeff Kingston. They both wear wedding rings, but I don't recognize the last names from anybody I go to school with, so I figure if they do have kids they must be middle school age or younger.

Anyway, this store is a flurry of activity and noise during rushes. The workers come in loud and happy, ready to head home or to the bars or wherever. My point is that working the rushes has made me an excellent listener, meaning I can hear pretty much anything from anywhere in the store, regardless of how many other conversations are going on. That's important, because Mr. Stevens and Mr. Kingston know I play football, and right now they obviously think the fact that they're three aisles away means I can't hear them.

"Hank says this year's team will be his strongest yet," Tom Stevens says. "Says the average weight of his offensive linemen is 260 pounds. That ain't bad for high school. It's amazing what he's done with that weightlifting program."

"That weightlifting program hasn't changed since I played for him," Jeff Kingston says. "Don't play dumb, Tom. Everybody knows what's going on."

"Whatever," Tom says. "The way I see it, those kids are just staying competitive."

"The coaches are involved."

"That's crap," Tom says. "Who told you that?"

"I hear things," Jeff says. "It's something I heard."

"It's just talk," Tom says. "That's all it is, meaningless talk."

They change topics after that, switching to their "asshole boss," but I've heard enough to know that I need to pursue the lead, because if what Jeff Kingston is saying is true, that football coaches actually supply the juice, then maybe I'm wrong about Big Dale giving his own son D-Bol. And my theory about Justin's departure from the team having something to do with steroids just gained some strength.

But don't get me wrong. None of this would change my opinion about Big Dale. Let's face it—the guy's a child-abusing, wife-stealing prick. But the fact remains that lately my best friend is showing some bizarre behavior and I think it has a lot to do with the workout junk he's putting in his body.

And whoever is supplying it needs to go down. Hard.

———

A few nights later, a Thursday, it's closing time and I'm rolling the beer-laden garbage cart across the empty parking lot, approaching the Dumpster, when I notice a car parked in the narrow alley behind the store, right in front of Huey's sealed back door. I see a figure in the driver's seat but it's too dark to see a face, so I play it cool and start emptying the trash, being careful to avoid the case of beer hidden at the bottom of the cart.

Seconds later I hear the car door open and close softly behind me. Looking over my shoulder, I spot Victor Hodge walking slowly toward me. He stops at the end of the alley. I'm relieved and pissed at the same time—relieved it's Victor as scheduled, pissed that he's breaking the established eleven-thirty pickup rule.

"What're you doing here?" I say. The night air is humid and thick, the parking lot silent save a few chirping crickets and the sounds of passing cars out on Michigan Avenue.

"Sorry," Victor says. "I'm heading to Ann Arbor to party with some teammates. I need to make an early pickup."

"Why didn't you text me or call? I can't just hand it to you right now."

"I know that." He shrugs. "But I knew you'd be out

here and your brother said it was cool. I'll just wait a few minutes after you go back in. Then I'll grab it and go."

"Whatever," I say, frustrated. "Don't make this a habit, and make sure Brenda doesn't see you."

"It's cool," he says, making a point of staying concealed in the dark alley. Anybody watching me right now would think I was some nut talking to himself.

Looking around, there isn't a soul in sight, so I lift the case of Bud out of the cart and slide it behind the Dumpster, keeping my back to Michigan Avenue the entire time. Then, knowing that Victor is a big-time college athlete and former Blaine Memorial superstar, I decide to take a risk and join him in the alley, leaving the empty cart on the side of the Dumpster.

"What are you doing?" he asks, giving me a look. "I already paid you."

"It's not that. I have to ask you something."

"Make it quick." He's tall and lean, all six feet whatever of him towering over me.

"Don't say anything to my brother, but what if I wanted some D-Bol?"

He stares at me for a few moments, sizing me up in much the same way he did with Tank that night in the school field.

Then he says, "I'd say somebody your size could use some D-Bol."

"Okay, so where do I get it?"

"It's not that easy."

"Can you hook me up?"

"Me?" he says. "Hey, I've always been able to throw a baseball fast and accurate. I've never needed chemical assistance."

"Victor, I'm not the Commissioner of Major League Baseball. I don't care what you put or don't put in your body. All I'm asking for here is a little direction." I pause. "Most of us don't have gifts like yours, so how do I get some D-Bol?"

There's a silence, deep thinking going on behind Victor's eyes.

"What I mean by it not being easy is that only certain people get it." He pauses. "And you're not one of them. Your best bet is to ask your wrestling buddy. He's one of them."

"How do you know?"

He rolls his eyes. "Dude, you can't be serious. All you have to do is look at him."

"But what if I was willing to pay big money for my own?"

"Zach, you don't understand. What I'm saying is that you can't buy it." He shakes his head. "Well, I suppose you could if you found the right source, but from my experience at Blaine Memorial, stuff like that isn't bought and sold." He pauses and looks around as if he's unsure of whether to say anything else. But he does. "It's provided to the guys who show the most potential," he almost whispers. "Guys like Tank Foster."

"And guys like you."

He shrugs. "Like I said, I've never needed it."

"But the offers have been there."

He nods, barely. "The offer was *always* there. Probably still is."

"Especially during baseball season, right?"

"Yeah, what a surprise, huh?" He raises his eyebrows.

"Is it a coach?"

Silence.

Then: "You're on your own, Ramsey." He takes a deep breath. "I'm done here. Go inside so I can get the beer I already paid for."

"What about Justin?" I ask. "Did he get offers?"

"You're on your *own*, Zach," Victor says again, this time with authority. He gives me a hard look that makes it clear he's serious.

I turn and go back to the empty cart. The rusty wheels squeak and moan as they roll across the cracked asphalt.

11

You can only stay away from your best friend for so long, especially when you totally want his twin sister, you're spying on his dad for cash, and you're seriously trying to bust whoever is giving him illegal drugs.

Don't get me wrong, I've been trying to contact him—I knocked on Tank's basement window a few times at night, but he never answered, probably had music blaring through his earbuds and couldn't hear me. I even sent a few texts and emails, but since his dad confiscated his technology I knew I wouldn't receive a single reply.

All of this, of course, means I really want to see Tank. What does a guy do when he's alone and grounded in the basement during the height of summer, anyway? Knowing Tank, he probably works out all day and watches Ultimate Fighting Championship DVDs.

Knowing Big Dale's off doing the undercover thing or

whatever this morning, I wake up extra early to avoid having to deal with my dad. In the bathroom, I'm about to jump in the shower when I realize I might run into Sarah this morning as well.

Which leads me to a confession: I've decided to save myself for Sarah Foster. There. I said it. I can't believe it, but I said it. I'm saving myself for Sarah.

That's my new slogan.

And if she tells me she's ready now, well, hey, that'd be wonderful. However, if she wants to wait until our wedding night, which, knowing my luck, is exactly how this thing will play out, then I guess that's fine, too.

Thinking about all of this makes me think about condoms. That's the one item I haven't been able to steal from Huey's. They're in the store, off to the side across from the orange lottery machine, and, strangely enough, right beside the adult magazine rack, but I just haven't felt the need to take any yet. Now, however, standing here in the humid bathroom and dreaming about Sarah, I realize I need to carry protection with me at all times.

So I take a good look at my body, which is nothing but skin and bones.

Man, Victor was right, I probably could use some D-Bol.

Anyway, what about my butt? Girls like guys with nice butts, right? Does Sarah like my butt? Has she even bothered to check?

I turn and look over my shoulder into the mirror.

Yeah, my butt sure looks good to me. A little flat and bony maybe, but it's still a fine male butt. I shake my hips back and forth. The flesh on my butt cheeks barely jiggles. I bend over and grab my knees, sticking my butt out as far as possible. How could a girl *not* like my butt? It's beautiful! The symmetry, it's perfect—nice and balanced, like two bowling balls resting beside each other.

Satisfied with my rear, I turn to survey my front, lanky but sexy ... I think.

I trace the curved outline of my ribs with my index finger. Then I raise my arms and flex my biceps. Man, screw the D-Bol, because I actually look fairly good in this pose. I start swiveling my hips like the male strippers do on the trashy morning talk shows. Fully into the fantasy now, I picture Sarah in the front row. Moving my hips faster, I smile at myself in the mirror and ...

... I hear a sound outside the bathroom door.

Damn. Back to reality. The door handle is turning.

Justin busts in and falls over laughing.

"Jesus, Justin, you heard of knocking?" I reach for a towel and wrap it around my waist.

"Where were you just now, a strip club?"

"Screw you. Get out of here so I can shower."

He stands there looking at my waist, then starts laughing again. "Be careful or you might bust through."

"Get out," I yell, cupping my hands over my midsection and turning to the side. "Mom!"

"Easy, big guy. They're not home."

"So get out."

"Listen," he says. "You're working tonight, right?"

"Yeah."

"I need a case. Bud cans."

"Ten dollars."

He cocks his head to one side and squints. "I haven't paid for a beer in my life."

"Guess you start now. Think of it as stimulating the economy."

"You suck."

"No, I'm a businessman," I say. "Now get out."

He stares at the towel. "So what's her name?"

"What? Who?"

"Whoever you're thinking about."

"Very funny."

"All right," he says. "I'll leave you in peace, but can I give you some advice?"

I roll my eyes. "Hurry, please."

"Tank's a loose cannon sometimes, isn't he?"

"That's hardly breaking news."

"But lately he's worse, especially when he drinks. Am I right?"

"What's it to you? You drink too much, anyway."

"Whatever." He studies me for a few moments. "I have a feeling throwing rocks at cars is just the beginning for him. But you, you've never gotten into much trouble before." He shrugs. "What I'm saying is, be careful who you hang out with."

"You sound like Dad."

"No, there's a difference. I know what it's like out there. Dad doesn't. I didn't learn much in high school, but I learned who my real friends were." He closes the door so that just a sliver of his face shows. "Remember that. During senior year, you'll learn who your real friends are."

"Yeah," I say. "And if *you* take another year off before starting college, you're about to learn what it's like to live in this hellhole your whole life."

He opens the door wide. "Zach, why are you so obsessed with my future?"

"Because there is no future in Blaine, Justin! Jesus, I don't know...I mean, I guess part of me is still pissed about you quitting football. That was your BEP, man. You had the ultimate Captain Rick, and it's like you just pissed it away without thinking. I look at a guy like Victor Hodge and realize he has it made. You had that same thing..." And here I pause. "But you totally screwed it up and won't talk about it."

True to form, he simply walks out and closes the door.

"Yeah, keep it inside," I yell. "That's real healthy, Justin." Silence. "You're a loser, you know it?"

Then, suddenly, the door swings open and slams the wall so hard that the whole house seems to shake. My brother's face is redder than blood, and I quickly regret making that last comment. It's been a while since our last brotherly fistfight, but I have a feeling we're moments away from ending the drought, and I'm pretty sure I'll catch the worst of this one. That's how pissed he is right now.

But instead, he stands there in the doorway, points at me, and let's some long overdue words fly.

"Listen, you little smartass piece of shit, you really want to know what happened with Coach Horton?"

"Yeah, I do, Justin. The guy's my football coach."

"Okay," he says, barely lowering his voice. "Horton blocked any chance of me getting a scholarship. I don't know what he said to recruiters, but he smeared me to the point where nobody was interested."

Silence.

"Why?" I say. "I mean, I know you guys never got along, but was it really that bad?"

"Blaine Memorial is a dirty school, Zach. And deep down you know that." Justin pauses. "Horton runs a dirty program, and I refused to get dirty." He shrugs. "I refused to get dirty several times. He let me play because I'm good, but in the end he screwed me. After community college I might walk on at Eastern," he adds, looking up from the floor. "But I don't know. That's at least two years away. I love the game, but I play by the rules. These people, Zach, people like Horton and his staff, they've gotten too damn competitive. I played football because it was fun, but those guys sucked the fun right out of it. Winning is like life or death for them."

"So Horton wanted you to cheat, but you said no."

"I said no over and over and over again."

There's another silence during which we stare at each other. I know exactly what he's talking about, of course, but I'd rather play dumb and hear it from him.

And he finally says it. "Steroids, Zach."

I swallow hard, heart racing.

"I know they're out there," I say. "And I've learned things about some coaches, but Horton?"

"He's the kingpin." Justin pauses again. "Horton only deals with the best athletes. Doesn't matter what sport."

"That's why you warned me about Tank being a loose cannon, right?"

"I'm guessing Tank Foster has put on at least twenty pounds of pure muscle since Christmas. How the hell does somebody do that?"

"Yeah," I say. "So why not go to the cops and nark on Horton?"

"With what proof?" Justin gives me a look. "Anyway, it's over. I'm done with that place." He points at me. "But you have one season left, so I guess that's another reason I'm telling you all this. Beware of Hank Horton. He's a sneaky, unethical son of a bitch."

I nod. But there's something more on Justin's mind. I can tell. "What else?" I say.

He studies me for what seems like an hour. "We're brothers, Zach. What I'm about to tell you stays between us. As brothers, okay? Dad doesn't even know, so don't breathe a word of it or I'll tear you apart, got it?"

"Okay," I say, unable to recall a time where he's looked and sounded more serious than now. "Swear to God, man. Just tell me."

"Blocking the scholarship isn't what made me walk.

What made me walk was when I caught Horton hitting on Mom."

"What?" My jaw nearly drops to my knees. "When?"

"It was during one of the summer work days, when the parents and players clean up the field and paint the goal posts. Somehow he managed to get her alone in the storage room beneath the stands...well, alone until I walked in to put away some paint cans and saw them. I'm just standing there, figuring he can see me, but he obviously didn't, because the next thing I know he's pulling her toward him and has his hands all over her. I swear if I'd had a gun I would've shot him right in his fat gut."

"Don't even tell me Mom gave in to him."

"Oh, no," he says with a smile. "She kneed him in the balls and ran out of there. That's when she saw me." He shakes his head and looks down. "God, Horton was on the ground in total pain, and I so wanted to at least get one kick in, but I knew I had to catch Mom, which is exactly what I did." He pauses. "We drove around for a while until she got it all out, then she made me promise never to tell Dad. I quit the next day. That surprised Mom, me quitting, because we never talked about me doing that. But she never asked me about it, either."

He's about to leave the bathroom when I say, "One thing I don't get. Why does Mom want me to play for that idiot after what he did to her?"

"That part's easy, Zach. She's trying to save her marriage."

"You mean it's that bad?" A sour, pit-like feeling spreads through my stomach.

Justin nods. "She can't take much more of Dad. All he does is sit around and drink and smoke. Start looking at things, like the fact that Mom barely smokes or drinks anymore." He shakes his head. "I never thought I'd say this, but I'm starting to think she deserves better than him."

"Think they'll split up?"

"I don't know, but prepare yourself, because if they do it'll be ugly." He turns and exits, saying over his shoulder, "And don't forget my beer tonight. I'll be at the Dumpster at eleven thirty."

"Wait. Justin?"

He sticks his head back inside. "What's up?"

"Knowing what I do now, I can't blame you for quitting. But don't get stuck here."

He forces a smile. "I'll do my best."

But the way he looks off to his right when he says it makes me doubt him.

Regardless, one thing I know is this. Hank Horton, my football coach, destroyed my brother's athletic future, made a move on my mom (which is just totally gross), and, if Justin has it correct, is the steroid kingpin of Blaine Memorial High School.

Which means Hank Horton is one king who needs dethroning.

12

After showering, I shove a pint and a pack of smokes down my pants and walk to Tank's, where I knock on the front door three times. Nobody answers, so I peek through the glass triangle into the kitchen. The room is empty but the lights are on. The remains of a big McDonald's breakfast lie strewn about the counter and table.

Walking around to the side of the house, I drop to my hands and knees in the dewy morning grass and look through the rectangular basement window overlooking Tank's lair. The basement is dark. Where the hell could Tank be so early?

I cross the lawn for a look up the driveway. As usual, Big Dale's blue pickup is nowhere in sight and the garage door is closed. The Foster estate is deserted.

Standing there at the foot of the driveway, the whole street seems lifeless, nothing but the endless droning of the assembly plant and its smokestacks in the distance. The sight of all the dirty bungalows, parched lawns, sagging maple trees, and general inactivity depresses me.

Where *is* everybody?

I'm about to take a lonely trip to the asphalt path to smoke a cigarette when I hear a girl's laughter coming from behind Tank's house. As I walk up the driveway, the laughter grows louder and my heart starts to dance. I stop at the chain-link gate that opens to the backyard and listen.

The laughter continues, innocent giggles followed by muffled conversation followed by more giggles. A smile crosses my face. Although I can't see her, I know Sarah's back there. I've memorized her voice as if it were a favorite song.

She's talking on the phone. When she says bye and the street resumes its silence, my thoughts immediately turn to Brenda and her worldly advice. This is my moment, my chance to spill it all to Sarah. I have no idea *how* to say it and my heart's thumping wildly at the thought of telling her, but it's here if I want it and I know I have to act quickly because Tank, or Big Dale, or both, could come home at any moment.

And the problem of choosing the right words is only compounded when the goddess herself emerges from the backyard wearing a two-piece bathing suit. She looks totally hot. The silky orange fabric of the suit shines like a Lake Michigan sunset. Her dark skin glistens with tanning oil, and her damp black hair is combed straight back over her head. She's wearing sunglasses and flip-flops. It takes everything in my power not to stare at her chest.

She sees me, and, somewhat startled and self-conscious, steps back behind the house, emerging a few seconds later wearing a white T-shirt and a beach towel wrapped around her waist. Damn. Anyway, she waves as she walks down the driveway.

My throat goes dry and I mumble something like, "From girl to woman in a single day."

"What?" She cocks her head as she draws closer.

"I said it's a beautiful day."

"I thought you were Tank or my dad."

She stops about three feet from the gate and slides her sunglasses atop her head. In the sunlight, her ivy-green eyes have a reflective quality that reminds me of stained glass.

"Where is he?" I ask.

"At a wrestling clinic. My dad took him. They'll be home any minute."

Awkward silence.

"Mind if I wait on the porch?"

"No." Pause. "I heard about what you guys did that night."

"Yeah, it was stupid. Won't happen again."

"I know it won't with Tank. My dad made sure of that."

"What do you mean?"

"You'll see."

She seems shy and distant now, looking off to the side, probably wondering what to say next. It occurs to me that she might be unsure of how to act around me. After all, until recently all I've ever done is pick on her.

"So," she finally says. "You ready for senior year?"

"Guess so. You?"

"I can't believe it's finally here." Pause. "Tank's worried about guys asking me out."

"Then maybe Tank should ask you to prom."

That makes her laugh, but I still sense an overwhelming nervousness about her. Then again, I detect it in myself as well.

"Look," I add. "He's your brother. He's proud of you and only wants the best for you."

"Oh my God, listen to how you put it," she says, rolling her eyes. "You know what he told me?"

"No, what?"

"He said he'll tear the lungs out of the first guy who asks me out."

"Come on," I say, picturing Tank reaching down my throat. "He just says those things because he cares about you."

"He has a funny way of showing it. I think he's serious when he says that stuff. He has anger issues, especially with my dad. You know that, right?"

"He's my best friend. Of course I know."

There's a long silence.

"At least he doesn't pick on me anymore. He hasn't done that since I got my braces off and everything."

"Sarah, you look great with contacts."

Jesus, where did *that* come from?

I think it takes a few seconds to register with her, too, because she just stares at me with this funny little smile that barely shows her teeth.

"Yeah," she finally says, embarrassed. "I have contacts."

My heart feels like it's out there dangling on a stick. I'm so nervous and have no idea what to say.

Awkward. Awkward. Awkward.

Sarah takes a deep breath and goes, "Well, I'll be in the backyard."

"And I'll be on the porch."

She turns and walks away.

"Hey, Sarah?"

She stops, turns. "Yeah?"

"You … you look really nice. And I just want to apologize for all the mean stuff I've ever done to you."

"I can't believe you think it's that easy." She rakes a hand through her hair. "You know what I'm thinking right now?"

"No, what?"

"I'm thinking we've known each other a long time, but this is the first time we've ever really talked like normal people."

"If that's the case, then I like talking to you, Sarah. And all the changes, with the hair and the braces and the contacts, they're nice changes, but the thing that makes them even nicer is you. You know, your personality."

She smiles, but I can tell she still feels awkward, probably trying to figure out what it means to have this new identity. It occurs to me that I might be the first guy to ever hit on her.

"Like I said, they'll be home any minute." She disappears behind the house.

I turn and walk toward the front porch, but halfway there I decide I'm crazy to just let it end like that. I mean, she's totally *alone* back there. Hello? It's now or never.

I turn, open the gate, and walk up the driveway.

"Sarah?"

She pops back out, still wearing the T-shirt and towel. "Yeah?"

"Can I tell you something?"

"I think you've said a little too much already."

"Just listen, okay?" She nods. Barely three feet separate us. "Sarah, my stomach does weird stuff whenever I think about you. That's never happened to me before."

"Zach, stop. You can't just … God, I can't believe this is happening. You're vicious to me for years, and now you think I'll just … " She trails off and stares at the ground.

"Okay, I get it," I say. "Fair enough. You're exactly right. But I'm not picking on you right now. I just want to ask you a question, and I need an honest answer."

She looks at me and nods. Barely.

"Okay," I say, heart pounding. "You obviously know how I feel about you." I force myself to take a deep breath. "So I just need to know if … Sarah … damn, this is hard … but … do you feel that way about me?"

She doesn't answer, just stares at me with those beautiful eyes that seem to melt something inside of me. It's as if she's frozen. I'm convinced this is the first time a guy has confessed his feelings for her, and the fact that it's me, Zach Ramsey, her psycho brother's longtime best friend...well, I'm surprised she hasn't passed out right in front of me.

After a few silent seconds that feel like hours, I decide to do something that will definitely give me an answer.

I reach for her hand and squeeze.

At first there's no response, just Sarah's soft hand resting in my own. But when I squeeze a little harder, she squeezes back. I feel a smile cross my face. I detect a hint of a smile on hers as well, but there's worry, confusion, and doubt there, too, which is totally understandable given the situation and our history. I promise myself that I will not screw this up. Sarah Foster is the last person I want to hurt.

"Sarah, have you ever—"

"No," she interrupts.

"Wait," I say. "How...how do you even know what—"

"I just know," she interrupts again. "Zach, this is all new for me."

"Me, too," I say. "Me, too."

I let go of her hand and place my right palm on the back of her head. There's an awkward moment as our faces come closer and we try to figure out when to close our eyes and how to tilt our heads, but I suppose such issues are standard when it comes to people experiencing their first kiss together.

We exchange quick smiles as our heads fall naturally to the right, and we each close our eyes at the last possible moment before our mouths touch. The feel of her soft lips pressing against mine seems to tickle every cell in my body.

And from that point forward human instinct takes over. Sarah's arms wrap around my shoulders and pull me closer. I bring my free hand up to the right side of her face and slide my other hand around to her left cheek. Soon afterward our mouths open. And although some couples' first kisses might be less than perfect, this one is fantastic and deserves a trophy. To me, it's like seeing Mt. Everest, the Grand Canyon, the Great Wall, and the Great Pyramid instantaneously. That's how majestic the moment is.

When our lips finally part, Sarah whispers, "Wow."

"Yeah," I say.

"What about Tank?"

"Give me some time to figure that out." I pause. "Don't say anything yet, okay?"

She nods.

We kiss again. Shortly into it, she pulls back a few inches and looks at me, worried.

"What is it?" I ask.

"What do you think he'll do when he finds out?"

I shrug. "I don't know. Let's not think about it right now."

There's a silence during which I imagine Tank at the wrestling clinic. He's probably tossing his opponents around as if they're mannequins. Does Sarah know about the juice? If not, does she need to know?

Yes, I decide. She deserves to know what's going on with her brother.

I mean, I'm totally in love with Sarah. I don't want to lie to her. Ever. I don't want to hide anything from her. Ever. I'm doing enough lying to other people right now, so I refuse to let deceit and dishonesty jeopardize my relationship with this beautiful girl. So that's why I decide to lay it on the table.

"I know something about Tank, something you might not know."

She stares me dead in the eyes and says, "Like what?"

"I hope I'm wrong, but you need to know. I want you to know. I can't hide anything from you." I glance toward the driveway, still empty. My heart starts pounding against my ribcage. "Downstairs." I pause and look at her. "In the crawlspace."

There's another silence. We stare at each other. Her lavender scent drifts toward me. I just want to keep kissing her, but I know that will have to wait.

She finally nods and turns, leading me toward the sliding glass door.

We step into the living room and she closes the door. As we cross toward the stairway, I glance at the old family photo tucked deep into the top corner of the dusty bookless bookshelf. Part of me wants to ask about her mom, but I know this is the wrong time.

Moving quickly down the steps, Sarah says, "What are we going to find, Zach?"

"Nothing, I hope."

"I don't like this." She sounds irritated, almost as if she thinks I'm using her just to sneak around down here.

I cut in front of her and head toward the paneled wooden door that opens to the crawlspace. The rusty hinges squeak as I open it. Reaching inside the dark space, I pull a little metal chain connected to an exposed light bulb on the ceiling. It's called a crawlspace for good reason. You have to climb into it, and, once inside, the distance from floor to ceiling is about four feet. As light fills the small space, I notice cobwebs caked along the concrete walls, especially in the corners, but the main path is clear, meaning Tank's been in here recently. Dozens of haphazardly stacked cardboard boxes line the far wall. The air inside is cool but stale.

"Some of that stuff is my mom's," Sarah says, peering over my shoulder. "Hurry. I'll wait here and listen for anything upstairs."

I squeeze myself through the square-shaped entrance, staying in a low crouch and constantly shifting my gaze from left to right, trying not to cough or sneeze as I move. The boxes are about ten feet away. When I reach them, I don't see anything of interest, and it occurs to me that I'll need a lot more time if I want to search through all this stuff. Suddenly doubting my hunch that Tank has a stash somewhere in here, I poke around a little more, desperately sticking my hand in the spaces between boxes and looking around the corners of the stacks.

Nothing.

Until I peek around the corner of the stack on the far right and see a fishing tackle box.

I mean, there it is, a green, newer-looking plastic tackle box, looking as out of place in this crawlspace as my dad inside a church. As I slide it toward me, my heart starts thumping like a bass drum. After a few deep breaths, I reach forward and open the box.

The top level is empty, nothing but little white plastic compartments for fishing tackle that isn't present. Raising the top level and inspecting the spacious bottom, however, I count four more amber pill bottles of Dianabol (D-Bol), but I also spot something that sends my worries about Tank to new levels.

Five small, clear, unused glass injector bottles rest at the bottom of a quart-sized baggie, each containing a slightly yellowish liquid. The bottles have silver caps with black seals, and the white label on each container reads "Decabol." The unused needles accompanying the bottles don't comfort me any.

"What is it, Zach?" Sarah calls from the entrance, startling me and causing me to bump the top of my head on the low ceiling.

"Hang on." I rub my head with one hand and carefully close and cradle the tackle box with the other. Shuffling toward her in my low crouch, I see the look of concern on her face as she studies the green tackle box in my left hand.

"What is it?" she asks again.

I don't say anything, simply kneel on the cement floor and place the box in front of me. Then I open it so that the empty top layer faces her. Sarah gives me a confused look. I feel like a seedy drug dealer about to show a buyer my goods. When I lift the top layer, Sarah's eyes bulge as she studies the contents.

"What is this stuff?" She's smart enough not to touch anything. I watch her eyes dart from left to right before settling on the needles and injector bottles.

"Take a guess, Sarah. Look at the labels."

She looks up at me. "I don't believe it."

"Well, I doubt these are your dad's. He has a bedroom to lock things in."

"No," she says, shaking her head. "What I'm saying is, I don't think Tank's using these. He's just selling them. He would never cheat at wrestling." She looks at me as if seeking confirmation.

But all I can do is give her a doubtful look.

"Put it back," she says. "I knew we shouldn't have come down here. Put it back exactly where you found it. This was a stupid idea."

"Sarah, I want you to know what I know." I nod toward the box. "And this is what I know."

"You need to leave."

"Fine," I say. "Whatever, but as his sister I thought you might want to know."

I scoop the box up and move as fast as I can toward the back of the crawlspace, frustrated with her refusal to accept the truth. I mean, yeah, I suppose she might be right. I guess there is a slight chance Tank is selling rather than using, but would that make the situation any better?

Doubt it.

Besides, Victor said only the *best* Blaine jocks (like Justin) get juice from Horton. Well, Tank's the best wrestler in Blaine history, so it only makes sense that Horton, probably working with Tank's coaches, is trying to make Tank even better.

After returning the tackle box to its original position and double-checking that nothing appears out of place, I waddle back toward the door, figuring Sarah probably just needs a little time for reality to set in.

"You need to leave," she says again.

"I know." I turn off the light and quickly exit the crawlspace. Dusting myself off, I give her a look. "You already told me that."

"No, I mean right now." She's looking up the stairway, wide-eyed. "They're home. I hear his truck."

"What? Shit."

Panicked, I slam the wooden door closed and race past Sarah and up the stairs, hearing her thumping feet close behind me. My throat goes dry and my heart wants to explode through my chest. Sprinting through the living room and sliding open the glass door to the backyard, I hear two thumps from outside—the truck doors closing.

"We'll talk later," I say, surprised to find Sarah right behind me.

"Okay," she says. "Go, Zach. Now!"

I sprint into the backyard, veering to the right to stay out of view of the truck. Looking over my shoulder, I spot the chrome grill of Big Dale's pickup in front of the open gate. From my angle I can't see the windshield, so I'm fairly certain they can't see me. Regardless, panic and worry race through me.

I head straight for the neighbor's fence.

Hopping over it, I hear Sarah in the distance. She's outside, talking to Big Dale and Tank, trying to play it cool. Nice move, a sound strategy.

Then I hear Big Dale asking her why the gate is wide open.

I don't bother sticking around to hear her answer.

13

Twenty minutes later I'm sitting on my crumbling front porch, lungs still burning from the madness of the Blaine backyard marathon. I'm waiting for Big Dale to leave again so I can go see Tank (and Sarah, of course). But when he finally drives past in his sparkling blue truck, he spots me and stops in the middle of the street, motioning me over with his index finger.

Damn. Sarah must have talked.

When I reach his window he gazes at me with disapproving eyes. The hairs of his mustache twitch like the legs of a nervous spider.

So, I say to myself, what did Sarah say? Did she spill it all, the kiss *and* the juice stash? I mean, after my involvement in the rock-throwing incident, I'm already on Big Dale's blacklist. What kind of cop wants his daughter going out with a guy who comes home handcuffed in the back seat of a police car? And what about Tank? Did she tell him, too? Oh, man, if that's the case I'm as good as dead, sneaking around in his basement lair *and* hitting on his sister!

As Big Dale stares at me with his pulsating facial hair, I have a horrible image of father and son tearing me apart limb by limb and storing my body parts in the crawlspace.

But when he says, "I'm gonna say something and leave it at that," something tells me Sarah hasn't dropped a word about us. Thank God.

"Okay," I answer, my heart racing.

"Tank's not grounded anymore. I let him off early for good behavior. But, Zach, if you two pull anything like that again, you guys are done. You won't be allowed over, and I'll make sure Tank never speaks to you. Understand?"

I nod.

And he goes, "Heard you're working at Huey's now."

"Yeah," I say. "To pay the deductibles."

"How is Huey?"

"He's ... uh ... he's interesting, I guess. How come I never see you in there?"

"I go to a store closer to my office." Dale pulls up his sleeves. The green dragon stares at me as if I'm its next meal. "What's it to you?"

"Mr. Foster, what kind of cop are you?" He raises his eyebrows at me. So I say, "Sorry. It's just something I've always wondered."

He checks his mirrors. "I'll put it to you this way. I do

the things people never hear about, and as long as people never hear about them, I know I'm doing my job." He shrugs. "That make sense to you?"

"Sort of."

We stare at each other for a few awkward moments.

"So what's really on your mind, Zach?"

"Do you have a girlfriend, Mr. Foster?"

"That's kind of personal, don't you think?" He says this with a smirk.

"Well, answer this then: what kind of man beats his kids and dates another man's wife?"

I know. I know. I can't believe I said it, but I just totally did.

And I immediately take a few steps backward.

But instead of punching me or grabbing me by my collar, he just laughs. "I don't beat my kids, Zach. And I can't believe that lush is using you to get his dirt." Looking me dead in the eyes, he adds, "You're seventeen. Don't be in such a hurry to grow up."

And then he drives off, leaving me coughing and choking on his truck's black exhaust fumes.

And I'm thinking to myself, man, what the hell is going on in this city?

Confused and semi-shocked, I head back to the sidewalk and make my way back to Tank's. Along the way, I keep my head down and make sure I step over every one of the lines that separate the concrete sidewalk squares. When we were younger, Justin told me I'd go to hell if my feet ever landed on one of those lines. That was at least ten years ago, and now here I am following the same rule even though I've matured enough to know that stepping on sidewalk cracks has nothing to do with life after death. I think about how pissed I feel about Justin's comments about the Blaine Memorial steroid ring, Mom and Coach Horton, and Mom and Dad.

That's when I decide how stupid it is to be avoiding sidewalk lines at the age of seventeen.

I stop in the middle of one of the squares. The sun beats on my neck as I stare at the next line in front of me. Raising my right foot as high as possible, I bring it down hard on the line and look back toward my house to see if Justin is watching. Of course he isn't, but I wish he were. I turn and smile, bringing my left foot forward and smacking it down on the same line. It's amazing how something so trivial can feel so liberating. Before taking another step, I rub the soles of my shoes back and forth over the line like I'm trying to erase it or something.

That's when I hear a familiar male voice say, "Hey, Ramsey, whatever it was, I think you killed it."

I look toward the street and see Coach Hank Horton sitting in the driver's seat of his silver sedan. The engine is running and he's stopped in the middle of the road. His face is plump and red, a drinker's face with a pleasant smile. He's clean-shaven with a full head of silver hair.

At first I wish I had a gun.

But then I get a better idea.

"How's it going, Zach?" His voice is deep and confident.

"Good," I say. "It's summer."

"Damn right it is," he says. He checks his mirrors for approaching cars, but the street is quiet. "Come here a second. I can barely hear you."

I cross the lawn and walk over. I have to shield my eyes from the sun to see him, but I notice his enormous beer gut hanging over his trademark pair of blue polyester coaching shorts. He offers to shake hands, which I reluctantly agree to do. His grip feels like a closed vise.

"I was thinking about your old man the other day," he says. "When we played high school ball together, he was the hardest-working guy on the team. And all that hard work paid off. He was small, but he was good. Damn good. He got better every day, never worse." I nod and think about how horrible of a player I am. "Then again," Horton adds, "anatomically speaking, the bumblebee isn't supposed to fly." He winks at me. "But nobody told the bumblebee that, now did they, Ramsey?"

"Come again?" I say, having absolutely no idea what he's talking about. That's the thing about Horton. He has all these ridiculous quotes that are supposed to pump players up and make us think positive and all that, but part of me wants to bust out laughing every time he spits one out. I mean, who really cares about bumblebees and their flight mechanics? Not me.

"The bumblebee," he repeats. "It's an expression, a

motivational saying. Come on, you've heard me use that one before." I shrug. He seems frustrated with my inability to grasp the meaning. "Never mind." He takes another peek up and down the street. "So, you getting in shape for two-a-days?"

"Working my butt off," I lie.

He smiles, wipes sweat from his upper lip and forehead. "Good, because with this kind of heat you need to be in tip-top condition. I mean, if you fail to plan, you plan to fail, right?"

"That's what I hear," I say, suppressing my laughter.

He looks me up and down. "You're a lot different from your old man, but I've always liked your attitude. It's … unique." He gives me the once-over—again. "So, why haven't you been coming to the weight room on Tuesdays and Thursdays?"

"Because I've been hitting my brother's weights like crazy. He doesn't use them anymore." That's another lie, of course, but it's an important part of my quickly developing plan.

And Horton totally takes the bait, saying, "How is Justin, anyway?"

"Beats me," I answer. "We don't talk much. I still can't believe he quit your team. I mean, I don't have anywhere near the football talent he has, but I swear I'll do anything to make myself better. I want to show him up, you know, show him how attitude, determination, and hard work can go a long way in making up for a lack of natural talent." I pause. "Kind of like how my dad did back when you guys played together."

"That's excellent, Zach." Horton smiles again. "I wish your brother felt the same way." He shifts into drive, keeps his foot on the brake. "You have enthusiasm, Ramsey. And you can do *anything* if you have enthusiasm."

"That's me, Coach. Call me Mr. Enthusiasm. I want to make my senior season count! I want to make it memorable!"

"Yes!" he yells, getting all fired up. "Another thing you need to remember, Ramsey. The person who said it can't be done is being passed by the person who is doing it."

"I get it!" I say, struggling to feign interest in this motivational bullshit. "In other words, nothing is impossible."

"Exactly!" He reaches into the back seat and turns toward me, holding a spotless white baseball cap with the Blaine team helmet (blue with a yellow B on the side) emblazoned on the front. "See this hat?"

"Yes."

"Take it." He dangles it out the window. "They're brand-new. I'm only allowing my seniors to wear them. I'm telling you, Ramsey. Our cheerleaders love guys who wear hats like this. And we have a fine-looking cheerleading squad at Blaine Memorial this season." He winks.

"Sweet." I grab the hat and put it on, a perfect fit. "How does it look?"

"Like it was made for you, son." He opens his mouth to say something, decides against it, but then changes his mind again, saying, "Listen, Ramsey, if you do the little things right, the big things will take care of themselves. Keep working hard and this program will reward you with everything you need." He nods and drives off.

I step into the middle of the street and wave goodbye.

He doesn't wave back, gives me a chubby thumbs-up out the window instead.

And I say to myself, I can't wait to watch this fat bastard fall.

———

When I get to Tank's, Sarah is nowhere in sight, so I go inside and walk downstairs. Tank is sitting on the blue sofa, wearing a pair of gray athletic shorts and watching season fifty of *Cribs* or whatever. The volume is up so loud he doesn't even hear me.

I stand at the foot of the steps, glancing at the crawl-space door every now and then, wondering what to say. I notice Tank's wrestling singlet, headgear, and high-top shoes lying off to one side of the sofa. He looks tired. I feel like I don't know him anymore. I mean, part of me wants to come right out and tell him about Sarah, the stash, his dad, and Huey, get it over with and take whatever beating is coming to me. But the truth is I'm too afraid to say anything right now.

When he sees me he raises both fists in the air and leaps off the sofa with a smile on his face.

"We're back, man," he says, laughing. "We are definitely back." He studies my forehead and squints. "Sweet hat, by the way." Then he hugs me and rocks me back and forth like an abused Teddy bear.

"Easy," I say, laughing with him, relieved he doesn't suspect anything. "Don't break me." Suddenly it's as if we've never been apart. "Let go a second. I have a surprise." He backs off. "Man, you stink."

"I haven't showered yet. Hey, I pinned three college dudes this morning. You should've seen their coaches' faces. I swear to God, I'm gonna shatter every collegiate record on the books."

"No doubt about that." Looking at his face, I notice his left eye is black and blue, but it appears to be well into the healing stage. Glancing down, I see a series of fading bruises along the outside of his left leg. "What's with the eye and the leg?"

It seems to throw him off, like he's forgotten about the wounds. He touches his left eye.

"Oh, those," he says. "One of the guys was a good match. He must've done it."

"They look like they've been there a while."

"No," he says. "They happened today."

And the look he gives me says it all. I need to avoid the topic.

Tank changes the subject. "Look, I've had a lot of time to think about that night, about how you took some of the blame. Thanks for doing that. I was pissed at you for confessing, but you were right. That guy on the balcony got a good view of us. So, I'm sorry."

"It's cool."

We shake hands.

Tank says, "So, what's the surprise?"

I lift my shirt and pull out the Jack Daniels and Marlboros, surprised they're both still intact after everything I've been through this morning.

Tank's eyes light up like Roman candles. "Sweet," he says. "My stock is totally dry. Where'd you get them?"

"Your dad didn't tell you?"

"Tell me what?"

"I'm a stock boy at Huey's."

"No way."

"My dad made me. I thought it was gonna suck, but Tank, it's the best gig ever. I can steal anything. I've been selling beer to guys like Tony Banks, Mike Foreman, and Victor Hodge for ten bucks a case." I yank out four crumpled ten-dollar bills from my front pocket and hand him two of them. "Dude, I'm known throughout the neighborhood as the Bootlegger of Blaine, and you can be a silent partner if you want. All you have to do is recruit some of your wrestling buddies as buyers. We'll split everything fifty-fifty."

"Hell, yes!" Tank puts his face in his hands and spins around three times. "My God, I love you, Zach Ramsey. This is incredible. It's the ultimate hookup." He walks over to the couch and plops down. "Get over here with that." He shuts off the TV.

I sit down on the recliner and twist the cap off the bottle. "But no more stupid stuff, okay?"

"Hey, you think I want to spend more time in solitary confinement?"

"Look, I have to work at three." I offer him the bottle. "Want some?"

"Yeah." He snags the pint and raises it to his lips, takes a swallow, and exhales deeply. "Man, that's good." He passes it to me. I take a sip. It tastes horrible so early in the morning, but I pretend to like it.

Then I decide to get down to business.

"I've been hearing some things in the party store." I hand him the bottle.

"Like what?" He takes a sip, gives it back to me.

"You're a big-time jock. You ever hear anything about Blaine coaches giving athletes steroids?" I take a big swig of JD, more to calm my nerves than anything.

"No," he says quickly, shaking his head and maintaining eye contact with me. "Who said that?"

"I overheard a couple of plant workers one night."

"Zach, those are Blaine factory rats. They make up shit out of sheer boredom."

"I guess." We stare at each other for a few uncomfortable moments. "Yeah, you're probably right. I just thought I'd tell you since we both play sports." I hand him the bottle.

He drinks and says, "You know I've always been a great wrestler. Dude, you should see the juniors and seniors at camp. They're all afraid of me. Why? Because of my reputation and my talent, that's why. I don't have to cheat, and, if it makes you feel any better, if the opportunity ever comes my way, I *won't* cheat. I promise." He passes me the bottle. "But thanks for the warning. Seriously."

"Like I said, just something I heard."

Looking at the ceiling, Tank totally changes the subject and goes, "She's wearing bikinis now, Zach. My sister is actually wearing a bikini. I saw it when we pulled in this morning." He shakes his head. "That's just wrong, man." He grabs the bottle from me and takes a long pull. "I saw something else when we came home this morning, too."

"Like what?"

"Like you."

In full liar's mode, I don't miss a beat, holding his gaze and saying, "Yeah, I came over looking for you, and when I went around back, I happened to run into Sarah."

"So why the hell did you take off like a jackrabbit when we pulled in?"

"I don't know. I was kind of freaked out, I guess. I didn't want you to get the wrong idea."

Tank studies me. I study him, two best friends lying through their teeth about some major issues.

"Are you up to something with my sister, Zach?"

"What? Hell no, Tank. Come on, you know me better than that. Besides, she's only seventeen."

"So are you, idiot."

"You know what I mean. I swear, nothing's going on."

"I hope not, because I remember what you said at the railroad tracks. The crack about being in love with her? I sure as hell hope you were joking."

"I was. I'm not in love with Sarah, okay? Don't worry about it." I stand, trying to add a little emotion to the act. "That's the stupidest thing I've ever heard, me having something for your sister."

He takes a deep breath and leans back into the blue cushions.

"Good answer, because if you ever do so much as hold her hand ... well, I'll hurt you, Zach, and I won't think twice about it." He makes a pained face and closes his eyes. "God, if she just could've stayed an ugly, greasy-haired, brace-face ... man, she'd be so much easier to deal with."

"Look at it this way," I say, trying to counsel him. "You can pretty much keep a constant eye on her our entire senior year."

"Yeah," he says, his spirits suddenly lifting. "And I'll tell you one thing. If she does go out with a guy, the dude better be Mr. Perfect."

"Hey," I say, desperately wanting another change of subject. "You want a smoke?"

"Yeah, we can go behind the garage, but I have to show you something first." He stands. "It's upstairs."

As we head up the stairs, it's as if I can feel the heavy weight of all these dueling secrets and lies, pressing harder down upon me with every step.

14

I stand behind Tank as he enters the combination to the lock on Big Dale's bedroom door. He's showed me the room once before, back in middle school, and I know it's full of guns. I've never stepped inside, just looked in from the hallway, but right now I have a good feeling I'll be going in to explore. I'm nervous because I hate guns. I've never handled one in my life, not even a BB gun or pellet rifle. I pray Big Dale isn't the kind of gun owner who keeps every firearm loaded, because the thought of Tank Foster around live ammunition isn't very comforting.

He's having trouble with the lock. Good. As he works it, I look to my right and stare through the open door of Sarah's small bedroom. She's made her bed, and the beach towel she had wrapped around her earlier now lies on the mattress with her orange bikini on top. There's a small dresser near the window on the far side of the room. I gaze at it, wondering what types of clothes are in the drawers.

Tank is swearing at the lock now, still can't open it.

My eyes drift back to the bikini. I study the two pieces of soft orange fabric in awe and have to force myself to look away.

That's when Tank says, "Dude, you okay?"

"Yeah, I'm fine." I wipe my forehead and tell myself to think about nursing homes or my grandparents. "It's kind of hot in here."

"The air's on."

"Must be the whiskey."

"Whatever." He dangles the lock in front of my face and pushes his father's bedroom door open. "Come on in."

From the looks of the place, Dale Foster is not an organized man. An unkempt full-size bed occupies most of the space. Loose change, wadded-up paper balls, and cologne bottles lie atop two dressers flanking either side of the bed. An old TV rests on a small metal stand at the foot of the mattress, a DVD player on the bottom shelf. The walls and ceiling are a dirty shade of beige.

But the gun racks stand out the most. Four of them, one mounted on each wall, each overstocked with powerful-looking shotguns and rifles leaning precariously against one another. Each rack has a glass door with a brass key lock, and I pray Tank doesn't know how to get into them. Boxes of shotgun shells and bullets, some open, most not, lie at the bottom of each rack. The place is a suburban arsenal.

"Is your dad expecting an invasion?"

Tank crosses to the far dresser.

"All cops like guns. But it's not the guns I want you to see." He lifts the flimsy mattress. "Check this out. I found the stash."

Turns out Dale Foster has more adult magazines hidden under his mattress than Huey has in his entire store. There they are, dozens of magazines strewn across the box spring, some in black and white, others in glossy color, all recent publications. And I have to give Big Dale some credit, because the quality of most of these magazines is far superior to that of *Michigan Cherries*.

Tank slides the mattress gently off to the side and walks over to me. We stand side by side and stare at the collection for a few moments.

"This is impressive," I say.

"Tell me about it."

"How'd you find it?"

"Snoop around long enough, eventually you find stuff."

"I still don't get why he just doesn't look at it online."

"Dude, I told you," Tank says. "He doesn't trust computers. He's busted a lot of people who use them to break the law, so he knows how easy it is to track people down online. It's like he's being paranoid and smart at the same time."

"I recognize a lot of these covers from the store. They're all new."

"What can I say? The old man keeps an updated library." Tank shrugs. "The girls are hot, Zach."

"I know," I say. "So, what's your dad do with all these?"

"I'd rather not think about that."

"Oh, yeah. Sorry, wasn't thinking." Pause. "Hey, how'd you feel when you first found these? I mean, with *Michigan Cherries* it was no big deal, you know, because it was just one magazine, but I think I'd be a little pissed if I knew my dad was looking at all this stuff."

"Guess I didn't feel anything. A little surprised maybe, but my dad's not married. If he was married I'd probably be pissed about the whole thing." He pauses. "What about you? You ever sneak through your parents' room?"

"No. And after seeing this I don't think I want to."

There's a long silence during which I find it interesting that neither of us reaches for a magazine. I mean, in a way, it's like all the hot women we've ever wanted are right here before our eyes—well, at least on paper, anyway—but we're both a bit too freaked to take a closer look.

"You know," Tank says, "I was wrong a second ago, when I told you I didn't feel anything." He crosses back to replace the mattress. "I was actually kind of relieved."

"Relieved?"

"Yeah. Before I started finding this stuff, I used to worry he might be gay."

"Tank, if there's one guy on this planet who's not gay, it's your dad."

"I know that now." He lays the mattress back in place.

"But a while back I started to think about stuff. How he never talks about women, never goes on dates...hell, the only people who call him are guys...except for that one woman I've heard him on the phone with." He pauses, scratches his head. "And to be honest, for a long time I wasn't even sure it was a woman."

What I want to say is, *Oh, it's definitely a woman, Tank. Her name's Helen Dawkins.*

But instead I say, "The guys who call him are just his cop buddies. You know that."

"Yeah, but can you see where I was a little worried? I started to think, hey, maybe the old man's a flamer. And that really got to me, because who wants a gay dad?"

"Not me."

"Exactly," he says. "I was so worried about it I decided to sneak around in here."

"It's a hell of a stash," I say, unsure of how to react.

But in reality the whole thing depresses me. Ever since I determined that Big Dale is more than likely not the one giving Tank steroids, I've been clinging to this tiny shred of hope that he might eventually redeem himself and emerge as a quality dad. As for his apparent fling with Helen Dawkins...well, I was beginning to think, beginning to *hope*, really, that maybe the two of them are totally in love and deserve each other. I mean, let's face it. Huey Dawkins is nothing but a drunk. Maybe his wife deserves better, kind of like how Justin feels Mom deserves better.

But no. Now it seems Big Dale Foster is just another

sick male with perverted sexual tastes. Gross. It's all just totally gross and disappointing. Why does one man need so many magazines? And why does a father feel the need to beat up his own son, anyway? It's all so beyond me. I don't understand any of it.

So Tank's going through the closet now, and I'm hoping, praying even, that he doesn't find anything else relating to his dad's personal life. I just want to go outside behind the garage and have a smoke and a drink with my best friend. I just want everything to be *normal* again.

"No treasures in the closet," Tank says. A wave of relief washes over me. "But give him time." He smiles. "Dude, I have to piss. Don't touch anything."

Tank leaves. I look around the bedroom, hoping this is all a bad dream. He's left the closet open. For some reason I can't quite figure out, I actually walk over and start checking the pockets of every piece of clothing I see, totally ignoring Tank's order not to disturb anything and kissing my own private wish for a return to normalcy goodbye.

Tank obviously did a rush job of inspecting in here, because as I reach my hand into the inside pocket of an old gray blazer hanging in the far left corner, my fingers touch what feel like three thin, square-shaped pieces of plastic. Removing the mystery items, I find myself staring at three photos, each featuring a semi-hot older blonde.

The woman is all smiles and completely naked. She looks about the same age as Big Dale, and is on a bed in what appears to be a hotel room. Despite the woman's ratted-out blonde hair, deep tan, and nice body, I'm not the least bit aroused. In fact, I'm embarrassed and sick to my stomach, even ashamed in a weird sort of way, like I know I'm *totally* invading somebody else's privacy.

So I'm about to put the pics back when it suddenly occurs to me who I'm *really* looking at.

An older woman with teased-out blonde hair, a deep tan, and a superb body.

I picture her lying on her side on a sandy white beach, wearing a yellow bikini and smiling at the camera.

It's official. The woman is Helen Dawkins.

Big Dale is having an affair with a married woman!

I mean, this is my best friend's *father*. This is *Sarah's* father! Something about seeing the actual proof in front of my eyes enrages me. He's nothing but scum. Scum of the earth. My heart plummets. I'm confused. I'm angry. I'm frustrated beyond belief.

I shove the photos back into the blazer and just stand there at the foot of the bed, slightly bent over, hands clutching my knees, feeling like I might puke. And that's when it hits me that the reason I'm so upset is because I'm actually no better than Big Dale Foster. In fact, I feel exactly like a Big Dale myself. He sneaks around with a married woman, right? And what am I doing? Oh, just sneaking around behind Tank's back, digging up all this steroid dirt on him and all this relationship crap on his dad. And to top it all off, as of this morning I'm having my own little secret affair with Tank's cherished twin sister.

I hear the bathroom door open, so I stand up straight and try to gather my thoughts, knowing I have to do something with all of this information exploding inside me.

"So at least he's not gay," Tank is saying, laughing as he enters the room. "I can relax about that." He looks at me. "What's wrong? You look kind of green."

There's a silence. Then I decide to make a stupid play involving yet another lie.

"Tank, there's something you need to know."

"Like?"

"I left something out earlier, when I was telling you about the plant guys talking about coaches giving Blaine guys the juice."

A brief silence.

"And what exactly did you hear, Zach?"

He steps closer, looking at me with one of those emotionless blank gazes he always gets before snapping and entering one of his psycho moods. I step cautiously past him and stand in the open doorway, relieved he's allowed me a clear path out of the bedroom and, if needed, the house.

"Tank, one of the guys told me Horton has you on the stuff."

"Shut up," he says, rubbing his forehead with his right hand. "Just shut up. That's a total lie. I don't cheat. I'll never cheat."

"Whatever, man, but people are noticing you." I take a step backward and into the hallway. "All I'm saying is that if a coach is involved, especially Horton, you need to take him down."

He paces back and forth at the foot of the bed, and I get really nervous when he eyes the gun racks.

Then he just stops and looks at me and says, "You need to leave, Zach. Now."

"Look, I'm sorry, but I figured you'd want to—"

"Just get out!" he yells, cutting me off. "If you stay, you'll get hurt, so get out. Now!"

And I'm totally out of that house in three seconds flat.

As I'm sprinting down the street, my new Blaine football hat flies off of my head and lands on a neighbor's dead brown lawn.

I don't stop to pick it up.

15

Four reasons why my life sucks right now:

1. I haven't spoken with either Tank or Sarah the past two weeks.

With Tank, well, he's the one who freaked out, so I figure he'll come around when he's good and ready. As for Sarah, she probably thinks I'm the biggest loser on the planet, kissing her and showing her Tank's stash, but then avoiding her all this time.

So why am I holding out on Tank with the Helen Dawkins thing, my knowledge of his crawlspace stash, and my hotness for Sarah? It's just that...well, as I've said, I don't feel like getting killed, okay? Besides, Tank's holding out and lying to me, too. Plus, telling him that his dad's involved in a secret relationship with my boss's wife isn't exactly what he needs to hear right now. And regarding the stash, I still have a plan for taking down Hank Horton, but if it doesn't work I'm kind of hoping Sarah either confronts Tank with the tackle box or steps up and tells her dad about it. I mean, Big Dale is a cop, after all.

2. Bootleggers of Blaine is totally out of control.

When I told Tony Banks and Mike Foreman to spread the word, they sure as hell did. I can't even keep up with the orders anymore. Economically speaking, demand is far greater than supply or whatever.

Anyway, apparently I've addicted dozens of my neighborhood peers to beer, and, like all diehard addicts, they're building tolerances that require increased consumption. Over the past two weeks, small pods of high school drunks have been gathering outside of Huey's, hoping to place orders with me. Sometimes I'll even see a group of rich kids from Blaine Heights hanging out, and they come up to me like we're all best friends, offering to pay double what my locals pay. But I can't stand those rich bastards, so I just say, "No way, dudes, hop in your BMWs and go back to the Heights and raid Daddy's wine cellar." And then they get all desperate and start begging like little street children in Calcutta.

It's hard being the local bootlegger. I'm starting to feel like a marked man every time I take the trash out. If the masses revolt, I'm history.

3. All my parents do lately is fight, fight, and fight.

There's an argument every night, and it's always Mom yelling at Dad about money and how much he smokes and drinks.

Hey, Dad, here's some breaking news: if you want to stay married, treat Mom like she's your wife rather than your house servant. I mean, when the summer began, she was all nice to me about it, telling me to make sure I stick with football for *him* and all that. But now... man, she's done being nice, and I don't blame her. I don't even want to go home at night anymore because of all the shouting.

4. I can't break the news to Huey Dawkins about Big Dale's photos of Helen, because all Huey does now is walk around the store drunk.

Okay, this is the one that's freaking me out the most. I think a husband has the right to know if his wife's sneaking around on him with an immoral child-abusing cop. But I won't tell Huey unless I'm lucky enough to find him semi-sober, and lately that's like trying to find a polar bear in Brazil.

So that's the kind of stuff running through my head when I arrive to work one day to find, big surprise, Huey hammered. And I mean he's blitzed beyond belief. He won't move from the stool behind the register, just keeps mumbling things and laughing. I'm having trouble understanding him, but I decipher enough to realize that he wants me to clean the top of the cooler between rushes. Damn. The one job Brandon warned me about. Looking around the store, I notice the two carts overflowing with empties, so I push them to the back room, happy to get away from Huey for a while.

After I sort the bottles and cans the trash cart is full, so I push it out to the main floor, where Huey has somehow managed to walk to the cooler. He's reaching inside for another six-pack when he sees me. He closes the door and, leaning against it for support, opens a beer and lays the others on the nearest shelf. His eyes look like red spider webs, hands trembling as he raises the can to his lips.

I'm a little afraid of him right now. That's how bombed he is. Like seemingly every other adult male I know in Blaine, he's really pissing me off lately.

"Hey, Ramsey," he slurs. "Come here with that cart."

"Sure, Huey." I make a U-turn and steer in his direction.

Keeping one hand on the door handle of the cooler, he sets his open beer on a shelf and pushes on the garbage in various spots like a customer inspecting fruit in a produce market. Then he digs deep into the cart, poking and prodding at different angles, using his forearms, elbows, and hands, examining the cart's contents like a doctor giving a physical.

"I think kids steal from me sometimes. I have to check every now and then. Don't take it personally."

"It's cool," I say, thankful I'm not smuggling anything out in this load.

Satisfied, he pulls his arms out of the cart, lights a cigarette, and reaches for his beer, stumbling as he does so.

He's a pathetic sight. His sour breath forces me to take a step back. He drifts off into silence, staring at the tile now, swaying from the alcohol.

"What do you know, kid?" He looks as though he might pass out, but he manages to pull out a fifty and dangle it in front of me. "Anything new?"

Finally, I say to myself. I can *finally* get this off my chest. And if he's too drunk to remember ... well, that's his problem.

"I confirmed what you already know," I say, not bothering to take the fifty.

"You did, huh?" He offers me the money again. I shake my head. "And what is it you think I already know?"

"That she's having an affair with Dale Foster. I saw some pictures."

He must think I'm holding out for more cash, because he reaches in for another fifty, offering me a hundred dollars now. It's all so disgusting to me. I'm totally jaded with adulthood as it is lived in Blaine. Screw these people, man. Screw them all.

"Keep your money, Huey. I'm not taking it."

"Why? You're doing great."

"I'm done. You have what you wanted. Proof. Now, if you don't mind, I have my own problems to deal with."

"Suit yourself, kid." He pockets the cash and leans back against the cooler. Then he slides slowly down until his butt hits the hard floor. "Don't ever get married, Ramsey." He looks at his wedding band, a thin ring of gold wrapped tightly around his finger. He tugs at it but it doesn't move. "I'd throw it away if I could get the damn thing off." He looks up at me through glazed, watery eyes. Then he closes them.

"You want some water, Huey?" I ask. He shakes his head. "Want some help back to the register?"

"I might be drunk, but I still know how to walk. Go on," he says, boosting himself up. "Take that garbage out. We got a rush to get ready for."

I wait for him to take a few steps on his own, which he eventually does.

When he's safely on the stool, I wheel the cart outside and empty the trash. In the process, I see Tony Banks and Mike Foreman smoking in the alley again. They give me these pitiful, desperate looks that make it obvious they want a case tonight.

So I walk over and go, "This parking lot's been like an amusement park lately."

And Foreman says, "You've got a sweet operation going, Ramsey."

And Banks adds, "Yeah, we've given you more buyers than you know what to do with, so how about bringing us in on things." He pauses. "From now on we want a cut for every customer we give you."

"Sorry, guys," I say, "but that's not how I roll."

Foreman smiles and says, "Well, maybe that's how you *should* roll."

"Yeah," Banks says, "or maybe we'll have to tell Huey about your little operation."

"So that's how you want to play it, huh?" I say, shaking my head in disbelief. "Okay, fellas, how about this. Truth is I already have a partner."

They look at each other and then back at me.

"Who?" Foreman asks, lighting a smoke and looking like a total idiot.

"Tank Foster."

They look at each other again. Foreman's cigarette falls out of his mouth and onto the steamy asphalt.

"So," I say, "would you like me to tell Tank about this little conversation, or would you rather pretend it never happened?"

Picking up his smoke, Foreman coughs and says, "No, we're cool, Ramsey. We didn't know you had a partner. Forget about it."

"Wise choice," I say. "But I have more bad news. The operation is shut down until further notice." I nod toward the store. "There's too much heat inside."

"Don't say that, bro. We need beer, man," Foreman whines.

I shake my head. "Sorry, guys."

And Tony Banks goes, "Okay, how about one more case, Ramsey. That's it." He manages to fish a bill out of his pocket. It's a twenty. "We'll pay you double."

I study them for a few moments to make it look good. Then I nod and say, "Okay, but this is it." I take the twenty. "Now, start texting people that I'm closed, okay?"

As they turn and walk down the alley in the direction

away from the store, I roll the cart to the Dumpster and empty the garbage. I'm feeling better. Huey finally knows what he needed to know, and, best of all, my career as a Blaine spy is finally over. Thank God. I've learned enough about the adult world to know I want nothing to do with it. Now all I have to do is one more beer run and I'll no longer have to worry about getting busted stealing and selling cases to minors. Yeah, I still have major issues with Tank, Sarah, and Coach Horton that need figuring out, but for the first time all summer some of that emotional weight pressing down on my shoulders is finally lifting.

So I'm rolling the cart back toward the entrance when none other than Coach Hank Horton himself pulls into the empty lot in his silver sedan. He parks in the space nearest the side of the building, almost sideswiping my cart in the process. He must recognize me, because he gives the horn a friendly blast as he shifts to park. I hear what sounds like arena rock coming from his speakers. For some reason that doesn't surprise me.

He kills the ignition and gets out, sporting those hideous tight blue polyester coaching shorts and a white polo with the Blaine team helmet on the left breast. He's not wearing a T-shirt beneath, and I can see a pair of doughy-looking man boobs that should be declared illegal. As for his gut, it resembles an inner tube for a semi-truck tire. Nasty.

"Zach Ramsey," he says, leaning his pale fleshy forearms on the hood of the car. "I thought that was you. Working for the summer?"

"No," I say. "I just enjoy pushing empty carts through parking lots." He squints. I smile. "I'm joking, Coach. Yeah, I'm working for Huey."

"That's good," he says. "Hard work builds character." He looks me over. "Still haven't seen you in the weight room. You still working out?"

"Like crazy," I lie, flexing a bicep that barely exists. "What, you can't tell?"

"Sorry, but no, not really. Maybe it's the program you're on. That's another reason you should come to the summer sessions. The coaches will put you on a training program that gets results."

I'm feeling pretty cocky about ending the spying thing and closing the black-market beer business, so I decide to make a play on Horton just to see how he handles it.

"Well, Coach, like I told you before, I really like working out at home, so can't you just give me the stuff that'll give me the 'results'?"

A long silence, Horton studying me, cocking his head slightly from left to right, trying to figure me out, I suppose. Behind him, the truck plant hums and hovers like some monolith from another world.

He removes his fat forearms from the hood and walks around the front of his car, stopping when he reaches my cart. Horton is three feet away from me, his face looking like a sweaty, uncooked hot dog.

"I'm afraid I don't understand, Ramsey. What 'stuff' are you talking about?"

"The same stuff my brother wasn't a fan of…but I am."

Silence.

Then, as if sensing a set-up or something, Horton backs off and shakes his head. "Like I said, I'm afraid I don't understand. Have a good day, Ramsey."

Damn! I was so close. I guess I went for the kill too soon. Knowing that he's onto me, I get a little desperate and decide to press him some more.

"So, is it a case of good things coming to those who wait?" I ask.

"This conversation's over." He turns and walks toward the entrance.

Frustrated, I say, "I know what you do, Coach. It can't last forever."

Over his shoulder he says, "What I do is coach football, Ramsey. That's what I do. And I know it won't last forever. I have to retire someday." He laughs as he passes through the door.

When the door closes, I shove the cart and kick it over onto its side. The sound of the metal smacking and vibrating against the asphalt echoes through the parking lot.

Then I put my hands on my hips and stare at the assembly plant across Michigan Avenue.

16

After helping Huey through the five o'clock rush, I pull all the red bags down from the top of the cooler and climb up for a look. I hear Huey cashing out in preparation for Brenda's arrival, and I want to finish this gross job fast.

Standing on the ladder and inspecting the bare cooler top, I realize why Brandon said this was the worst task imaginable: dozens of sticky pools and trails of liquid meander across the top surface. It's like looking at an oversized map of the local waterways. I press a finger lightly against what I think is a dry spot, but even the "dry" spots are sticky. I have no clue where to begin, so I climb down, grab all the sponges and towels I can find, and toss them onto the cooler. Then I climb back up and basically throw myself onto the towels.

I'm crawling around up there, the different mystery liquids soaking through the knees of my blue jeans and reaching my skin within minutes. My bare hands slip forward with every new reach, so I create a pair of makeshift gloves out of two towels. I look like a wounded soldier who's just lost both hands.

But the smell is the worst part, like beer puke with some rotten garbage mixed in. I tie a clean rag over my nose and mouth and hold my breath until I'm forced to exhale. I decide to begin at the far wall and work my way backward, wiping and soaking up as much of the beverage sludge as possible. I figure it'll take at least an hour to do a decent job, but twenty minutes later I'm already out of sponges and towels and I haven't even cleaned half the space.

I decide to take a quick break.

And that's when I hear Brenda yelling.

I crawl toward the front of the cooler. Fake ivy winds through the lattice, concealing me from view. Years of dust cover the ivy, and I have to fight the urge to sneeze. Gazing down over the store, I see Brenda standing near the entrance, Huey standing behind the register. Brenda has her purse over her shoulder, held tightly against her ribcage. I picture the handgun lying at the bottom.

"You need to leave, Huey," she yells. "Go sleep it off. I'm not staying here with you like this."

"Come on, baby," he slurs. "I'm just playing around."

"Go home," she shouts. "I'm giving you the benefit of the doubt here. I've never seen you like this before. You need to get help. If you want *me* to stay, then *you* need to leave."

"Fine, fine, fine," he says and laughs. "I'm going. I'm going." He grabs his keys and a bank bag.

Brenda walks further into the store, keeping her distance from Huey as he exits. When the door closes, she throws her keys across the store.

"I'm sick of this shit," she yells.

I climb down and run out to see her. She's sitting behind the counter.

"Hey," I say. "You okay?"

She looks at me, notices my soiled knees, and scrunches her nose. "Zach, you smell like death."

I tell her about the cooler job.

"You mean you actually listened to him today?" she asks.

"He told me to do it. I can't afford to get fired."

"Zach, tomorrow morning that man's not going to remember a thing." She gazes up at the cooler. "Did you finish?"

"No."

"Well, consider the job done."

"Thanks."

———

Twenty minutes before closing, I finish my tasks and enjoy my usual beer and cigarette in the cooler. The only thing left to do is the final trash run, which, of course, means the final beer run ... well, at least for a while, anyway.

For some reason, as the big moment draws near, my

nerves increase. But I know failure is impossible. I mean, I've stolen at least thirty cases of beer the past few weeks. Plus, Brenda is totally pissed at Huey, so there's no way she'll bother checking the cart.

I eat a few beef sticks and keep an eye on Brenda from inside the cooler, waiting for her to put down her novel and get busy restocking the booze and cigarettes. She finally starts at ten minutes before eleven.

Perfect.

I turn, grab a case of Budweiser cans, and step into the back room, where I've already created a nice hiding space deep within the trash-filled cart.

As always, I lay the case over a thick bottom layer of cardboard and paper bags and cover it on all sides, packing it in there as if it's a fragile piece of art. After double-checking every possible angle, I push the cart out onto the main floor. The thing is so full I have to keep one hand on top of the garbage heap to prevent debris from falling out.

She stops me three feet from the entrance, telling me to wait as she fetches the small trashcan at the opposite end of the counter.

Damn.

My chest tightens and my stomach sours as she jogs toward me with a smile on her face and the trashcan held in her outstretched hand. I know I'm busted as soon as she tips the can over and rams it down hard onto the garbage heap to make some space. A loud thud echoes through the store as the metal trash can collides with the case of beer.

"What's that?" she says, squinting into the cart.

She uses the trash can as a type of hammer, pounding on the garbage in different spots. Each time she does so, that depressing thud repeats itself.

"Zach, what the hell's in here?"

"Garbage," I mutter, backing up a few steps.

"And?"

I say nothing.

She sets the trash can aside and reaches into the cart, where she quickly finds the cardboard carrying handle of the Budweiser case and pulls it out. Loose paper, plastic bags, and cardboard spill onto the floor as she does so.

"Zach," she says, gazing at the case in disbelief. "Who is this for?"

"Me," I lie.

She lets the case fall gently back into the cart.

"How many times have you done this?"

"This is the first," I lie. Again.

"Look at me." I look. "I trusted you," she says. She looks around the store. "I can't believe this. So what am I supposed to do, call Huey and get you fired?"

Silence.

"Brenda, if you do that, then I'll have to narc on you."

"What?" she says. "What did you just say to me?"

"I know about the cigarettes," I say. "And the Diet Coke...and why do you have a gun, anyway?"

A furious look crosses her face as she puts it all together. I've never seen a woman so angry. She reaches down for her purse, looks inside as if to make sure everything is still there, and slings it over her shoulder.

"You went through my purse?"

I shrug, feeling like I'm a bigger Big Dale with every passing second.

"Damn you, Zach. I feel like punching you right now. You're lucky you're a minor."

"Sorry," I say. "It was just there one day and I looked through it."

"Jesus." Her face reddens.

"Anyway, about the stealing, we both do it, so what's the big deal? Let me just roll this out and we'll pretend you never looked inside."

"You're unbelievable."

She opens her purse and tosses two unopened packs of cigarettes onto the counter. Then she opens the register and removes a piece of white cardstock from beneath the change drawer. Somebody has scrawled some notes on it in tiny blue letters, but I'm too far away to read them.

She holds the cardstock closer to my face.

"Do you see this?"

I nod.

She hands it to me. "Take a closer look."

The notes are for cigarettes and sodas, the price of each listed to the right. I don't say anything, because I know exactly what's coming.

"I haven't stolen a damn thing in my life," she says. "Everything I take from this store gets deducted from my paycheck."

There's another awkward silence during which I feel like burying myself in the Dumpster and never coming out.

"Well, what about the gun?" I say, handing back the cardstock. "What's that all about?"

"I don't have to tell you about the gun, Zach...but I will, because for some weird reason I can't figure out yet, I think you should know." She replaces the cardstock and shoves the cigarettes back into her purse. "I'm allowed to carry this gun for reasons having to do with my ex-husband." She pauses. "There, that's all you need to know. Does it satisfy you?"

I lean my hands on the side of the cart. "I'm sorry. It won't happen again."

"Leave the beer and take out the garbage," she says, shaking her head and looking around the store. "I can't deal with this right now. I have to get out of here on time tonight."

I prop the door open and push the cart outside. My head hangs low and I wonder if I'll ever be able to look Brenda in the eye again. Glancing at the assembly plant across the street, part of me suddenly doubts I'll ever make it out of Blaine.

Do I even deserve to make it out? I wonder.

Out at the Dumpster, I decide I'm going to quit my job as a stock boy. Well, maybe not quit, but at least take some time off, fake sick or something. Everything's just too awkward now. Once again, I feel as if I've reached rock bottom.

As I'm tossing ideas around in my head about how to handle the Tank-and-Sarah mess, I sense something in the alley behind me. Figuring it's Foreman and Banks coming for their beer, I gently close the sliding door of the Dumpster and wipe my dirty hands on my jeans, fully prepared to inform them that Bootleggers of Blaine is gone forever.

However, when I turn to face them, they're not there. Instead, I see a large and shiny green pickup truck roll to a stop in front of the sealed back door of the store. The driver is facing me, but his face is dark and unidentifiable. The engine is running and the vehicle is about twenty feet away.

The driver reaches his left hand out of the window and waves me over. I abandon the empty cart and approach, thinking he's some late delivery person looking to use the back entrance. However, when I'm parallel with his window I realize I know the man. In fact, I just saw him in the store less than an hour ago. He's a regular customer during the ten o'clock rush, a quiet guy in his forties who buys a quart of malt liquor and a pack of cigarettes nightly. He's tall and lean and always has thick razor stubble covering his face and neck.

"How you doing, kid?"

His voice is gruff. His breath smells of cigarettes and alcohol, typical for a Blaine factory rat.

"I'm okay," I say. "Day off tomorrow?"

He raises a paper bag to his lips and takes a long drink from a quart of beer, wiping his mouth with the back of his hand. Despite the air-conditioned breeze escaping through the open window, beads of sweat coat his forehead and upper lip.

"They gave me a permanent vacation," he says.

"Who did?"

He points in the direction of the factory's smokestacks. "They did," he says, holding a pink piece of paper in front of me. I can't read the fine print, but I know it's a layoff notice. Dad and his buddies talk about the "pink sheets" often.

"Sorry."

He drops the paper onto the passenger seat. "Sometimes I have a dream that I get to line up all the CEOs of American car companies and shoot them between the eyes."

"I'm sorry you lost your job, sir."

"It's Barry," he says. "Barry Deck. You look about my son's age. His name's Barry, too."

"I know him," I say. "We've been in school together since kindergarten. I mean, we don't hang out or anything, but I know who he is. He's a cool guy. I'm Zach. Zach Ramsey."

"Oh yeah," he says. "Ramsey. Your parents have been working there a while, huh?" He nods toward the factory again.

"As long as I can remember. So, how's Barry been?"

"He's good. Barry's good. Stays with his mom most of the time. He's excited about his senior year." He runs his palm over the spotless dashboard. The truck smells brand-new. "I'm gonna have to get rid of this baby, you know that? Talk about humiliating." He shakes his head.

"Well, I should get back inside."

"Hey, how's Huey doing?"

"I think he's been better."

"He's going through hell." Barry pauses. "We're all going through hell around here. If Detroit doesn't learn how to build a decent car, I bet Blaine's a ghost town by the time you're twenty-five."

Silence. The truck's engine purrs smoothly. I can feel its heat against my thighs and shins.

"I hope things turn around for you. Tell Barry I said hello."

"Thanks," he says and nods. "Hey, you like subs?"

"You mean like the sandwich kind?"

"Yeah."

"Who doesn't?"

"There's a great little place up the road in Ypsi." He points toward Michigan Avenue. "Best subs you've ever tasted. They're open past midnight, Friday through Sunday. Maybe one night after work I'll take you up for one. How's that sound?"

Okay, so my freak detector instantly goes into high alert and I'm thinking to myself, get away from the pedophile. Fast.

"No," I say, "but thanks anyway."

I turn and walk back toward the cart, totally grossed out.

"Wait," he says. "Just hang on a second."

He shifts to drive, catches up with me at the Dumpster.

"I really have to get back inside, sir."

I grab the cart, ready to slam it into his door if necessary.

"It's Barry," he says, "and don't get the wrong idea. I'm not a weirdo, okay?"

I stare at the asphalt, both of my hands white-knuckled to the handle of the cart.

He says, "It's just…I never get to see my son, and you remind me of him. That's all. I didn't mean anything weird by it, so don't go telling your old man I tried to pick you up."

I refuse to look at him, convinced he's one of those sick old pervs they catch trying to hook up with middle school students in chat rooms.

"See you around, Ramsey," he says and drives off.

I push the cart as fast as possible toward the front entrance.

———

I end up faking sick to avoid work for the next week. During the seven days I spend alone in my bedroom, I basically wait for my parents to somehow find out what happened that night. I figure either Brenda will change her mind and go to the police, or she'll tell Huey and he'll fire me.

My anxiety level seems to increase daily. I hate everything right now. Everything about life sucks big balls. I've yet to see Tank since the day I confronted him in Big Dale's bedroom, so he's obviously still pissed about that. He hasn't even called or texted. As for Sarah, I'm totally in love with her and think about her all the time, but I can't muster the courage to tell Tank about it, especially with the steroid thing still clouding the air. Man, part of me wants to go out to the old fort, lock myself inside without food or water, and die a miserable, slow, agonizing death. That's exactly what I deserve.

So you know how sometimes you reach a moment when it seems life can't possibly get any suckier, but then, of course, something happens to elevate the "Life Sucks" scale even higher? I mean, that's how it works, right? Well, one night my dad makes this quiet entrance into my room, saying he really needs to speak with me.

He sits on the edge of my bed with a can of beer and a half-smoked cigarette. I stand up and lean against my dresser, noticing the worried look on his face. I'm thinking he's about to break the news of a divorce. But instead, he stands, pops the cigarette between his lips, and reaches into his back pocket.

"You need to know that your mother and I received these today," he says, not making eye contact. He shows me two pink layoff notices from the assembly plant. My stomach does this total drop, like I'm going down the first steep hill of some massive roller coaster.

"Why?" I ask. "You two have been there forever. It's where you met."

"I know, Zach," he says. "Believe me, I know, but twenty years isn't exactly forever. A lot of those guys have been there close to thirty." He tucks the notices back into his pocket. "But that's how far they decided to go back, twenty damn years." He looks over my shoulder toward the only window in my bedroom, one that happens to offer a view of the brightly-lit assembly plant and its smokestacks in the distance. "When I got that job, I figured I was set forever." He shrugs.

"Sorry, Dad."

"Me, too." Before turning to leave, he says, "Look, we'll be two of the first people called back, but I have no clue when, or if, that'll happen, so you need to be ready for some changes, okay?" I nod. "Like this house," he says, gazing around my room. "We might have to move." I nod again. "And money. I mean, I know we've never had any, but now things will get really tight. Put in as many hours as you can before football starts. You'll need the money during the season."

I take a deep and confident breath and say, "What if I just don't play football? That way I can work after school and help you two out even more."

"Out of the question," he says. "You're a player, Zach." He pauses. "Besides, football takes everybody's mind off of reality."

And I so want to argue with him and get all pissy

right now, maybe even tell him what Coach Horton did to Mom and why Justin *really* quit football, but even I know this isn't the ideal time to do that.

Then he says, "I talked with your brother. He's agreed to hold off on that community college idea for another year and get a job."

"What?"

"We need his help, Zach. I talked to a guy from the plant. He installs carpet on the side. He's taking Justin on as an assistant. I think it's the right step. Maybe Justin will learn something ... for once."

I look down, shake my head, and whisper, "The trap has sprung."

"What was that?" Dad asks.

"Nothing," I say, looking up. "It's just that you can't pull a Captain Rick installing carpet in Blaine."

Silence.

"Yeah," Dad says. "Good ol' Captain Rick." He draws hard on his cigarette and exhales a cloud of smoke. "He's one of the lucky ones."

He drops his cigarette butt into the beer can. The room is so quiet I can actually hear the fizzy sound of the lighted end landing in his backwash.

When he leaves the room I feel my cell vibrating against my hip.

It's a text from Tank. Finally.

TANK: Wuts up w u & s?

My stomach drops. Not exactly the kind of message I was hoping for. Great.

ME: NOTHING! WTH? RUOK?
TANK: Y IS SHE ASKING ABOUT U?

She's asking about me? Really? Cool.

ME: NO CLUE. MAYBE SHE LOVES ME. JK
TANK: DPWM. STAY AWAY FROM HER OR IKU
ME: DON'T EVEN KNOW HER #. UR PARANOID.

This is true, by the way. The thing about not knowing her number.

TANK: HOPE SO. L8R

End of chat.

I go to bed feeling like the biggest loser on the planet.

AUGUST

17

So I eventually go back to work and all that, but I still don't see Tank, only now I think it has more to do with his wrestling obligations than him being pissed at me. I mean, I *think* we're still best friends and everything, but the demands on an all-state athlete, especially one of Tank's caliber, increase dramatically during the month prior to the start of the school year.

Huey hasn't said much at all to me since the night I confirmed the Helen–Big Dale affair. Actually, he barely speaks to *anybody* now, not even the customers, and he always looks at me out of the corner of his eye, like he knows *something* bad has happened but can't remember exactly what. He's the same way with Brenda, too. I can't even believe she still works here. The only good news is that she never narced on me for trying to steal the case.

Anyway, on the first Friday night of August, I finally

decide it's time to speak to Sarah. It's been weeks since I've seen her, and I'm fully prepared for the worst, but I need to talk to her about the crawlspace stash and explain why I haven't told Tank about us yet. Basically, I have to convince her that my recent absence has nothing to do with her and everything to do with me and my lack of courage or whatever.

Knowing Tank's away at a weekend wrestling camp, I dress and sneak out through my window around midnight. Three minutes later, I'm standing on the damp lawn on the side of Tank's house, just outside Sarah's bedroom window.

The blind is closed. I listen to crickets sing and watch fireflies dance for several minutes before deciding to tap lightly on her window.

She doesn't answer.

I knock again, harder this time, and after a few seconds, the blind lifts and a tired but beautiful Sarah Foster rubs her eyelids and stares at me, clearly surprised at my presence.

She lifts the window. Only the screen separates us.

"Let me guess," she says, irritated. "You're here to explain yourself."

"It's been an odd few weeks." I place my open palm against the screen. "Hi, by the way."

She stares at my palm, doesn't bother pressing hers against mine.

"Hi," she finally says, looking beyond me toward the side of the neighbor's house.

"Look, I'm sorry, okay?" I withdraw my hand from the screen. "There's a lot going on."

She stares hard at me. "Zach, why are you here?"

"I wanted to see you. I always want to see you. Every night. You're all I think about."

"You have a strange way of showing it," she says. "You pick on me my whole life, and then one day, out of nowhere, you decide to kiss me. And then what do you do? You disappear. I mean, is that how you treat somebody you care about, Zach? You take off without saying a word?" She pauses. "I realized something the other day. I've known you for years, but I've only trusted you for about fifteen minutes. That was the day in the backyard." She jabs an index finger into the screen and gives me a look. "You have no right to hurt me, Zach. No right at all. We're not little kids anymore."

"The last thing I want to do is hurt you, Sarah," I say, feeling heat building up behind my eyes. "I swear to God. I'm sorry for staying away. That day in the backyard, you said this was all new for you. Well, guess what? This is all new for me, too."

We stare at each other for a long time. She's pissed and has every right to be, but I can't help getting lost in those green eyes.

Finally, she says, "What are you going to do?"

"About what?"

"About *this*," she says.

"I'll talk to him. I promise."

"You're afraid."

"Maybe," I say, shrugging. "But it has to come from me. It's something I have to do."

She looks behind her. The bedroom door is closed.

"My dad likes you," she says.

"Really?"

"He talks about you sometimes. He likes your attitude."

"Sarah, does your dad hit Tank a lot?"

"It's not what you think," she says. "Dad gets mad sometimes, so they fight. Tank fights back, but he always loses." She pauses. "Funny thing is, the next day they're like best friends."

"Has he ever touched *you*?"

"Never."

"Thank God."

"My dad's my best friend," she adds. "Tank and him, the fighting, I don't know exactly how to say it, but it's not abuse. It's almost like they enjoy it, like they both know that one day Tank will get the best of him. And when that day comes, the fights will stop." She stares at the windowsill. "They make me go to my room before they start. Can you believe that? It's like a reality series I'm not allowed to watch."

There's a silence.

"Have you thought about the stash at all?" I ask.

"I've done more than think about it. I checked it yesterday when he left for the camp."

"And?"

"It's bigger now. Some of the bottles are empty." She pauses, looks away. "Some of the needles have been used." Looking back at me, she says, "You were right. I just didn't want to believe it."

"So what now?"

"What do you mean?"

"You want him to stop, right? It's cheating."

She shrugs. "Is it?"

"He doesn't need that stuff, Sarah. He's good enough without it."

"I've been thinking a lot about that," she says. "And it comes down to this. I'm lucky enough to have a brain that will get me out of Blaine and into a good college. That's my...what do you call it?"

"Your BEP. Blaine Escape Plan," I say. "And when it actually happens, you've pulled a Captain Rick."

"Right," she says, smiling. "I like that. So that's my BEP, and, hopefully, my Captain Rick. But all Tank has is wrestling. His athletic talent is the equivalent of my academic talent. So that stuff he's using is like added insurance for his BEP. I don't think he's doing it because he wants to. I think he's doing it because he feels he *has* to."

"And you're smart enough to know that you're totally rationalizing his behavior, right?"

"Maybe," she says. "But think about this, Zach. If there was a brain drug that would boost your chances of getting into Harvard, would you take it?"

Silence.

"I've never thought about it like that."

"Well, I have," she says. "And if something like that existed, I sure would be tempted to buy it."

"What if you didn't have to buy it?"

She squints. "Then how would I get it?"

"What if your favorite teacher supplied it?"

"What are you saying?"

I take a deep breath.

"I'm saying it's coming from coaches."

She studies me hard, thinking. Then: "Coaches are supplying athletes?"

"Only the really good athletes."

"To make them even better."

"Bingo."

"And you're sure about this?"

"I have two solid sources," I say, not mentioning Justin and Victor Hodge by name. "It's happening, Sarah. Tank's getting it from a coach."

"I'm not sure how I feel about that." She looks over my shoulder into the dark and humid night. "Zach, I don't want to think about this right now."

We listen as crickets chirp away.

"I know one thing," I say. "If Tank was home right now, I'd wake him up and at least tell him about us. I want everything out in the open."

She smiles. Finally.

"You want to go for a walk or something?" I say.

"Right now?"

"Why not? It's a nice night."

She looks toward the bedroom door and then back to me, saying, "I've never done anything like this before."

"You're seventeen, Sarah. I'd say you're overdue for a little mischief. Tank sneaks out all the time, says your dad basically hibernates when he sleeps."

She laughs and takes a deep breath. Then she reaches for the top corners of the screen and feels around for a few seconds before popping the sliding latches. The screen falls slowly toward me. I catch it, lift out the bottom half, and lay the screen gently on the moist grass.

"Hang on a second." She slips on a pair of black flip-flops and comes back to the window. "Get ready. I might need help." She boosts herself feet first through the open window. I cradle her waist and help her out. She's wearing tight red short shorts and a black tank top. Beautiful. There might as well be fireworks filling the entire Blaine sky.

"Where to?" she asks as we head toward the sidewalk.

"I think I know a spot."

We cross through the backyards and end up on the brush-filled slope beside the railroad tracks. I can't believe I'm actually back here, but the circumstances are so different this time that I guess it doesn't matter. I show Sarah the entrance to the fort. She asks why the door is lying off to the side, so I tell her about Tank drunkenly ripping it from its hinges. She wants to go inside. I explain about nasty insects, falling dirt, and sweatbox-like temperatures. Still, she wants to go in.

"Look," I say, "I've outgrown this fort." I gaze at the apartment complex beyond the brick wall. "I guess I've outgrown a lot of things lately."

"Please, Zach," she says, "just for a minute, so I can see it. You're the one who brought me here."

"It's too dark to see down there."

"I don't care. I'm not afraid."

"Fine, but just for a minute." I lower myself to a pushup position and stick my head inside the rectangular opening. A damp, musty odor greets me. I wave my hand in front of my nose and rise to a kneeling position. "Smells worse than I remember."

"It can't be that bad," she says.

I haven't actually been down here in four years, since the summer following seventh grade. Stepping through the narrow doorway and down onto the loose wooden planks, I feel a wave of nostalgia, kind of like when you go back to visit your elementary school and suddenly remember things you thought you'd forgotten.

I duck inside and see the four milk crates pushed together in the far corner. I also see the empty pint bottle Tank tossed down here after he tore the door off. I kick the bottle into a corner.

Funny, but the space isn't as dark or as warm as I thought it would be. Basic shapes are visible and the night air is cooler at this depth. I reach my hand up through the entrance and help Sarah down.

"Be careful," I say. "You have to stay low."

Loose dirt cascades down the entrance shaft like a waterfall as she makes her way in. Once inside, I push a milk crate toward her. We sit in the middle of the cramped floor. She looks around, taking it all in.

"So, what did you guys do down here?"

"Ate candy and drank pop." I pause. "It's cool when a train passes. You shake like crazy."

"Maybe one will come."

"We'll see."

Pointing up through the open door, she says, "Look, you can see the sky."

"Yeah, not much to look at though."

"Only if you decide there isn't."

"Huh?"

"Nothing." She shrugs. "It's something my mom used to say." She traces a figure eight on the floor with her foot. "She should've taken more of her own advice."

"Tank says she's still messed up."

"Yeah, my dad's tried everything to help her, but I think he's pretty much given up. Guess I can't blame him." She runs her palms over her thighs.

I scoot my crate directly beside hers until they touch. I look up through the entrance and study the Blaine sky, nothing but clouds. Our thighs brush against each other now and then. She might think nothing of it, but my entire body tingles every time we touch. I'm nervous in an excited way, unsure of what to do or say next.

"I've never looked out from this angle," I say.

"Can I tell you something I haven't told anybody except my dad?"

"Anything."

"I really miss my mom," she says. "I hope she's okay, wherever she is."

"You know what I think?" She's silent. "I think you'll see your mom again. Soon." There's a rumble in the distance. "Hear that?"

"A train?"

"Yeah. Close your eyes when it passes. It can get messy down here."

We listen in silence as the locomotive moves closer and the horn grows louder. After a few minutes, we feel the vibrations shooting out from the steel rails. I reach for Sarah's hand and squeeze. She squeezes back. As the train thunders past, she squeezes harder, and we laugh as the fort shakes and more dirt showers down on us from the earthen ceiling.

Afterwards, as Blaine resumes its nighttime summer silence, Sarah and I tilt our heads back and stare up into the dusty sky. At one point there's a brief clearing, and we both agree that we've never seen so many stars above our city.

———

We don't say much on the walk back, just hold hands and listen to the chorus of crickets, enjoying the moment. I feel a warm, slick sweat forming between our hands, but I refuse to let go. I want to hold her forever.

Standing by her window she says, "Okay, I've thought about it. If it's coming from a coach, then we have to do something. Tank probably feels like he has no choice. He worships those coaches. He'll do anything they tell him to do."

"I have an idea," I say, wiping sweat from my brow. "You said some of the injector bottles are empty, right?"

"Yeah, at least five."

I pull out my cell and flip it open. "You snuck *out*. Any chance I can sneak *in* and take some pictures?"

"In the crawlspace?" she asks. I nod. "Right now?" she says. I nod again. She looks horrified at the thought.

I shrug. "Your dad hibernates, remember?"

"Yeah, but it's one in the morn—"

"Sarah, it's now or never. Tank comes home tomorrow morning. You might not have another chance to get down there for weeks."

She thinks about it and finally nods, saying, "Okay. But if my dad wakes up and hears somebody in the crawl-space . . . well, I'm not responsible if he shoots you."

"That's comforting," I say, raising my eyebrows. "Thanks, Sarah."

She turns toward her window, waiting for me to give her a boost, which I gladly do. She's amazingly silent as she slides through and turns, looking down at me from inside her bedroom now, motioning for me to join her.

It's one of those rare times when I'm actually glad I'm a skinny beanpole, because I'm able to prop myself up and through the window rather gracefully for a dude.

She opens her bedroom door without a squeak and leads me into the hallway, where I steal a glance at the locked door to Big Dale Foster's Room of Weaponry. My skin turns to gooseflesh at the thought of him waking up and coming at me with his arsenal. Part of me suddenly wants to dart back into Sarah's room and dive out the window to safety, but all that would do is prove how uncourageous I actually am.

We reach the basement without making a sound, a couple of high school ninjas. The crawlspace door squeaks as usual when I open it, but there's no way somebody sleeping above and at the opposite end of the house would hear it. Sarah gestures with her hand, waving me onward as if to say, hey, you're on your own on this one.

Knowing the terrain, I turn on the light and enter the tight space quickly and expertly, shuffling forward in that same crouching position I used before. I find the green tackle box in the exact same spot, around the corner of the stack of boxes on the far right. Opening it, I check the bottom and see that Sarah was right. Five empty Decabol bottles and accompanying used needles rest at the bottom of a separate baggie. Another baggie contains several unused bottles and needles. I don't see any D-Bol pill bottles this time, leading me to believe that Tank is done with the oral stuff and sticking with injecting.

So I take out my cell and snap two pictures showing the whole bottom layer of the box and its contents.
Then I take two close-ups of the bag with the used items,
another two of the bag with the unused stuff. At first I'm a
little worried about the lighting, but the results on the cell
screen look clear enough.

Then, making sure my back is screening Sarah from
seeing the box, I open the bag containing the used stuff,
carefully reach inside, grab an empty injector bottle, and
shove it deep into my front pocket. It's a total spur-of-the-
moment move. I have no clue what I'm going to do with
the bottle, if anything, but something's telling me it can't
hurt to have at least one piece of physical evidence just in
case I have to confront Tank in the coming days.

After being sure everything's precisely back in place, I
scoot back toward Sarah and give her a thumbs-up as I exit
the crawlspace. She turns off the light and gently closes the
door.

"Mission accomplished?" she whispers.

"Done," I whisper back.

"What are you going to do with the pictures?"

I shrug. "I'm not sure."

"What?" She gives me a look. "You said you had an
idea."

"My idea was to take pictures. That's what I did."

"How do the pictures incriminate the coaches?"

"They don't," I admit. "But they sure incriminate
Tank."

She rolls her eyes. "We already know about Tank."

"And now we have proof to confront him with, if necessary." I pause. "Sarah, he's lied to me twice about not using."

"Fine," she says, massaging her forehead with both sets of fingertips. "It's late. You should get going."

I gaze across the basement and spot Tank's laptop resting below his sixty-inch TV.

"There has to be something else down here," I say, walking toward the TV. "You ever check his computer?"

"No." She sounds worried as she follows me.

We stand above the laptop for a few moments as if it's a dangerous landmine or something. Sarah keeps giving me looks of doom.

"If I touch this he'll know," she says.

"There's probably nothing on there. Just log in and see what comes up. We'll never have another chance like this."

"I don't know any of his passwords."

"Just check the recent files. Maybe he keeps a diary or something."

"My brother, keep a diary?" She covers her mouth to keep from laughing out loud. "Yeah, right."

As she sits down on the sofa and goes to work with the laptop balanced on her knees, I glance around the living space, looking for anything of interest. I study his dresser drawers for a few moments but decide to stay away because it would be too easy for him to notice something out of place. However, remembering Big Dale's mattress magazine stash, I cross over to Tank's bed and carefully raise one side of the mattress several inches, finding nothing but the box spring beneath.

I'm about to check the other side of the mattress when I hear some crackling audio coming from the laptop. Sarah quickly turns down the volume and says, "Oh my God. Come here and listen to this."

"What is it?" I rush over and sit beside her.

"Just listen. It's transferred audio from his phone. It's the only clip in the folder. Look at the file name."

Squinting and leaning in toward the screen, I see a file name that actually excites me. The file name is *Horton*. I've never been so happy to see that idiot's name.

"Play it," I say, my heart racing wildly.

We both lean in close to the speakers and listen to a surprisingly clear sixty-second recording of Coach Hank Horton and Tank Foster.

The highlights:

> *HORTON: "So you like what you're seeing, huh?"*
>
> *TANK: "I've put on ten pounds in four weeks. A few more cycles should do it."*
>
> *HORTON: "I don't see why people get so worked up about this stuff. I look at them as advancements in athletic training. They don't hurt you as long as you use them responsibly, which is exactly what we do here."*

TANK: *"Some schools are randomly testing student-athletes."*

HORTON: *"That will never happen here. Trust me."*

We listen to it three times, our jaws dropping closer to the basement floor with each playback.

"What's the date on the file?" I ask.

She checks. "Exactly two weeks ago."

"Oh my God. He actually listened to me," I say, feeling a wave of relief spread through me. "Unbelievable." I smile.

"What do you mean?" she asks, browsing for more files.

"The second time he lied to me was right after I told him I'd heard coaches were involved. He told me to leave the house or else he'd hurt me. Right before I ran out I told him that if it was true, if a coach *was* involved, especially Horton, then he needed to do something about it." I pause and almost break out in laughter. "And he did. Jesus!"

"Yeah, he sure did," Sarah says. She squints at the screen again. "No way."

"What now?"

"A video file." She points at the file, this one again titled *Horton*. "Imported from his phone." We look at each other in disbelief.

Then Sarah clicks the file name.

It's blurry, quick, and unsteady, but somehow Tank

rigged the exposed camera eye of his phone somewhere on his chest area and captured video of Horton sitting across from him and gently pushing a small brown box across the desktop. The audio is all garbled and unclear, but the footage is clear enough to make a positive ID on Horton, and, judging from the trophies and framed photos on the wall and shelves behind him, to prove that the setting is Horton's office. It stops after twenty seconds and cuts to a crisp segment of Tank filming himself in a boys' john at Blaine Memorial. After staring into the camera, he aims it down at the small cardboard box resting near the sink. Tank's free hand then comes into frame and opens the top of the box, which houses ten small glass injector bottles. Removing one of the bottles, he gets a great close-up of a Decabol label.

And then it's over.

"This is insane," I say.

"My brother's smarter than I thought."

She's about to shut the laptop down when I say, "Wait. What are you doing?"

"I've seen enough. He obviously knows what he's doing."

"At least go online and email me the files."

"What?" She gives me a look. "No. Why do *you* need them?"

"So I can have a copy. So *we* can have a copy, Sarah. What if something goes wrong? What if Tank screws up? I mean, I don't know if this stuff would hold up in court or anything, but don't you think it's important enough that somebody should have a second copy?" I pause. "He'll never know. Just send them as attachments and clear the browser history."

Sarah bites her lower lip and looks away. Then she calmly shuts down the computer, stands, and crosses to the TV, where she returns the thin laptop to its exact original location.

"I think it's time for you to leave, Zach."

I stand. "Why won't you send me the files, Sarah? We need backup copies."

"You just listened to and watched the backup copies," she points out, her face flushing with anger. "Think about it. The originals are on his phone."

"And if they're not?"

Silence.

Then she says, "I'm beginning to think you're a very selfish person."

"Selfish? I'm trying to help your brother. We don't know what his plans are. We should form a plan of our own. Just to be safe."

"Tank's clearly building his own case against Horton. Let *him* do it. *He's* the victim, not us."

"Whatever," I say.

"Whatever," she says, mocking me. "Are you using me?"

"Using you?" I say. "No! I…I think I love you, Sarah."

She makes a little grunting sound and shakes her head.

"The last two times I've seen you you've managed to talk me into coming down here to sneak around." She pauses. "Are you using me, Zach?"

"No," I repeat, louder but still aware of the sleeping, gun-toting maniac one floor above. "All I'm trying to do is bust a football coach who has done some bad things. You don't even know the whole story." Now *I'm* getting pissed, thinking of Horton hitting on my mom and ruining Justin's chances of a football scholarship.

"Get out of here," she says, suddenly fuming. "I can't believe I didn't see this coming. I can't believe you did this to me."

"Did *what*?" I say, holding my arms out, palms facing up.

"Follow me and don't make a sound. I want you out of here."

She turns and leads the way back upstairs, through the kitchen, down the short hallway, and into her bedroom, all very quickly and quietly. I follow her the entire way, confused and wondering what I've done wrong. She won't even look at me as I pass her and head toward the open window.

"The screen," I say, hoping for some type of acknowledgement. "Want me to—"

"I'll get it," she hisses, avoiding eye contact and leaning against the far wall, arms wrapped around her shoulders, staying far away from me as if I'm some sort of deadly communicable disease. "Just leave," she adds. "Now."

I can't think of anything else to say, so I hop out the window and make a point of stepping hard on the screen.

Then I jog home.

18

A few days after the Sarah debacle, Mom and Dad have a huge blowout.

It's early afternoon, and I'm in my bedroom getting ready for work. Ever since the layoffs they've made a point of discussing their differences in private, but today emotions run too high for them to sneak away.

I place my ear against the door. Their voices are muffled but audible.

"And all you did was spend it when you got it," Mom is yelling. "You never thought to put some away for a rainy day."

"I don't *have* anything to put away," Dad fires back.

"My God, you should hear yourself," she says and forces a sarcastic laugh. "The reason you never have any money to put away is because you smoke and drink it all away." She pauses. "Just cut back, Bill, cut back and start saving. Lord knows it'll help your body, and it might just get a kid through college."

"That's the stupidest thing I've ever heard," he says. "You expect me to save money after getting laid off? Even if I did, there'd never be enough to send them through college. Let's just put Zach's work money away after those damn deductibles are paid."

"You can't do it, can you? You're so addicted that you can't imagine quitting."

"Karen, shut the hell up, will you? You sound like some know-it-all counselor. Just shut the hell up, okay?"

"I want you to listen to me," she says. "I want you to hear this. I managed to quit, so I'll be taking that saved money out of my check—unemployment or whatever—and depositing it elsewhere. And if you can't do the same, if you don't love me enough to give this a try . . . well, I don't know what else to say."

Dad loses it like I've never heard him lose it before.

"We need that goddamn money, Karen!" he screams. "We need every cent of it to live on!"

I have my hand on the door handle, ready to barge in.

Mom says, "No, Bill, *you* need it to live on. *I* can make it work. The big question here is *you*. Can Bill Ramsey stop killing himself?"

"Don't talk to me like that, like I'm your goddamned son or something. That kid of ours will get a football scholarship. He won't need a penny of our money. And Justin . . . well, I don't see Justin lasting long at any college. He's never lasted long at anything."

I hear a loud crash, like glass breaking, followed by a long, uncomfortable silence. That's when I decide to open the door.

Mom has her back to me, but Dad sees me right away. He raises his eyebrows and massages his temples with his fingers. They're both staring at the kitchen window ... well, what's left of the kitchen window. One of them has just thrown a full can of beer and shattered the glass into dozens of pieces. Dangerous-looking, knife-like shards surround the frame.

Dad says, "Way to go, Karen. Pay for that with your newfound savings."

"Shut up, Dad," I say. Mom turns, surprised at my presence. "Just shut up. Both of you."

"Excuse me," Dad says and takes a step toward me. "You don't tell your parents what to do, son. We tell you." He's trying to remain calm, but I can see him totally shaking. "And right now I'm asking you to leave this house, Zach. Go to work early. There's no need for you to be around this."

"Oh, let him see it, Bill," Mom says, still staring at the window frame. "Let him see it. Let him hear it. There's no use hiding anything. He's not a little kid."

"I did hear it," I say.

"Your mother and I, we're having some problems is all. It's nothing that can't be solved, but every day isn't a good day."

"It's your father who has the problems, Zach, not me."

"Christ, Karen. Not in front of him, okay?"

"Dad," I say loudly, "you need to get it through your head that there's not a chance in hell of me getting a football scholarship. I hate the game and I'm horrible at it. You know that, but you refuse to admit it."

Mom turns toward me. "Wait, Zach. I talked to you about—"

"And you're the one who just said there's no use hiding anything."

She looks down, turns away.

I say to Dad, "The only reason I play is because of you, to please you." I pause, finding it hard to believe the words are coming out of me. "Only now, Dad, I really don't care if I please you or not."

"That's it," he yells, his face red with anger. "I'm out of here. This is a family of goddamn quitters. You and your brother quit everything you try. Quit, quit, quit. Well, I'll tell you something. You're both on your way to Loserville real fast."

"And what about you?" I bite back. "You proud of your life? I mean, what do you really do, Dad? Hey, I'm sorry you got laid off or whatever, but maybe in a way that's a good thing, because Mom's right, after working inside that factory all day, all you do is come home and smoke and drink in front of the TV all night."

"Stop it, Zach," Mom says. "That's enough."

"I'm leaving," Dad says.

He turns and walks toward the front door.

"Divorce," I yell.

Dad stops, turns.

"That's what's gonna happen, isn't it?" I ask. "You two will get a divorce, like everybody else around here." I turn to leave. Walking past Dad I say, "By the way, Coach Horton's not the man everybody thinks he is. You'll know that soon enough."

I walk to work with my head down.

———

I'm rolling a cart into the back room when Huey comes in and tells me about Brenda, saying she called to let him know she was finally quitting, not even giving him the standard two weeks' notice. My heart skips a few beats, but I continue working because I still don't feel comfortable speaking with Huey about anything. As for Brenda, I'm actually happy she's left this depressing place. I mean, I hope I see her again and all that, but I sure as hell hope it's somewhere other than inside this party store. I guess she never did tell Huey about me stealing the case. She saved my job, and I'm totally in debt to her for that.

Anyway, because of Brenda's sudden decision to ditch this joint, Huey ends up taking her shift, something he handles by drinking beer for the next six hours. He darts off for a final piss just before the ten o'clock rush, so I take the opportunity to sneak behind the counter and steal another pint of Jack Daniels and a pack of Marlboros. Then I march over to the magazine racks and stare at the small selection of condoms. I grab a three-pack in a small orange box and stuff it into my front pocket. Not because I think I'll need them any time soon, but just because I figure Tank will think it's cool the next time I see him.

Shortly after eleven I walk home slowly, not wanting to deal with Mom and Dad's fighting.

I think about going to Sarah's window and trying to patch things up, but I decide against it because I know Tank's home tonight. We've texted a lot the past few days. Thankfully, he hasn't said anything about that missing bottle of Decabol I swiped from his stash. I can only hope he never noticed. We've resorted to texting because he's been at wrestling camps all week, and he says he's too exhausted to go out at night, which is fine with me because I really don't feel like seeing him right now. Based on our texting it sounds like everything is still cool between us, but if I see him in person I'll have to tell him about Sarah—something I still can't bring myself to do.

The night is warm, the summer almost over.

I lower my head and walk on, feeling alone and depressed. I turn down a side street to make the trip longer. Then I light a cigarette and take a sip of Jack Daniels, laughing to myself at the thought of a seventeen-year-old kid roaming the streets at night with a bottle of whiskey, a pack of smokes, and a three-pack of condoms. Maybe Dad was right. Maybe I am heading to Loserville real fast.

Passing the old bungalows, I listen to the Saturday night sounds of my neighborhood: televisions blaring, people yelling, babies crying, all of this drama playing out before me. I gaze at towering maples, dark windows, lighted windows, drawn curtains, open curtains, newer cars, older cars, and wonder how many of these people are truly happy with the hands they've been dealt. Who's faking it and who's being honest? Is there any way to really tell?

Probably not.

That's when I decide that life here in Blaine feels like something along the lines of having permanently slit wrists.

I imagine a giant suction tube falling from the sky and slurping me up and out of Blaine, then spitting me out into some clean, sterile city free of smokestacks, lay-off notices, fighting parents, and drug-dealing football coaches. I picture myself as the only male in my new city, surrounded by three hundred Sarah Foster clones. In fact, I decide to name the city Sarahtown, population three hundred one. The Sarahs roam freely in Sarahtown, never confined to a house occupied by an abusive cop father and a psycho twin brother. In Sarahtown, my Sarahs meet every physical and domestic need of mine, and in return I treat each Sarah like a queen, buying them anything they want, regardless of cost. I even decide on a citywide holiday, The Day of the Sarahs. On this day, the Sarahs tell *me* what to do for a period of twenty-four hours. I mean, I have to give them *some* freedom, right? But after that, I resume control for the next three hundred sixty-four days.

I'm contemplating the concept of polygamy in Sarahtown when I hear a car approaching from behind. Thinking it might be Mom or Dad looking for me, I flick my cigarette onto the sidewalk, step on it, cap the pint, and shove it down my pants. I sense the car slowing as it draws nearer. When the vehicle is parallel with me, I look to my left and see Barry Deck riding high in his green pickup, a smile on his face as he parks curbside and waves me over.

Great. Mr. Pedophile is soliciting me. Why does this shit always happen to me?

I cross a small patch of lawn and stop at his passenger-side door. The window is down. I take a quick look around the neighborhood. Many homes still have interior lights on. Thank God.

"Hey, Barry."

"What's happening, Ramsey?" His happy tone hints at his drunkenness. He has a half-smoked cigarette dangling from one corner of his mouth, his trademark quart of malt liquor tucked inside a paper bag and wedged between his thighs. "A beautiful night, isn't it?"

"Not bad."

"My boy wants to play football during his senior year," he says proudly. "You play, right?"

"For now."

That seems to confuse him. He adjusts his baseball cap and gives me a look.

"He says practices start on Monday, the double sessions."

"Yeah."

"I like that Coach Horton," he says. "Now there's a guy who can make a man out of a boy. He's a hell of a leader, don't you think?"

"Actually," I say, feeling the onset of a whiskey buzz, "I think he's a prick."

"What'd you just say?" He squints and takes a swallow of beer, rubbing his razor stubble with his palm.

"I said Coach Horton's a prick." I'm *really* feeling the whiskey now, and I begin to wonder how much I drank during the Sarahtown fantasy. "You won't believe this, but one day he made a move on my ... oh, never mind."

"You been drinkin', Ramsey?"

"A little bit," I say. "Maybe a lot, I'm not sure. Hang on." I pull out the pint and hold it in front of my face. It's half-empty. I tuck it away. "Looks like I've had a lot, Barry. You mind if I smoke?"

He looks at me and shrugs.

"Cool," I say, and light a cigarette.

"You need a ride home?"

I think about it. Truth is my legs are a little rubbery, and the alcohol has totally impaired my judgment and decision making. Suddenly, the simple task of a ten-minute walk home seems daunting.

So I say to Barry, "Yeah, if you don't mind."

"Hop in." He reaches over and opens the door.

I grab the handle for support and step up into Barry Deck's green pickup.

As soon as I'm in he says, "You really want to go home right now? You might get in some trouble."

"I can handle it. Just take me home, okay?"

He shuts off the radio and draws hard on his cigarette, the orange tip brightening to an intense red for several seconds. As he pulls away, the silence is uncomfortable and I realize I should've just stumbled home on my own.

A few minutes later we come to my street. Barry turns, idles past the first few houses and parks along the curb. The street is dark but I can see my house, five up on the right.

"I'm thinking of leaving it all behind," he whispers.

"What do you mean?"

He waves me off. "That pint of yours," he says. "You want the rest of it?"

"Not really."

"I'll take it. I need it."

I fish it out and hand it to him. He takes a long drink.

"That's more like it," he says. He wedges the bottle between his legs. "What I mean, kid, is that there's nothing left here for me—no wife, no kid, no job."

"Look at it as your Blaine Escape Plan," I say. "Hell, I'd jump at the chance to get out of this place. Soon as I'm eighteen, I'm gone. Captain Rick style."

"You know how many people say that and never do it?"

"I'll do it, Barry. No question about that."

He takes a few more drinks in silence. Finally, he says, "I'll tell you one thing. It's hard being a man."

"Yeah," I say, a little creeped out with how weird this is getting. I tell myself to trust him, yet at the same time I have my right hand on the door handle just in case.

Outside, crickets chirp wildly.

"Hey, kid, I don't know why I'm telling you this. Maybe it's the alcohol talking, but I just want you to know there's nothing like having a wife and kids. It's the best goddamn feeling in the world."

"My parents," I say, "they've been fighting. They both got pink slips, too."

"Yeah, I heard. It's like the whole damn town got laid off." He pauses. "Do they love each other, your parents?"

"I don't know. Doesn't seem like it. But they're both good people."

"Men have a way of screwing things up, Ramsey. And when a marriage falls apart... well, it's usually our fault. Trust me. I know." He pats my thigh a few times like I'm his dog. "You have a girl, Ramsey?"

"Yeah."

"You love her?"

"More than life."

He laughs. The odor of malt liquor and cigarettes fills the cab.

"That's good," he says. "That's real good." He looks straight ahead. "I did some bad things when I was married, some real bad things. Thought I was smart enough to get away with them, but it's hard to cover your tracks these days. All I'm saying is that if you find love, don't mess with it. Respect it for what it is."

"I think my dad needs to hear that."

"I'm no role model," he says. "I'm just speaking from

hindsight, but if I had a second chance, that's how I'd go about it. I'd respect it and work to keep it alive."

Silence.

"Take care, Barry. Thanks for the ride."

I push the door open a few inches. The dome light illuminates the cab.

"All right, Ramsey," he says. "Thanks for listening to my drunken babble." He laughs again.

I hop out and close the door.

Barry Deck drives away.

Walking along the sidewalk, I step on every line and decide that Blaine, Michigan, might just be the strangest city in the world.

19

Sarah's email came two days ago but I just saw it this morning. As I've said, Justin has the only computer in the house, but he's always on it when he's home and he keeps his door locked when he's out.

Except this morning he forgot to lock it. Actually, this has been happening more and more with him, and I attribute this carelessness to his commitment to staying drunk all summer, a goal he's well on his way to achieving.

So I go in there and check my email and see this quickie from Sarah:

> Z,
>
> *Tank's acting really weird lately. 'Unstable' is a better word. I'm worried. Not sure he will act on the Horton thing. Files are attached, but promise me one thing: we'll work together. Tank has to stay anonymous. Think it over and we'll talk. DON'T*

MAKE A MOVE WITHOUT ME. Sorry about
snapping on you that night.
    Love, S

So of course I'm thrilled when I finish reading it. Not because she's attached the audio and video files, although that's a nice surprise, but because she's used the *L* word.

Sarah Foster loves me.

Man, something good has come my way.

Finally!

20

My summer explodes on Saturday night, August 10th. It's a night when fears and hopes collide at full speed, changing the lives of everybody involved, young and old, for better or worse or both. A summer full of seemingly unrelated events come together like puzzle pieces. Tank is involved. So is Sarah. Dale Foster and Helen Dawkins play prominent roles. Hell, even Hank Horton pops up.

But in the end it's me, Zach Ramsey, who catches the worst of the blast.

There's a hard knock at my bedroom window shortly before midnight. I've just slipped into bed after a sweaty shift at Huey's, my hair still damp from the shower. I've been avoiding Mom and Dad since the day of the big blowout, and from the looks of things they've been avoiding each other as well. In a way we're all on our own now, a divided family forced to live under the same roof. Justin's never around (unless he's passed out on the couch), and it seems Mom, Dad, and I do our best to take separate paths wherever we go.

Life in the Ramsey home is totally touchy.

I'm actually thinking about sneaking out for a cigarette, but when I hear that knock on my window I figure it must be Sarah stopping by to talk about the Horton plan. I scramble out of bed and hustle over, not paying any attention to the fact that I'm wearing only underwear.

My hopes deflate when I see Tank outside, smiling his devious smile, clearly ready to explore the neighborhood.

"Get dressed," he whispers. "We're going out." He looks excited and definitely has something on his mind. Damn. I start to panic.

Wait a second.

Sarah was right. He doesn't look excited. He looks *unstable*. There's this disturbing glaze to his eyes I haven't seen before.

Does he know about Sarah and me?

Did Sarah talk about the stash?

Does he know about the missing injector bottle?

"Where to?" I ask, my mouth going dry.

"It's a surprise. I haven't been out in over a month, so get out here." He checks his cell for a text or something. "You're gonna love it."

"Hang on."

I go find some clothes, feeling a little more at ease with the situation. From his tone, I'm fairly certain Sarah hasn't said anything, which means this is my big chance to do the right thing. It's time for *me* to tell Tank about Sarah. It's time for *me* to confront him about the stash and show him the empty bottle and the crawlspace pictures on my phone.

He presses his face to the screen. "Hey, did you get any more liquor?"

Slipping into my blue jeans, I smile and say, "I have enough whiskey and cigarettes to last a month. I stole some condoms, too." I hold up the orange three-pack and put it in my front pocket, not because I think we'll need them, but, again, because I know Tank will think that's cool.

He gives me this look like I'm reading his mind.

"You're a good man, Zach Ramsey," he whispers. "You're a damn good man."

I smile again. Moments like this make me wonder how I've gone a day without seeing or speaking with Tank. His sense of humor, his daring personality, they always have a way of sucking me in. I'm a perpetual passenger on his life ride, and when it comes down to it, I'll do anything to help him. Tank's my best friend, my brother, and my father all rolled into one.

I take a fresh pint, an unopened pack of smokes, and the empty Decabol bottle from my closet hiding space, tucking the latter deep into my front pocket. Then I pop the screen and hop out into the sticky August night.

"Don't think I'm weird or anything," I say as I secure the screen back in place, "but I've missed you." I give him the Jack Daniels and the Marlboros, both of which he tucks into his front pockets. "Life's been pretty boring lately."

"How do you think I feel?" he says. We're walking across the lawn now. "Every night I come home, I tell myself I'll go out and have some fun, but once I sit down I collapse." He pauses. "I slept twelve hours last night. You believe that?"

"How's wrestling going?"

"I pinned a former state champion yesterday. The guy went to Iowa on a full-ride and I pinned him in less than two minutes." He shrugs. "You know what's funny? I can't do fractions without your help, but I'll get to handpick my college because of my body."

"I guess," I say, staring at my feet as we walk. The neighborhood's a ghost town at this hour. "You want a smoke?"

"Yeah, light me up." I light it. He snags the cigarette from between my fingers, saying, "You're not going to believe what we're about to do."

"Oh yeah, what?"

He keeps checking his phone and reading texts. "Are you still nervous around girls, virgin boy?"

My stomach starts to bounce. "Of course not. Why?"

"Because we're on our way to meet a special one."

I feel my Adam's apple rise as I swallow.

No wonder he gave me that weird look when I showed him the condoms.

———

Her name is Mandy Frack. I don't know her. She attends a private school in Dearborn and lives on the other side of Michigan Avenue in snobby Blaine Heights. According to Tank, she's been showing up in the bleachers at wrestling clinics all summer and is totally hot for him. Apparently, some of his fellow teammates noticed her constantly eyeing him and recently decided to set them up.

"And tonight's my night," Tank says to me just after we cross Michigan Avenue, about to enter the city known for its tri-levels, colonials, swimming pools, and white-collared men with high-paying jobs. "Her parents are out of town. She told me to meet her in the backyard around twelve-thirty. She's been texting me all night. She has a pool, Zach." He rubs his hands together, excited. "Man, I haven't been with a girl since June. Feels like years ago."

"So what do you want me to do, watch?"

"No, idiot. I told her I had a friend . . . a virgin friend."

"What?" I say. "Dude, I can't believe you said that." I pause. Tank's laughing. "Yeah, very funny, Tank . . . so what'd she say?"

"She said she loves making virgin wrestlers happy."

"I don't wrestle, so I guess that counts me out."

"Oh, you wrestle, Zach," Tank says, laughing again. "You do now, anyway. I lied a little to help you out, told her you wrestled but hurt your ankle back in May and have been rehabilitating all summer."

"Uh . . . thanks," I say and fall silent, trying to brainstorm a way out of this mess. Here I am, a seventeen-year-old virgin with what appears to be a golden opportunity to finally have sex, yet I can't go through with it because I'm saving myself for my one true love, who happens to be the twin sister of the guy who's working so hard to hook me up right now.

Tank says, "You'll have to limp a little when we get there. You know, just to make it look good."

"Fine, but what happens when school starts and she finds out I don't wrestle?"

"Who cares? At least you won't be a virgin anymore. Anyway, this girl won't mind. She's gets around. It's not like I'm in love with her."

I nod. Barely.

Tank says, "I can't believe you actually have rubbers. That's a message from above. Tonight's our night, man." He pauses. "You ever used one?"

"No, haven't had a chance yet, remember?" I give him a look. "But I've read the directions on the back of the box about a thousand times. I'll be okay when the moment arrives."

"It's not the same," he says. "It's like science class. You learn best through hands-on experiments. I used to practice a lot with some of my dad's."

"That's sick," I say.

"Why?" he says, laughing. "I had to make sure I knew how to put one on."

"Look, Tank. Like I said, I'll be fine when the moment arrives."

"Zach, the time is now." He throws his hands above his head. "Mandy Frack is waiting for us, and I don't want you embarrassing yourself, and me, by taking an hour to put on a condom."

There's a brief silence as Tank turns and leads us down a long, tree-lined street with a wide grassy median. It's a nice street with houses three times as large as our Blaine bungalows.

"This is her street," he says. "You have a three-pack, right?"

"Yeah."

"I think you should practice with one before we get there."

"What?" I gaze around the stately neighborhood. "Where?"

"In there," he says and points to a trio of large, tightly spaced evergreens towering over the median. "It'll only take a few minutes. Nobody's gonna see you. I'll stand guard out here."

"And what am I supposed to do to get excited, look at you?"

"I don't know," he says. "Think of someone hot. Who's your dream girl?"

Your twin sister.

But I can't say that, of course.

So instead I say, "I don't know. Any *Maxim* girl, I guess."

"Okay, so go in there and think about *Maxim* girls or whatever. Then make sure you can put a condom on."

"This is crazy." We cross the street and step onto the median. "I can't believe I'm about to do this."

"You'll thank me later," he says. "Trust me." He gives me a gentle push in the back.

I wedge my way between the evergreens, being careful to avoid the prickly needles. Once I'm through, the area widens and there's more space than I thought. A thick layer of fallen needles coats the ground, and they make crunching sounds every time I shift my feet. It's dark in here and smells like Christmas wreaths.

"Can you see me?" I ask.

"No. You're good."

"Tank, I just had a strange thought."

"You're stalling."

"No, really, just listen. Do you think Hugh Hefner uses condoms?"

"What?"

"Just answer the question."

"I don't know," he says. "No, probably not. Hugh Hefner doesn't use condoms."

"Then why should we?" I remove a condom from the box and tear off the top of the orange wrapper.

"Because I don't want a baby or an STD during my senior year, do you?"

"No," I say, stalling on purpose now. "Hey, if we had kids now, we'd only be thirty-four when they turned seventeen. That's weird."

"Zach, shut up and think about *Maxim*."

I shut up, but I think about Sarah instead. After a few minutes of wonderful scenarios, I'm ready to begin. I drop my pants to my knees and slide the moist and slippery circle out of its wrapper. I try squinting to get one last look at the directions, but it's too dark to see the pictures or the text. For some reason, I decide to smell the condom before putting it on, which is a bad move because the strong odor of skunked latex catches me off guard and gags me. I wonder if I'm handling an expired batch, so I make a mental note to check the expiration date when we come to a streetlight.

I hear Tank laugh.

"Just got another text," he says. "She's waiting for us in the pool and says to hurry. Come on, Zach. You're supposed to wear it, not eat it."

I don't respond. All of my energy is devoted to the task at hand.

However, the problems continue.

Next thing I know, the lubricant is all over my fingers, and I damn near drop the condom onto the needle-covered ground. Who knew preparing for safe sex could be such a chore? Frustrated, I pull down my underwear and try forcing the thing on, but I can't get the latex to unroll. I push and push with everything I have, but it's like trying to cover a tree stump with a small balloon. Impossible.

"This one's defective," I whisper. "And it stinks." The odor's growing more nauseating by the second.

"That doesn't happen," Tank whispers back. "They all get inspected. It says so on the package."

"Well, they missed this one. It won't slide down."

"Jesus, Zach, I'm glad we did this. I bet you have it inside out. It's a common rookie mistake. I did it a couple times myself. Reverse it and try again."

"Okay," I say and take his suggestion.

He's correct. The condom unrolls like a latex Slinky, hugging my skin all the way down as if it were custom-made for my body. The smell is atrocious, but I'm smiling.

"It worked, Tank."

"Good, but you ruined it," he says. "You can't use one if you don't put it on right the first try."

"What should I do with it?"

"Just dump it in there. Nobody'll find it."

"Why's it smell so bad?" I reach down with both hands and begin pulling it off.

"Must be the lubricant," he says. "I can smell it out here. It reeks."

"Maybe they're expired."

"Just hurry the hell up, Zach. She won't wait all night." He pauses. "Dude, there's a car coming."

I have the condom halfway off when I hear something scurrying about in the needles behind me. I turn and look down, where I notice two wide bands of white fur against a background of black. It's not the condom that smells like a skunk. It's a real goddamn skunk, standing there barely three feet away, rocking its body gently back and forth, fluffing its fur and stomping its feet, trying to decide if I'm a threat or not.

I freeze.

That's right. I freeze with my pants and underwear down to my knees and a condom wrapped around my slowly deflating…well, you know.

Unable to see me, Tank says, "The hell's going on in there?"

I whisper, "Tank, there's a skunk in here. Don't move."

"What?" he says. "I can't hear you. I'm coming in. The car's getting closer. Might be a cop."

"Tank, no!"

But he never hears me.

As soon as he busts through the evergreens, I yell "Skunk!" and make a break for it, coming at my stunned best friend with my…well, you know…bulging forward. The terrified skunk lets out a growl and finally decides to lift its tail. I push through Tank and force him backward through the stand of trees. The skunk sprays like a broken water main, but luckily for us, the evergreens seem to bear the brunt of the damage.

But the humiliation isn't over.

Stumbling backward and out of control through the evergreens, Tank ends up falling and landing on his back in the grassy median. I follow him down, landing directly on top of him. It's not a pretty scene. Making matters worse is the fact that at the precise moment I land on Tank, the car he was so worried about is a mere twenty feet away and approaching quickly.

So here I am, naked and wearing a condom, my body resting between my best friend's spread-eagled legs.

The look of disgust on Tank's face is unforgettable, and he immediately does what anybody in that situation would do. He pushes me off. But the timing is horrible, because as I battle with my pants and scramble to my feet, the car passes.

And it's not a cop as Tank had feared, but it is a silver sedan, meaning it's ... no way ... yes ... shit ... it's Coach Hank Horton, and the look of horror that spreads across *his* face is worse than the one I just saw on Tank's.

Horton slams on the brakes, coming to an abrupt stop in front of us. He rolls down the passenger-side window. I stand there, trying to pull my underwear up and over the condom, which barely clings to my ... well, you know.

Tank looks defeated. He rolls onto his belly and stares at Horton's car.

"Well, Jesus Christ," Horton says. "I figured you might be a homo, Ramsey." He's wagging an accusatory finger at me. "Wait'll I tell your old man about this." He scrunches his nose and frowns. "And what the hell's that smell? Man, you two stink." He looks at Tank. "As for you, Foster, I have to say I'm a little shocked. I never pegged you as gay."

"I'm not gay, coach." Tank bounces to his feet and dusts himself off.

"Whatever," Horton says. "Have a good night, ladies."

"Hey, Coach," I say, totally pissed as I toss the condom into the evergreens and manage to pull up my underwear and pants. "Guess what?"

"What is it, Homo? I mean Ramsey." He laughs.

And I say, "Enjoy yourself tonight, because you're about to go down."

There's a long silence, Tank shifting his gaze between Horton and me, Horton shifting his gaze between Tank and me.

"Is that right?" Horton finally says. "And what makes you say that, Homo Ramsey?"

"Guess you'll just have to wait and see."

Another silence.

"Yeah right," he finally says. "You don't have anything on me and you know it."

He drives off. We listen to him laughing to himself all the way down the street.

As Tank stands in the median with his hands on his hips, staring at Horton's taillights, I come up behind him, cautious. I know he's about to totally call me out on what I just said, so I put my hand in my front pocket, relieved to feel my phone and the empty injector bottle.

Trying to keep it light, I say, "I guess Horton thinks we're gay."

"Yeah, looks that way."

"Think he'll really tell my dad?"

"No," Tank says. "He's bluffing."

"What's he doing out here in the Heights so late, anyway?"

"Beats me."

I inhale deeply, smelling nothing but skunk spray. "Hey, I think the skunk got us a little."

"Zach, don't ever say a word about what just happened."

"Don't worry. It was kind of weird, wasn't it?"

"It was the weirdest thing ever," he says. "So don't talk about it, okay?"

I nod.

He says, "At least you know how to wear a condom now."

"True."

We cross to the sidewalk and continue on.

A few moments later Tank says, "So what the hell were you talking about when you told Horton he was about to go down?"

And I still have my hand in my pocket, grasping the Decabol bottle, and I'm just about to take it out and simply hand it to him, when suddenly I get cold feet and decide to go with another fact instead. Tank just looks too unpredictable and crazy tonight. I seriously consider the fact that he might break a bone of mine or kill me altogether if I confront him with the stash.

So this is what I give him: "Horton forced himself on my mom a few years ago. I just found out about it. Justin saw the whole thing. That's the real reason he quit playing."

It's something.

It's true.

Not exactly the whole story, I know, but it's not a lie, either.

"Damn," Tank says. "That sucks. Did he hurt her?"

"More like she hurt him." I smile. "She kicked him in the balls."

"Sweet. So what now, they've decided to go to the police?"

"Yeah," I lie. "Horton's history."

"Sounds like it," Tank says, not offering any information of his own but changing the subject instead, saying, "Well, Horton was right about one thing." He sniffs the air. "We stink." He pauses. "I hope Mandy's still interested."

And I say, "Well, if she likes skunks, we're all set."

21

We reach Mandy Frack's house, a huge colonial, and cut across the dewy lawn, walking alongside the home until we come to a tall wooden privacy gate. The gate is unlocked. We push it open and enter an enormous backyard. A tall fence matching the gate surrounds the yard. To our immediate left, an ornate plywood deck borders the rear of the house. I see two outdoor speakers mounted above the sliding glass door. Hip-hop music plays quietly.

The swimming pool is clearly the jewel of the Frack estate. It sits in the center of the yard, a fancy, aboveground, Kayak-style rectangle with a wooden deck surrounded by a fiberglass privacy wall. We can't see the water, but we hear some light splashing, like somebody's hands smacking the surface. Tank and I look at each other, shrug, and walk over to the short ladder leading to the deck.

She's waiting for us, Mandy Frack, wearing a black

two-piece and lying on her back on a raft in the middle of the pool, showing the kind of body I thought only existed in movies. She's seventeen going on twenty-five, with long black hair combed back over her head. Beads of water cover her bronze skin.

No wonder Tank's so excited.

Despite her beauty, however, I'm thinking only of Sarah, because the sight of this teen goddess in a swimsuit transports me back to that unforgettable morning behind Tank's house when I kissed Sarah for the first time. I want *Sarah* to be on that raft right now, not this wrestling groupie. If she were Sarah, I'd be in the water already. But she isn't Sarah, and the realization that I have to figure out some way to avoid this girl hits me like an oversized hailstone. My stomach rumbles at the thought of being with any female other than Sarah Foster.

Standing on the deck, I notice her eyes dancing over Tank. She doesn't seem interested in me. Good.

"Hey, Tank," she says in a high voice. "Thought you two would never show up."

"Had a short delay," Tank says. He nods toward me. "This is Zach. The guy I was telling you about."

She finally looks at me, paying close attention to my feet.

"So, which one is it?" she says.

"I'm sorry?" I ask, clueless.

"Which ankle did you hurt? They both look fine to me."

"Oh, it's my right one." I reach down and massage it for dramatic effect. "Hurts bad tonight. I think climbing that ladder made it worse."

Tank gives me a look.

Mandy says, "You two gonna stand there or get in?"

"Oh, we're coming in," Tank says and starts to pull off his shirt.

"There's a rule for guys," she adds. "No clothes allowed."

"No problem," Tank says, ripping off his shirt as if it's on fire. He's careful with his pants, though, gently removing the pint and cigarettes, then turning away from me as he slowly pulls off his jeans and underwear, folding them neatly and stacking everything on a small table near the ladder. He lays the pint on top of the pile like it's a paperweight.

He asks me for a condom. I give him one. Then he jumps in and swims toward Mandy.

I'm still fully dressed.

Mandy says, "What's the matter, Zach? Come on in. I don't bite."

"My ankle's really bad," I say, adding a limp to the act. "Give me a few minutes to walk it off." Tank's behind the raft now, throwing his hands in the air as if to say to me, what, are you crazy, Ramsey?

I turn and hobble down the ladder.

When I'm on the lawn, I hear her whisper to Tank, "Is he gay?"

"Just nervous," Tank says. "He'll be ready in a few minutes."

"There must be a skunk around," she says. "Something stinks." I hear her slide off the raft and into the water.

So I pace back and forth on the lawn, listening to the disgusting sounds coming from the swimming pool. At one point I have to plug my ears. The whole scenario is too disturbing. I mean, she's expecting *me* next, and if I don't go through with it, Tank and everybody else at Blaine Memorial High School will hold it over my head for my entire senior year. The hallways will be a living hell.

On the other hand, if I go ahead and join Mandy, Sarah will eventually find out and our relationship will end, and there's no way I can risk that. The student body of Blaine Memorial can taunt me all they want, but if it means saving my future with Sarah, I'll take it like a man.

So I'll have to be honest and tell Mandy I'm not interested, tell her I'm saving myself for somebody special. Sarah Foster is the only girl I can imagine being with. Of course, if I say that to Mandy, the thing about saving myself, Tank will wonder who I'm talking about and prod me until I tell him.

And maybe that's exactly what I need right now. Finally.

The more I think about it, the more it makes sense. The timing will be perfect. What better time to tell Tank about his twin sister and me than right after he's been with Mandy? I mean, he'll be in a great mood, right, having just done it and all that? Maybe he won't beat me to death after all.

I don't have a watch, but Tank's been in there close to five minutes now. The annoying sounds, combined with Mandy's periodic complaints about the skunk that must be hiding under the deck, further sicken me.

And that's when my stomach decides it can't handle the stress any longer.

I bend over and vomit onto the white landscape rocks bordering the pool, the burn of bile and whiskey stinging my throat and esophagus as the puke spills out. After wiping my mouth with the back of my hand, I hunch forward and spit out several long and sticky strings of saliva. Feeling much better, I straighten and listen. Mandy and Tank don't seem to have heard me puking. Good.

I'm about to continue my nervous pacing when a pair of hands surprise me from behind and cover my mouth and eyes. I try screaming, but only a muffled grunt emerges. Next come several more hands and arms, lifting me like a roll of carpet and carrying me several feet before dropping me onto my stomach.

What the hell?

Now two heavy people, have to be guys, are straddling my back, one of them pushing my face into the lawn hard enough for me to taste grass and smell the fertilizer Mr. Frack must have recently applied. This same person pins my arms behind my back, pushing them up at an agonizing angle. The other guy immobilizes my legs, and I'm afraid to move, afraid of more pain. I listen as a flurry of footsteps trot around me and throughout the yard. Then

I hear some light laughter and whispers followed by an uncomfortable silence.

A male voice close to my ear says, "Relax, man. It's just a joke." The two guys suddenly decide to get off of me and I scramble to my feet, where the flash of a portable spotlight instantly blinds me. Shielding my eyes, I turn away and stumble toward the pool.

That's when I hear Mandy Frack laughing.

"The hell's going on out there?" Tank yells from the pool.

"Welcome to senior year, Tank," Mandy says. "Surprise, surprise!"

Tank, angry now: "Who's out there?"

From behind the spotlight a series of male voices say, in unison, "Yeah, welcome to senior year, Tank!"

The spotlight goes out.

Ten members of the Blaine Memorial High School wrestling squad, all upcoming seniors like us, stand in the yard, laughing and giving each other high fives.

Chad Billings, the second best wrestler on the team behind Tank, stands in the middle. He holds the spotlight and is clearly the ringleader. He's taller and bigger than Tank, a rare sight. Regardless, Tank can't stand the prick, says Chad's always been jealous of his superior skills on the mat.

I look down and notice Tank's clothing bundled into a small pile on the lawn, inches from Chad's feet. The cigarettes and pint still rest atop the pile. Chad Billings reaches for the bottle, takes a gulp, and passes it to a teammate.

"You drink good booze, Foster," he says. "Now get out here and let's go party." He looks at me. "You can bring Ramsey, too, I guess."

Billings gives me one of those cocky jock looks, and then I hear Tank say, "Is that you, Billings?"

Billings says, "No, it's your mom."

His cronies laugh.

Mandy Frack laughs.

Tank and I don't laugh.

Chad Billings has just made a horrible mistake. Tank's mom is off limits.

I hear Tank lift himself out of the water. He walks to the edge of the privacy deck and stares out into the yard. The deck's side panels conceal him from the waist down. He looks toward the ladder and seems puzzled for a moment. Then he fixes his gaze on Chad Billings with that disturbing look of rage in his eyes that I know all too well. I saw it the night he played chicken with the locomotive, saw it again during the Big Dale Foster Bedroom Tour.

"Where'd my clothes go?" Tank says.

"See, that's the thing," Billings says, his buddies still laughing. "You'll have to come and get them." He points down at the pile.

Tank studies his clothes as if something isn't right. He has that puzzled expression again. Weird. Tank never seems puzzled.

"Okay, fine," Tank finally says. "Here I come."

Mandy Frack laughs. "Oh, you go get them, big boy."

"Shut up, bitch," Tank yells. His eyes are on Billings as he crosses toward the ladder.

The team stops laughing.

So does Mandy.

"Hey, relax, Foster," Billings says. "We're just playing around here." He pauses. "Dude, we're here to tell you we want you to be our senior captain."

"Screw you, Tank," Mandy says. I hear her getting out of the pool. She's wrapped a towel around her waist and stands on the far side of the deck. "And by the way, you smell horrible."

Tank climbs down the ladder and steps onto the grass. Billings and his crew snicker and mutter things under their breath. Tank walks past me like I'm not even here. It's awkward seeing him like this, walking nude in front of so many people. I wonder why he didn't simply challenge Billings to walk the clothes over to him at the pool. I mean, that's what I've come to expect from Tank when he gets like this. He doesn't take shit from anybody, and the last thing he wants is to embarrass himself.

But that's exactly what he's doing right now, humiliating himself, walking around like this in front of his wrestling peers.

So I follow him, worried.

When Mandy sees me, she says, "Thought your ankle was hurt, Zach."

"Guess it got better," I say over my shoulder.

"Suppose you're ready for me now, huh?" she says. "Well, too bad. You were never in the plan."

I stop and turn. "That's good, because I wouldn't touch you even if we were the last two people alive."

I continue trailing Tank. He doesn't say anything, just keeps walking toward Billings. Billings looks nervous.

Tank's about ten feet away from him, silent but determined.

Billings kicks the clothes.

"Don't touch them," Tank orders. "Don't touch my stuff."

"You challenging me, Foster?" Billings says.

"Just don't touch them."

Billings glances to his left and right, smiling at his buddies. Then he reaches down and picks up Tank's jeans.

"Drop them," Tank says, barely three feet away from Billings now.

"Christ, Foster," Billings says, smelling the fabric, "you do stink." He feels the front pocket. "What's in here, anyway, free weights?"

But before Chad Billings can check, Tank raises his right foot and kicks the jeans out of Billings's hands, his foot hooking the pants in a way that sends them floating back toward him, where he snags them in mid-air, all of this done in one swift motion. It's the kind of fight move you see in movies, yet here it is going down in a backyard in Blaine Heights, Michigan.

Incredible.

Stunned, Billings steps back and stares at his empty hands, shaking the sting out of them. Tank quickly steps into his pants, pulling them up and zipping them. His underwear is still on the ground, but he doesn't seem to care.

"The hell's your problem, Foster?" Billings says.

"You are," Tank says, and reaches into his front pocket.

The gun is tiny and looks like a toy, but I know it's real. Tank obviously took it from his dad's collection.

Everything makes sense once he pulls it out and aims it at Chad Billings. The reason he acted so oddly on the deck was because he couldn't believe the wrestlers didn't find the gun when they took his clothes, too caught up in their own prank to notice. Now I understand why Tank so willingly swallowed his pride and walked across the lawn to get his pants. I mean, the last thing he wanted was Chad Billings getting his hands on the gun.

The only problem now is that Tank has snapped, and I have a feeling he might actually shoot Billings because of the comment about his mom. Jesus. Our first night out in what seems like forever is turning into a nightmare, and I have a feeling it's about to get worse.

Call it 'roid rage or whatever, but the fact is that right now Tank Foster looks like a deranged psycho with a total chemical imbalance, standing there wearing only jeans, waving the gun back and forth over the wrestling team. A wet spot emerges on the front of Chad Billings's khaki shorts, and I watch it spread until it's the size of a mini-Frisbee.

"Hey, I'm sorry, Foster," Billings pleads. "Jesus, it's just a prank. We want you as captain, man!" He points at the gun. "That thing loaded?"

Tank says, "You want to find out? How about I stick it in your mouth and make you pull the trigger? Ever suck on a gun barrel, Billings? My dad tells me they used to mess with captured Iraqis that way in the Gulf War, stick it down their throats and make them squeeze the trigger."

I watch Billings's Adams apple bob as he swallows. He says, "Christ, you're crazier than I thought."

Tank extends his arm until it locks out. Twelve inches of air separate the gun from Chad Billings's face.

"Tank," I say, moving closer to him. "It's over. Just put it down, man. He apologized."

Billings starts to cry. "Yeah, man. Jesus Christ, I'm sorry, Foster. Please don't shoot me."

Tank doesn't answer, cocks his head from left to right, eyes on Billings. I'm convinced I'm about to witness a homicide, and judging from the looks of the other nine guys, they must feel the same way. They remind me of electrocuted ghosts, shocked and white.

From the pool deck, Mandy Frack yells, "That thing's a toy. Kick his ass, Chad."

Bad move, Mandy.

Tank lowers his arm across the front of his body, making a large U shape as he raises the gun toward the pool and steadies it on Mandy Frack. A yellowish-orange flash of light explodes from the end of the gun's short barrel, followed by a loud cracking sound that reminds me of one of the M80 firecrackers Justin blows up in the backyard every now and then when he's drunk.

The weapon's kickback has no effect on Tank. He stands his ground like some stoic marble statue. A putrid odor accompanies the thin streams of smoke hovering above the barrel. Mandy Frack's backyard suddenly smells like skunks and smoke bombs.

With the exception of Tank, everybody drops to the grass upon hearing the blast. When the smoke clears, I sit up to check on Mandy. She's nowhere in sight. I picture her lifeless body floating in the pool, the water stained red with her blood. Moments later, however, I'm relieved to hear the sound of her crying somewhere on the deck.

Tank says, "Still think it's a toy, Mandy?"

She's crying harder now.

"My God," a terrified Chad Billings says. "You shot her."

"I didn't shoot her," Tank says, finally lowering the gun.

"How do you know?" Billings asks.

"Because I know how to shoot," Tank says. He turns toward Billings. "I went wide right on purpose."

Billings sits up. Tank walks over and presses the barrel to his forehead.

An overwhelming silence descends upon Blaine Heights.

Tank notices. "Why's everybody so quiet? I feel like I'm at a convention for mutes."

For some reason, that almost makes me laugh.

Shifting his gaze between Billings and his petrified crew, Tank says, "Not much to talk about now, huh, Billings?" To his crew: "Not much to laugh at now, is there, guys?" To Billings and his crew: "Funny how the prospect of death silences even the biggest of assholes."

Billings is on his knees now, arms limp, all of his buddies still lying in the grass, arms over their heads like they're participating in one of those old Cold War duck-and-cover drills. Looking at Chad Billings, I see a guy who thinks his life is about to end. He's too afraid to speak. Snot dangles from his nostrils like silly string, eyes closed as he awaits Tank's kill shot.

"Tank, don't do it," I plead. "You'll go to prison forever. Just breathe and let's get out of here."

Billings whimpers like a helpless puppy. Tank doesn't acknowledge me. He's in another world, some possessed state I know nothing about. His chest rises and falls rapidly, his brow furrowed. I think back to the railroad tracks again and how close he came to getting killed that night. This Tank Foster is a stranger to me, a terrifying stranger who is impossible to reason with. Despite all of his athletic gifts and bright future, my best friend has some psychological scars that need serious professional attention.

"Tank," I say again, trying to sound calm. "Put the gun down." Again, he doesn't respond. I watch his finger apply added pressure to the trigger. Another little squeeze and Chad Billings gets a bullet lodged in his brain.

Luckily for him—and for Tank—a siren saves his life.

There it is, the unmistakable high-pitched wail of a nearby police cruiser. Tank hears it, too, and it somehow yanks him out of his psychotic trance. Maybe the sound reminds him of his father, or maybe it just startles him. I have no idea, but I'm relieved to see him shaking his head and rubbing his ears, back from that dark place.

He lowers the gun and scoops the rest of his clothing toward him with his foot. Chad Billings hangs his head, puts his face in his hands, and cries like a newborn, thanking God and Tank for not killing him.

"Shut the hell up, Billings," Tank says. He studies the empty Jack Daniels bottle lying on the grass. "You owe me a pint of whiskey. I want it within a week." Shifting his gaze between Mandy on the pool deck and the other nine guys scattered across the lawn, he yells, "Listen up, kiddies. Don't ever mess with Tank Foster again. If anybody talks about tonight, I'll hunt you down one by one and eat you for dinner."

The siren is getting closer.

Tank notices, grabs his clothes and the cigarettes. As we pass through the gate and reach the front yard, he stops to put his shirt and shoes on. When we're on the sidewalk, I expect him to want to go run and hide, but he's as casual as an old lady strolling through her flower garden.

"I like the feel of not wearing underwear," he tells me, tossing his bunched-up briefs into a neighbor's bushes. "I think I'll roll this way from now on."

"Tank, I think those sirens are coming for us."

"What makes you think that?"

"Well, you just fired a gun in Blaine Heights."

He lights two cigarettes, hands me one.

"Big deal. Nobody got hurt." He smells his shirt. "Mandy was right about one thing, though. We smell."

"You wanna go home? Wash up in some tomato juice?"

He thinks about it, looks himself over.

"Yeah," he finally says, tucking the gun in the back of his waist and pulling his shirt loosely over it. "That's probably a good idea."

I breathe a deep sigh of relief, lower my head, and follow, knowing it's not exactly the greatest time to bring up the stash and Sarah.

I mean, think about it. The guy has a loaded gun and has shown his willingness to use it.

22

Maybe it's because we're suddenly in a hurry to get out of the Heights and away from the cops, but somehow we lose track of street names and find ourselves lost. The only good news is that the sirens quickly come to a halt, and I wonder if the police have showed up at Mandy Frack's. For all I know, Tank Foster might be the city's most wanted man.

Tank seems to know this, because he turns off his cell and orders me to do the same, which I immediately do.

We find ourselves on a street called Glendale. The homes here are even fancier than the ones on Mandy's street, bigger colonials on double lots with well-groomed lawns and mature willow and maple trees. There are no streetlights. We avoid sidewalks, using trees and the sides of houses for cover. As we navigate the street, I wonder what these people do for a living to afford such luxury.

We stay silent for a few blocks until we feel somewhat safe from the police.

However, we still don't know where we are.

That's when Tank says, "I scare myself sometimes."

"You scare everybody, Tank."

"I'm not joking."

"You have a loaded handgun in your pants. That should tell you something about yourself right there."

"I'm a responsible marksman. My dad taught me well."

"You call firing at a girl on a pool deck responsible?"

"I knew what I was doing."

"What about when you had the gun on Billings's forehead? You remember that?"

"I was in total control."

"Whatever. I know when you lose it. Your face says it all." I pause. "You don't remember, do you?"

"Bits and pieces. That's why I scare myself. I know when it's coming, one of the moods. Sometimes I can stop it, other times I can't."

"Maybe you could at least take the bullets out of the gun."

"No. It'll be tricky enough replacing the one I used. If I don't put it back exactly how I found it, my dad will know."

A few minutes pass in silence. Then we come to Birch Street and can't help but smile. We know where we are. Finally. Birch is the wealthiest street in Blaine Heights. We turn left, knowing Michigan Avenue is only ten minutes away. Massive brick Tudors line Birch Street, most of them built by wealthy auto executives back in the glory days of the industry. The homes are set back atop a natural rise, each one overlooking a lush green lawn that seems larger than a football field.

"Wow," I say, craning my neck to get a view of each house we pass. "Trump could live back here."

"You think they have it all," Tank says. "But my dad says rich people are more screwed up than average people."

"I wouldn't mind finding out for myself. I want to be rich. I *have* to be rich."

"Why?"

"Because I'm sick of being poor."

"Yeah, me too."

"You know, if Mandy and Billings tell the cops, you'll get arrested."

"They're too scared to tell."

"But what if they do?"

Tank ignores the question, stops and points toward a house up the street.

"Looks like a party," he says. "Check out all the cars."

The house is about forty yards away. We walk toward it.

I count four vehicles in the driveway, a few more parked along the curb. The street is silent. For some reason, Tank quickens his pace and walks ahead of me, coming to a sudden stop about ten feet from the driveway.

Catching up to him, I say, "Hey, maybe this is where Coach Horton was coming from. I bet some rich football boosters live here or something."

Staring at the street, he says, "Recognize that truck?"

I look.

I nod.

A sick, sour feeling fills my gut. A blue Ford truck is parked curbside. The shiny chrome grill means it can belong to only one man: Big Dale Foster.

That's when it hits me that Big Dale might well be here with his girlfriend, one Mrs. Helen Dawkins.

Damn.

Tank says, "What's my dad doing at a party in the Heights?"

"I don't know. Let's just go home."

"Are you kidding?" He walks up the driveway. "We totally have to check this out."

And all I can do is shrug and follow.

The silence is deceiving. Despite the vehicles out front, we don't see or hear any evidence of activity inside the house. Moving up the long driveway, we eventually veer left and walk alongside a stand of trees running the length of the lot that serves as a natural privacy fence from the neighboring home. I'm out of breath by the time we reach the top of the rise, wondering how I'm going to make it through a single football practice without throwing up a summer's worth of alcohol and tobacco.

We stop and stare at the side of the house. Every window is dark, curtains and blinds drawn. Tank studies the layout and steps out from the shelter of trees. We cut across the lawn until we reach a cobblestone path hugging the side of the home. Walking the path, I look up and notice thick ivy blanketing a huge chimney. The house reminds me of some aristocratic cottage in the English countryside. I look down and see several rectangular windows along the foundation, but these are dark as well.

Where *is* everybody?

A six-foot-tall, black iron fence borders the backyard. Each fence post has an ornamental spike on top. The gate is latched, so Tank reaches his hand through one of the wide spaces between the posts and opens it from the inside. The gate creaks as it opens. We continue along the cobblestone path, which takes us to a large concrete patio surrounding an in-ground, kidney-shaped swimming pool. No one is in the pool, and the underground lights give the undisturbed water a glasslike quality.

Tank stops and rubs his chin, thinking as he gazes into the water.

The more I look at the pool, the more its beauty stands out. This is a work of art compared to Mandy Frack's pool. Waiting for Tank to decide on his next move, I imagine Sarah and me owning this house and swimming together back here, Sarah in her orange bikini, smelling of lavender as she swims toward me and ...

... and I pull her close, the two of us kissing in the shallow end as music plays through the best outdoor speakers on the market.

Then I picture our kids—twin daughters named Ashley and Katelyn—running onto the patio wearing their diapers, giggling at Mommy and Daddy kissing in the pool. Sarah and I laugh and lift our angelic offspring into the water. Sarah grabs Ashley. I take little Katelyn. We hold them high above our heads, our hands under their armpits as they laugh from the excitement of being so high in the air. They scream with joy as we lower their little legs into the cool water and spin them around in quick circles until they're dizzy and exhausted. After a few more minutes of valuable parent-child bonding time, I summon the nanny to come and put the twins to bed.

Next, I tell Stuart the butler to put on some steaks and to be sure the Budweiser is cold and the music loud. He smiles, bows as always, and heads inside to meet my simple requests. When I turn around, Sarah is smiling and swimming toward me.

After dinner, Sarah and I decide to take the Ferrari out for a late-night cruise. I navigate Michigan Avenue as if it's the Autobahn, cranking the bass and laughing at every car we pass, including police cruisers.

We're pulling the Ferrari into the driveway and getting ready to jump back into the shallow end when...

... Tank elbows me and says, "Hey, look up there."

Fantasy over.

Still slightly dazed, I stare at the stained-glass-like water and say, "Tank, there's something you need to know about me and—"

"Not now," he interrupts. "Look up there."

I look away from the pool and follow his outstretched

index finger. He's pointing at the back of the house. An outline of dim light borders the edges of a drawn curtain in a room on the second level. The room has a walkout balcony overlooking the pool.

"It's too high," I say.

"So we climb. All we have to do is get to the balcony."

I scan our surroundings. "I don't see a ladder."

"We don't need one."

"What are we supposed to do, jump?"

"The chimney," he says and heads back toward the gate. "We can use that chimney."

I shake my head and flip him off behind his back.

"You're gonna get us killed tonight."

He laughs and opens the gate.

———

Being taller and wider than me, Tank cups his hands and boosts me as I step into his linked palms. The chimney has a series of small step-like indentations up the side. The width and spacing of the "steps" look safe enough to walk up, as long as we keep our bodies against the chimney for balance.

Problem is, the first step is at least ten feet off the ground, meaning I have to pull myself up once I get hold of the ledge. The thick ivy isn't making the task any easier. Hanging there, I realize this is the equivalent of trying to do chin-ups in a rainforest canopy. And sure enough, my reach falls short on the first attempt. My palms scrape brick all the way down. Tank has to break my fall. I'm in pain and my forearms itch from the ivy, but I don't say a word, just put my foot back into Tank's palms and let him shove me skyward again.

This time I make it, digging my fingertips into the brick and pulling myself up until I'm standing on the first ledge.

"Good job," Tank whispers up at me. "Can you make it on your own?"

"Think so." The steps are wider than I thought, and I'll only have to climb four more before being able to leap onto the roof. "I hope so."

"Get going," Tank says. "I'll be right behind you. We'll have a smoke when we get on top."

I take a deep breath and scale the second step with ease. But then the angle between the ledges changes and I have to bear-crawl my way up the next two. When I look down, Tank has already lifted himself onto the first step with effortless grace. He's obviously done a lot more chin-ups in his life than I have. Anyway, my stomach whips around a bit as I realize the distance between the roof and the last step is greater than I'd anticipated.

Feeling Tank closing the gap below, I take a deep breath and dive for the roof.

I land on my side, my body hitting the thick slate tiles with a dull thud. The pain in my ribs is intense. I groan. Sitting up, I see Tank standing on the top ledge, eyeing the roof with a doubtful look on his face.

"I think I'm too big," he says.

"And you'll be too loud," I say, rubbing my side. "If anybody's sleeping, I just woke them up." I lift myself to my feet. "I'm coming down."

"No," he whispers, and launches himself toward the roof. He lands in front of me, barely making it onto the slate. The roof shakes like an active fault line. I lose my balance and nearly fall to a premature death.

"We could get shot up here," I say. "You realize that? Whoever lives here can shoot us and get away with it, say they thought we were breaking in."

"I'll shoot back," he says, patting the gun. "Light me a smoke. We don't have much time."

I light the cigarettes and follow Tank toward the back of the house and around to the balcony. Here we are, smoking cigarettes as we try to keep our balance on the roof. It's all so funny that at one point I have to bite my tongue to keep from laughing.

Anyway, despite our tiptoeing and my near-laughter, I'm convinced somebody inside can hear us and will emerge at any moment. But I have to admit, there's an element of excitement to the danger. Yeah, I'm scared of what I'm about to see, but the adrenaline flowing through my body seems to override the fear, forcing me onward like some soldier of the suburbs.

We hop the balcony's short guardrails with ease. The view of the pool is magnificent. I'm tempted to continue my fantasy with Sarah, but Tank has other things on his mind. I turn to say something and notice him standing in front of the window already, staring at it like he's afraid to go any further. Inside, the dim, filtered light still shows around the edges of the drawn curtain. The gap between the curtain and the window frame is barely an inch, meaning Tank will have to press his nose against the glass to see inside.

He takes one last big hit off his cigarette and flicks it over the balcony. I watch it land on the patio, the lighted end splintering off into dozens of tiny orange particles. Tank gives me a look, cups his hands around the left edge of the glass, and peers in. Seconds later, without turning, he reaches his right arm behind him and motions me over to the opposite side. I toss my cigarette butt and step forward.

What I see makes me want to puke.

A man and a woman are naked in bed, no sheets covering them. The bed is fancy, a king-size four-poster. The man is lying on his back in the middle of the mattress, but we can't see his face because the woman is straddling his mid-section, her back to us. The woman has a stellar body, a dark tan, and long, ratted-out blonde hair, three features that convince me she's Helen Dawkins. I've never seen anything like this, and it's totally upsetting and gross, so I close my eyes.

Tight.

None of it seems to bother Tank, though. I can hear him laughing.

He says, "You think that's my dad?"

"I don't know." My eyes are still closed, my stomach churning. "Tank, I don't like this. I think we should—"

"Dude, it's my dad," he interrupts.

I open my eyes, but I still can't see the guy's face.

"How do you know?"

"His Gulf War tattoo," he says. "The green dragon."

He's right.

Dale Foster has his hands clasped together behind his head in a way that flares his elbows out to the side, making his forearms visible, and the green dragon is looking at us through the window. The woman on top suddenly runs her hands through her hair and turns her head to the right. At that moment, I see enough of her face to realize she's definitely Helen Dawkins.

Tank sees her too.

He says, "Wow. She's pretty hot."

Silence.

"It's Huey's wife," I say, swallowing hard and looking away, somewhat shocked as the reality of it all sets in. Up until now I'd only seen pictures of her stashed away in Big Dale's closet. But something about actually witnessing them together sends me to new lows.

"Huey's *wife*?" Tank says, still watching but sounding concerned. "Are you sure?"

"I'm sure." I watch Tank watching them. "I recognize her from a picture." And that's really all my best friend needs in terms of proof, because there's no way I'm telling him about the three photos I found in the closet.

"My dad's with Huey's *wife*?" Tank says in disbelief. "A married woman?"

Another silence.

I don't know what else to say to him. Truth is, we're both pretty bummed out.

Tank punches the glass door. Hard. I can't believe it doesn't shatter.

Helen Dawkins turns toward us as the unmistakable face of Dale Foster appears just to the left of her torso.

Damn.

Tank bolts past me and hops back onto the roof before I can even react.

I follow, more worried about him now than I was in Mandy's backyard.

When I reach the chimney, he's somehow already made the dangerous return leap and is descending the bricks and ivy with little regard for his own body. By the time I summon enough courage to make the jump, Tank's on the ground, running toward the front of the house.

I land hard. Pain shoots through my feet. I look toward the front yard and Tank's nowhere in sight, so I run for the street, figuring I'll meet up with him back home.

But that never happens.

I'm nearing the long driveway when I hear another loud, M80-like crack echo through the night.

Tank is shooting at something... or someone.

Another three shots ring out by the time I've reached the street. Tank's standing in front of his father's truck, staring at the grill, the gun dangling from his limp right hand. The overwhelming smell of cordite permeates my nostrils and mouth. I stand beside him and look at the pickup. He's shot all four tires, the bottom of each looking like a big wad of melted tar.

Before I can try to calm him down, the front doors of the house open and Dale Foster runs toward us, a white robe hanging loosely from his body. Helen Dawkins and a few other robed adults stand on the wraparound porch, gawking. The sight of all those robes makes me wonder what *really* goes on in this house, but I don't have time to ponder that thought, which is probably a good thing.

Tank shoves me out of the way and raises the gun toward his father.

Dale Foster stops on the lawn and puts his hands in the air. He's about twenty feet away from his son. I get up from the hard cement and retreat to the sidewalk, the sting of the concrete snaking through my body like a fast-growing spider web.

"Put it down, son," Big Dale says, in a voice that is half cop and half parent.

"Why should I?" Tank says. "You're nothing but a lie."

"Son, I know you're upset right now, but don't make things worse."

"Why can't you just be a dad? You drove Mom away and you're nothing but a goddamn fake."

Sirens sound in the distance.

Some of the adults on the porch are on their cell phones.

Neighbors are out on their lawns now.

"Tank, put the gun down," Dale pleads. "This is wrong and you know it."

"I don't know what I know," Tank shouts. He turns to his right and fires a bullet through the truck's windshield.

People scream. Many retreat indoors.

Tank drops the gun onto the hood of the truck and takes off down the street past me. I think about following him but decide against it.

Dale Foster sprints out into the street and grabs the gun. Watching his son vanishing into the darkness, he says to me, "Zach, does he have any other guns on him?"

"No," I say, pissed off at this miserable excuse for a father.

So I march toward Big Dale and glimpse what look like flashing blue lights moving quickly up a neighboring street. On the lawn, Helen Dawkins jogs toward us with a look of concern on her face. She hugs Big Dale and looks at me.

"You're in a lot of trouble, young man," she says.

"Nice to see you tonight, *Mrs.* Dawkins," I say.

She squints and studies me.

"Do I know you?"

"I work for your husband. You know, the guy you're *married* to?"

She turns and walks back to the porch.

Big Dale shuffles his feet and shakes his head.

"Mr. Foster, can I tell you something?" I ask, totally fuming.

"After tonight, Zach, I think you can tell me anything."

Pointing at him, I go, "Well, sir, I…" And here I trail off for a moment, struggling to organize all of this flaming anger into the right words. "I…I used to really hope you would end up being different from everybody else around here." I pause, shaking my head. "But you're not." I stop pointing and shove my hand in my front pocket.

"Nobody's perfect, Zach," he says calmly. "Especially in Blaine."

"Here," I say, handing him the empty bottle of Decabol.

He holds it up, inspects it. "Where'd you get this?"

"Hang on," I say, taking out my phone and loading the pictures I took of Tank's stash. "You need to check the green tackle box in the crawlspace." I hand him my phone. "Take a look."

"Jesus," he says, squinting and studying each picture. "Tank's on this stuff?"

"Come on, Mr. Foster," I say, rolling my eyes. "Take a good look at your son." He hands me my phone without saying a word. "Get Coach Horton," I add. "He's the kingpin."

Holding my gaze, Dale Foster says, "You should probably go home now, Zach."

"Right," I say and take a deep breath. "Just one more thing, sir." I clear my throat and notice the flashing blue lights closing in on us. "You need to know that I'm in love with your daughter and she's in love with me."

And he just looks at me and says, "We already know that, Zach. We've known since June."

"*We?*"

"Tank and me," he says, at which point my stomach seems to drop to the pavement. "He hasn't mentioned it to you?"

"No," I say. "I mean, not really. I had a pretty good feeling he knew, but … well, no."

He shrugs. "Well, that's kind of surprising, because we're both fine with it."

"You are?"

Two police cruisers pull up beside him. He waves to the officers and gestures toward his bullet-ridden pickup. Then he hustles over and says something to them, pointing in the direction Tank went. I recognize the two men in the first car as the same officers who escorted Tank and me home the night of the rock-throwing incident. As their cruiser speeds past me to go find Tank, the two officers spot me and shake their heads like I'm the biggest loser on the planet.

"Listen, Zach," Big Dale says, jogging back toward me. "Sarah could do a lot worse. Those were Tank's exact words, 'Sarah could do a lot worse.'" He looks up the street in the direction Tank ran. "Just give him some time to cool down."

He puts his hands on his hips, gazes up and down the street.

Two more police cars arrive. Mr. Foster heads over, says something to them, and the two cruisers speed away. Then a wrecker arrives to get Big Dale's truck. A fat guy gets out and shakes Dale's hand before cranking the useless pickup onto the rear deck and driving away.

After the wrecker leaves, Dale asks me how I'm planning on getting home. I tell him I feel like walking. He says that's fine with him. I light a cigarette. He doesn't say anything.

"I suppose you'll tell my parents about tonight, huh?"

"Why?" he says. "As far as I can tell, you didn't do anything wrong."

He turns to join Helen and the others on the porch.

I stand there, sort of stunned, watching the flashing blue lights atop another arriving cruiser flicker and spin, the beams hitting my face every few seconds. I mean, it feels good knowing I've finally spilled the news about the stash and Horton's role. And it's cool knowing I have Big Dale's blessing with Sarah or whatever, but somehow I know the biggest hurdle still lies ahead.

Think about it: if Tank approves of Sarah and me, why hasn't he said anything?

23

The walk home is uneventful.

I reach my street at two o'clock and stand on my front lawn, staring at the dark house. I look around for Justin's car but don't see it. I'm tired, exhausted even, but I don't want to go inside yet. Because of all the fighting, Dad's been sleeping on a sofa in the basement. And that's such an uncomfortable feeling, living with parents who hate each other so much they can't even share a mattress at night. I wish they'd just divorce and get it over with.

I think about going to Sarah's window, but I can't take the chance of pissing off Tank. He's been through enough tonight. I've never been more worried about him, physically and emotionally.

So I light a cigarette and sit on the porch, gazing at the homes across the street and the railroad tracks beyond, reliving the time I spent with Sarah down in the fort. I feel helpless, like there's *something* I'm supposed to do but can't figure out exactly what it is.

Sarah Foster.

Tank Foster.

Girl of my dreams.

Best friend since elementary school.

After several minutes it finally hits me.

"Screw it," I whisper, and stand to go inside, flicking my cigarette onto the dead lawn and knowing that what I'm about to do will come back to bite me in the ass.

Regardless, it's the right thing to do.

Because right now it's all about helping Tank Foster, my best friend.

————

True to recent form, Justin has left his bedroom door unlocked. As I sit at the computer and wait for it to start up, every organ in my body seems to tremble with nerves.

I send two identical emails, one to the Blaine Police Department, the other to the Detroit Police Department. Between those two places, I figure Big Dale will either get a call or a forward pretty quickly. To be certain, I type *Attention Dale Foster* in the subject header.

This is what I write:

> *To Dale Foster and All Others Concerned,*
> *I think you'll find the attached audio and video files interesting.*

Sincerely,
Zach Ramsey

There. Simple and to the point. Between the video and audio files incriminating Horton, the empty Decabol bottle I already gave Big Dale, and the crawlspace tackle box stash, Dale Foster and his law enforcement pals should have more than enough information to begin looking into this mess.

And if not... well, at least I feel comfortable knowing I've finally revealed everything to somebody who can definitely get the job done.

Big Dale isn't a perfect man.

But he's one hell of a powerful cop.

24

The bite in the ass comes six hours later.

Sarah raps on the edge of my window screen at eight o'clock the following morning. It's Sunday and I can tell from the sweat covering me that today will be the hottest day of the summer.

I don't want to go to the window. I know exactly what's coming, and I suppose I deserve it, but I can't think of any plan that doesn't carry positives and negatives.

But, man, this particular negative is going to suck big-time.

So I pop out of bed and dash to the window, hoping her constant pounding hasn't awakened Mom or Dad.

When I lift the shade, I see Sarah Foster with a look on her face that makes it clear she would love nothing more than to punch through the dirty screen and tear my head off.

I can't even get the first word in.

She jabs her index finger against the screen. "Screw you, Zach. Screw you. I told you we had to work together, but you went off on your own. Do you have any idea what you've done?"

"Sarah, I'm sorry, but I had to do it. It couldn't wait. He's out of control. You would've done the same thing. You wouldn't believe what I witnessed him do last night."

Still jabbing the screen, she says, "It's not *what* you did, jerk. It's *how* you did it. You sent them to my *dad* and two *police departments*." She holds her hands up. "What the hell were you thinking? There was no reason to get them involved."

"Then who's supposed to take down Horton, Sarah? Got an answer for that one?"

"I was thinking *we* would, you idiot. That's why I said not to do anything without me. I'm not dumb, Zach. We could have confronted Horton on our own and forced him to stop supplying Tank." She makes a fist with her right hand and punches her open left palm. The smacking sound makes me flinch. "I sent you those files thinking I could trust you. I *wanted* to trust you. Look where that got me." She pauses. It's hard to hold her gaze. That's how pissed she is. "The most important thing was to keep Tank out of it, to keep him anonymous," she adds. "Well, congratulations, you just totally screwed that up."

"It's not just about Tank!" I yell, not caring if I wake anybody up now. "Jesus, Sarah, don't you see that? It's not just Tank. It's *everybody* Horton's supplying. I stand by what I did. The cops needed to know." I pause. "And now they know."

"Yeah," she says. "Let's talk about what they know. Now my dad and the police know that Tank Foster, all-state wrestler bound for greatness, maybe even Olympic gold, uses steroids supplied by a legendary high school football coach. I mean, my God, when the media gets hold of this—and you know they will, Zach—they'll have a field day. It's too juicy to resist."

"I don't know what's going to happen, Sarah. And neither do you, so stop speculating."

"Oh no," she says, shaking her head and pointing at me again. "Don't you dare tell me what and what not to think. Right now I'm telling *you* what to think. So think about this. When the story breaks and Tank's name surfaces, what college is going to offer a wrestling scholarship to a guy involved in a high school steroid scandal?" Silence. "Got an answer for that one, Zach?" Silence. "The answer is *none*. So there you go. That's what you've probably done. You've probably ruined Tank's ... Blaine Escape Plan ... or whatever the hell you call it."

"Again, you don't know any of that will happ—"

"But what if it does? I mean, how will you feel, Zach?" She pauses. "You should have waited for me."

Silence.

Then quietly I say, "I didn't want it to come to this, Sarah, but would you like to know the real reason why I did it?"

"Yeah, Zach. I think that's the least you could do for me."

"Okay." I pause and take a deep breath. "I did it because Tank's my best friend...and you're not."

She looks at me for several moments. I'm waiting for her next verbal assault, but it never comes. She opens her mouth to say something but decides against it, shaking her head slowly a few times as if in disbelief.

Then she turns and walks away.

Watching her go, I can't help but wonder if she's right. Have I initiated a chain of events that might result in Tank Foster losing his only chance of pulling a Captain Rick?

Man, I hope not.

Talk about a plan backfiring.

———

After scrubbing myself raw in the shower to get rid of what's left of the skunk odor, I put on shorts and step into the kitchen around nine. Mom's sitting alone at the kitchen table, drinking coffee and reading the paper. Dad's nowhere in sight.

Without looking up from the paper, she says, "You went to bed early. How'd you sleep?"

"Like a log," I lie. But it doesn't matter what I say, because I can tell from how she asked the question that she knows I snuck out. So I go to the fridge and take a slug of milk from the carton. "Justin home yet?"

"Not yet." She looks up. "Zach, at least pour it in a cup."

"Sorry." I put the milk away and close the fridge. "It's hot today."

"It's supposed to crack a hundred." She folds the paper and pushes it aside, takes a deep breath, and stares at me.

"What's wrong, Mom?"

"Your father left last night. He's at a hotel, but he didn't say where." She's fighting tears. "I'm sorry, Zach, but I think you saw it coming."

I walk over and hug her.

And she totally loses it.

Within seconds, I feel her tears trickling down the back of my shoulder. She shakes like a child for several minutes. I've never held my mother for this long. But just when I think she might pass out from the breakdown, she somehow manages to pull herself together.

"God," she says. "It was never supposed to end up like this."

"It'll all work out, Mom. If you're supposed to stay together, you will. If not, then why should you stay miserable? He's the one who needs help, not you."

She wipes her face with her hands, takes several deep breaths, and leans back in her chair. I sit beside her and hold her hand.

"At least I have my boys," she says. "Whatever happens, at least I'll always have my boys."

"That's right," I say, and pause. "So, you think he's coming back?"

"Beats me. He's never done this before." She taps the fingers of her free hand on the table. "I never thought we'd grow apart, but that's exactly what's happened."

"Mom, you wanna go get some breakfast or something?"

"The way I look right now?" She feigns a smile. "Not a chance."

"What about lunch?"

"Maybe," she says, thinking about it. "I'm going to see some friends this morning, but lunch with my son sounds nice."

"Lunch it is then." I stand and let go of her hand. "I have to see Tank for a few minutes. It'll be real quick."

My heart starts pounding as soon as I say it, and I wonder what kind of mood he's in. As for Dad's absence, it's a weird feeling that's actually more liberating than troubling. I know this might sound horrible, but I sort of hope he doesn't come back.

"Go ahead," Mom says. "Your brother just called. He's on his way. I have to get cleaned up. You still plan on going to practice tomorrow?"

"Guess so." I shrug. "Why, you don't want me to?"

"No," she says. "It's not that." She studies my eyes for a moment and smiles. "I'm proud of you, Zach. Whatever happens, I want you to know that."

"Proud of me for what?"

"For being you."

"Thanks, I guess." I look at the front door, then at her.

"How is Tank, anyway?" she asks. "I haven't seen him in a while."

"I'm not sure. Seems like he's got a lot on his mind."

"Boy, do I feel for that family. My situation's nothing compared to what they've been through."

"Tank's strong. He'll be fine."

"And what about you?" she asks. "How are *you* doing?"

"I'm not sure, Mom. Right now, I'm really not sure."

"Be careful, okay?"

"Always."

I turn and walk out the door.

————

Big Dale and Sarah are eating breakfast—McDonald's—at the kitchen table. Looking through the glass triangle, I watch the back of Sarah's head sway back and forth as she talks. She has on a pink tank top that shows off her slender shoulders and delicate neck. Regardless of the argument we had, truth is I could watch her from this angle, or any other, for hours, but my business here this morning concerns Tank.

I knock on the door. Big Dale's eyes shift up toward me. He nods as if he's expecting me. Sarah gets up and walks to the door. She won't look at me, but I swear she gets more beautiful every time I look at her.

She reaches for the handle and gives me a quick, neutral glance as she opens the door. Stepping out onto the porch, she closes the door behind her and screens her father in the process, a move that surprises me.

I say, "Sarah, look, the last thing I said came out wrong. I made it sound like you didn't matter to me, but you know that's not the case. I was mad at you for being mad at me and I just said it the wrong—"

"Zach, shut up," she interrupts. "I know what you meant, okay? That's why I turned around and left without saying anything. There was nothing left to say. We spoke our minds and had it out. That sure beats keeping it all inside."

I stare at the glass triangle. "Has he said anything else to you this morning?"

"My dad?"

"Yeah."

"He said you declared your love for me last night."

"That's how he put it? Oh my God."

We stare at each other for several seconds.

"Okay," I say. "Guess it's time for the hard part. Did you know Tank already knows about us?"

She nods and points her thumb back toward the door. "My dad told me that, too. What we can't figure out is why Tank's never brought it up with you."

"Is he awake yet?"

She nods. "He's in the basement."

"Can you tell him to come out here?"

She nods and goes inside. I sit on the porch and gaze at the empty street. Seconds later, Big Dale steps out and stands beside me.

I look up and say, "Mr. Foster, do you think it's fair to talk to him today? I mean, after everything he went through last night?"

He stares at the street, thinking. The green dragon seems much brighter now that I'm seeing it in daylight for the first time.

"That's your decision," he finally says. "Thanks for that email, by the way. Things are already happening." He looks at the sky and squints. "Christ, it's hot out here today."

Then he steps back inside and shuts the door.

Tank comes out two minutes later, wearing nothing but a pair of mesh gym shorts. Despite living in air-conditioned splendor, a thin film of sweat covers his body. He walks past me toward the middle of the lawn, stretches his arms high above his head, and yawns.

"You interrupted my workout, idiot," he says. "How could you possibly want to be outside in this heat?"

Sitting there looking up at him, I feel like a dwarf gazing at a giant. "Hell of a night last night, huh?"

"Yeah," he says. "Hey, those same two cops drove me home again. You believe that?"

"Were they cool about it?"

"That's the thing. They didn't say a word. I guess my dad wanted it that way."

"You remember everything?"

"You mean about Mandy, and the gun, and my dad's truck? Yeah, I remember it all. I did what I had to do. It's over now and I can't change it."

I'm surprised how calm he is.

"Look," I say, unable to return eye contact, "about the Horton thing. I just did what I thought was right."

"You mean like lying to me and sneaking around my basement all summer?"

"Don't play it like that," I say. "You've been lying and sneaking around all summer, too, just in different ways."

"Whatever."

"Can I ask why you think you need that stuff?"

"You know why, Zach. In fact, you're obsessed with the very reason why."

"To escape, right?"

Tank nods. "But your little email has probably ruined that."

Silence.

"Were you planning on doing anything?" I ask. "With the files, I mean. Did you have a plan?"

"Not yet," he says. "But that doesn't mean your plan was the right one, because it wasn't. Trust me."

There's a silence. The morning heat intensifies and seems to burn clear through my skin. We listen as a train passes. When it's gone, the only sound I hear is the hum of the air conditioner.

I say to my best friend, "I'm in love with your sister."

"I know."

"I know you know. What I'm wondering—hell, what everybody's wondering—is why you haven't said anything."

"Because I've been waiting for this moment."

"What moment?"

"Right now," he says. "For you to actually have the balls to say it to me."

"Well, I just did," I say, feeling quite relieved. "I'm serious, Tank. She feels the same way. Sarah loves me. I'm glad to see you feel—"

Mass confusion.

There's a headlock first—I feel *that*, Tank's left arm wrapping around the back of my neck and jerking my head toward his chest. Next comes a sickening smacking sound as his right fist collides with my cheek. The tinny taste of blood fills my mouth as he drags me onto the lawn and body-slams me face first into the grass. His fists press against my ribs as I hit the ground, knocking the wind clear out of me. Gasping for air, I feel the next punch land on my opposite cheek with a dull thud. Fresh blood pours out of my mouth and coats the green grass.

Tank continues delivering powerful lefts and rights to the sides of my face.

That's when I black out.

25

When I come to, he's still punching me, but I hear Sarah's screaming and Big Dale's booming voice as they struggle to pull him off of me. Next thing I know, Sarah's rolling me onto my back and crying as she wipes blood from my mouth with a dishtowel or something. For some reason, the pain hasn't registered yet. My face and mouth feel numb, like I've just had major dental work under heavy sedation. Sarah keeps saying how sorry she is. Over and over again, all I hear is "I'm sorry. I'm sorry. I'm sorry." I try telling her she has nothing to be sorry about, but the words come out in an inaudible blood-and-saliva-filled mumble.

Then it's like somebody suddenly gives me an adrenaline shot.

Fearing Tank might pounce on me again and resume the beating, I push Sarah away and scramble to my feet.

That's when my brain and nerves decide to deliver the news. Agony replaces the numbness and I have to struggle to remain standing. My vision blurs and my head feels like one massive bruise. Rubbing my temples with my palms, I scan the yard and, squinting, see that Big Dale has his son pinned to the ground. To my right, Sarah's sitting on the lawn, holding the bloody towel. She looks dazed, stunned even. I notice blood splatters, *my* blood splatters, across the chest of her pink tank top and feel bad that I've ruined such a nice piece of clothing.

It's weird, the kind of stuff you think about after getting your ass kicked for the first time.

Mr. Foster's shouting now, yelling for me to go home. Below him, Tank's screaming every profanity imaginable and squirming like a hooked fish as he tries to escape. There are so many things I want to say right now, to Tank *and* Sarah, but it's impossible to speak under such pain.

I stumble over to Sarah and touch my palm to the side of her face. She doesn't react, just stares blankly at the blood-soaked towel as if she's a mannequin.

I turn and run.

Somehow I get home and stagger into the kitchen, where I black out again after hearing Mom's terrified voice. When I open my eyes, Mom and Justin are carrying me toward my bedroom.

I wake up on my bed several minutes later. It suddenly feels like winter, and I quickly realize Mom has ice-packs pressed against my stinging cheeks. Surprisingly, I've escaped any major damage. I mean, my cheeks feel like erupting volcanoes and my ribs ache something awful, but the rest of my body seems unscathed, not even a black eye to accompany the facial bruises. Justin says something about me being lucky, like a boxer who takes a savage pounding but seems fine right after the fight ends.

I take the icepacks from Mom's hands and manage to sit upright. Remarkably, I don't even have a headache. I look back and forth between Mom and Justin. My vision slowly clears.

"My God," Mom says, her eyes red and swollen. "What happened?"

"Tank beat me up."

Justin says, "The hell you doing fighting with Tank Foster? That's suicide."

"Sarah," I say, leaving out the stash and Coach Horton. Mom and Justin look at each other, then at me.

"What about her?" Mom asks.

"We're in love."

"Man, that explains it," Justin says. "Mom wanted to take you to the hospital, but I talked her out of it. I think he went easy on you. You're lucky." He pauses. "But good luck at football practice tomorrow. I don't know how you're gonna put a helmet on. You look like a chipmunk with your cheeks like that." He shakes his head and exits the room, closing the door behind him.

"Are you sure you're okay?" Mom asks, pulling herself together a bit.

"Yeah," I say. "It's not as bad is it looks."

I can see the relief on her face as she says, "I know he acts tough around you, but your brother was scared to death when you came in. I don't know what I would've done without his help."

"He's a pretty good brother."

She sits down and puts her arm around me. "How come you never told me about Sarah?"

"You've had a lot on your mind lately." I shrug. "We all have."

"She's a sweet girl."

"The best," I say, and smile. Soreness ripples through my cheeks, but I don't care. "My stomach jumps around whenever I'm near her."

"That means you're in love."

I think about Dad and wonder what Mom's life was like before him.

"Did you ever love anybody before Dad?"

She looks at my face and winces. "Zach, are you sure you want to talk about this right now?"

"Yeah, yeah," I say. "It'll take my mind off of my face. What was his name?"

"Rick North was my first love. Seventh grade."

Silence.

"Are you kidding me?" I finally say. "You were in love with Captain Rick?"

"Yes," she says, like it's no big deal. "The first boy I ever kissed ended up becoming a space shuttle pilot." She laughs.

"You actually kissed Captain Rick? Holy shit!"

"Watch your mouth."

"Sorry," I say, laughing despite the pain it causes. "So what happened? I mean, why'd you two break up?"

"High school came. That's when I met your father."

Another silence.

"Do you ever wish—"

"No," she interrupts. "I suppose Rick North could have been my ticket out of Blaine, but if you start second-guessing the past you'll end up torturing yourself for life."

"Sounds like something Coach Horton would say."

"No," she says, smiling. "Hank Horton's not smart enough to think of something like that."

I take a deep breath and say, "I know he touched you in the storage room. Justin told me."

"Oh, that," she says, as if it's no big issue, but I can tell from her sudden frown that it is. "Well, thank God your brother showed up when he did that day."

"Mind if I spit in Horton's face tomorrow?"

She laughs and says, "You mean you're actually going to practice with your face like that?"

"I'll at least watch."

She nods and stands. "So, where do you go from here? I mean, with the Tank and Sarah thing."

"Beats me," I say. "But it's funny. The more I think about it, the more I realize Tank was in total control of the situation. He acts all crazy when he snaps like that, but I think he knew exactly what he was doing, like he coordinated every detail of the fight ahead of time and was holding back on purpose." I exhale deeply and shake my head. "Justin's right. Tank could've done a lot more damage if he'd wanted to."

"Well, he is your best friend."

"Guess so."

She gives me that worried mom look.

"Any news on where Dad is?"

"No," she says. "And you know what, Zach? Right now I really don't give a shit."

And that makes me laugh, hearing Mom swear like that.

She shows a hint of a smile. "I'll be in here every twenty minutes or so, and don't you dare complain about it." She gives me the once-over. "God, I can't believe he did this to you."

She leaves the room and closes the door.

I hold the icepacks firmly against my cheeks and fall asleep, dreaming about what I'll say to Coach Horton tomorrow.

————

A few hours later I wake up to take a pee. Sitting up and then standing, I'm relieved not to feel any excruciating pain. But once I start walking, my head throbs with each step.

Leaving my room and entering the hallway leading to the only john in the house, I notice Justin's door is open several inches, the light on and Metallica coming from inside. Poking my head in, I see my brother sitting at his computer, bobbing his head up and down to the beat of the music.

I knock on the open door.

He turns, sees me, and nods.

Turning the music down, he says, "Bet you feel great right now, huh?"

"Very funny." I open the door wide and step inside. "I have to show you something."

"So show me."

"I need to get to my email."

He gives me an irritated look, shrugs, and stands, motioning for me to sit in his sacred throne.

"Hurry," he says. "This better be good."

"Oh, it's good." I walk over and sit.

What I do, of course, is play the Horton video and audio files for him. He's speechless and plays each one three times, his smile growing wider with each playback, stunned but thrilled at the thought of Horton falling from grace. There's this awesome look of delight on his face as I tell him about last night's email and what Big Dale told me this morning, his comment about things already happening.

"Man," Justin says, staring at the monitor. "If they can get Horton... well, that would be beautiful." He looks at me. "Nice work, bro."

He gives me a high five.

"Thanks, but it wasn't all me," I say, thinking of Victor Hodge, Sarah, and of course Tank. "Anyway, he's going down. It's just something I feel."

Justin gives me a concerned look. "What about Tank and his wrestling?"

"I'm not sure," I say, shrugging. "It's a play I had to make, but something tells me Big Dale will find a way to protect his son's future."

"Yeah," Justin says, nodding. "I have to agree with you on that one."

I turn and leave, closing the door gently behind me and not bothering to tell him that he's been leaving his door unlocked a lot lately.

26

At seven the following morning, Mom drops me off at the coveted football locker room entrance behind Blaine Memorial High School. As stated in Coach Horton's annual summer letter, players must arrive an hour early on the first day of practice for helmet and shoulder pad fittings.

A long wooden bench spans the width of the brick wall outside the locker room. As Mom drives away, I cross the asphalt road and see about fifteen players sitting on the bench. Some of them point at my battered face and snicker. I stop and turn, taking a good look at the well-manicured turf and impeccably maintained grounds of Hank Horton Stadium, arguably one of the finest high school football venues in the Midwest.

Approaching the bench, I notice Barry Deck's son, Barry Deck, Jr., sitting at the far end, his hands clasped together in his lap and looking like he isn't sure whether he wants to go through with this football thing. He's tall and thin like his dad, and he gives me a look and a nod as I sit beside him. I wonder if his dad mentioned me.

"What's up, Ramsey?" he says in a gravelly voice similar to his dad's.

"Hey, Barry." I realize he even looks a lot like his dad. "You're giving this a try, huh?"

"Yeah. There's not much else to do around here." He stares at the stadium. "So how was your summer?"

"Eventful."

"That's nice. I was bored to death." He coughs. "What happened to your face?"

"Skateboarding accident."

"Yeah, right."

"Look, I'd rather not talk about it."

"Fine. My mom says she sees you working at Huey's a lot."

I find this interesting, because I have no idea what his mom looks like.

"Yeah," I say. "I started this summer. It's an easy job, great gig for senior year."

"Word has it you sell beer."

"Not anymore." I pause. "Why, you interested?"

"Not really. I don't drink. My dad's a drunk. I'm worried it might run in the family."

There's an awkward silence.

"But I'll tell you what, Ramsey. If I don't like football, I'll be looking for a job. Think you can put in a good word for me with Huey?"

"No problem."

Knowing how unstable his dad is, helping this guy get a job is the least I can do. I want to ask him if he's seen his dad lately, want to know if Barry Deck, Sr., has actually left Blaine behind.

God, I sure hope so.

───────

After the equipment managers issue helmets, shoulder pads, and locks, we pick our lockers, store our gear, and gather in a large space outside the showers for our team meeting with Coach Horton. It's a traditional pep talk from the head coach, Horton's futile attempt to pump us up for the grueling double sessions that await us.

The other coaches order us to form a semicircle and kneel on one knee, which, despite the uncomfortable tiled floor, we all do. When we're silent, Hank Horton walks out of his office and saunters into the middle of the semicircle, one hand on his hip, a football tucked under his opposite arm, a ridiculous act I've seen far too many times. He has one of his new Blaine football caps pulled down tight over his forehead. His white polyester coaching shirt is way too tight and his gut totally jiggles and bounces like Jell-O with every step. I have to bite my tongue to keep from laughing.

As he looks us over, I study the faces of the players, sickened with the expressions of awe that adorn them. They look as if they're waiting for God to speak. Horton always seems to sense this, too. He scans his disciples in silence, milking the attention for at least two minutes before finally deciding to talk. I feel like I'm in some sort of twisted, modern-day athletic version of a Hitler Youth rally.

Then Horton clenches his fists and says, "Men, you can do anything if you have enthusiasm." The other coaches look at each other and nod. "And whatever you do, men, remember this: never give up. No matter how bad it gets, you must never, ever give up. You must never surrender."

Players nod in agreement. I cock my head and squint, gazing around the room in disbelief. How many times have I heard this same speech? My God, I say to myself, at least a dozen, and each time he delivers it, the players act as if they're hearing it for the first time. Unreal!

He says, "Whether you think you can, or whether you think you can't, either way, you're probably right."

Affirmative grunts echo throughout the room.

The assistant coaches clap.

Taking this as their cue, the players join in the applause. But I don't.

Truth is, I'm really confused, baffled even, so I raise my hand, which is a total Blaine football cultural blunder. Within seconds the room falls silent and every set of eyes descends upon me. And I really don't care, because at this point I know my career as a Blaine football player will be over in less than five minutes.

"What is it, Ramsey?" Horton barks.

"Coach, maybe I'm missing something, but I don't really know what you mean by the 'think you can, think you can't' thing."

Horton shakes his head and stares at the floor. "Well, you will in time. It's a new one. I have new material this year. Just listen and learn." Anxious to resume his gridiron rhetoric, he says, "Gentlemen, winning is contagious, but so is losing."

I raise my hand again.

"Christ, Ramsey, what now?"

"No offense, Coach, but I'm afraid I can't buy that. I mean, I don't know anybody who likes losing so much that they try to spread it to other people."

A series of impatient sighs fills the room.

"Will you just hear me out, Ramsey? It'll all make sense if you take the time to listen." He pauses. "Maybe your head's cloudy from your late-night date with Foster the other night." He grins.

Players and coaches laugh.

"Whatever you say, Coach," I say. "By all means, fire away."

He sucks in his gut, cocks his head from left to right, and jams his thumbs inside his belt loops.

"Men," he says, "I want you to know that *anything* is possible ... it's just that the impossible things take a little longer to accomplish." A cocky smile crosses his face.

Players and coaches applaud again.

But I can't buy his motivational bull any longer, so I raise my hand for the third and final time.

Moans fill the room. A few players tell me to screw off under their breath.

Horton points at me.

"I'm about done messing with you, Ramsey. Last question."

"Coach, I have to tell you. That last thing you said was just plain stupid."

Coaches and players lower their heads in embarrassment.

"Know what, Ramsey? I'm beginning to think you're no longer Blaine football material."

"Coach, I've known that since I was a freshman, but just hear *me* out on this one." I stand and rub my sore knee. "First of all, it's just downright cruel and unusual punishment to make us take a knee on a floor like this, but that's not my point. What I'm really wondering is, if *anything's* truly possible, how come I can't lift a full-grown elephant above my head using only my pinky?"

A few people laugh.

"Son," Horton says, "what the hell are you talking about?"

"I'm talking about your little slogan, Coach. You just said *anything's* possible, but I seriously doubt that statement."

Horton lifts the bill of his cap and rubs his forehead as if he has a migraine.

"What are you trying to say, Ramsey?"

"Well, Coach, I guess what I'm trying to say is that

you need to research your material before springing it on your flock, because all I've ever heard come out of your mouth is a lot of bullshit."

I scan the room. Besides a shocked Coach Horton, nobody's looking at me.

"Damn, it sure got quiet in here," I continue. "So let me leave you fine people with the following brief statement. A couple of nights ago, some interesting audio and video footage of Hank Horton providing steroids to an anonymous customer somehow showed up at two nearby police departments." I smile. Horton's face is beet red. "Now, I'm not saying I had anything to do with that, but I *can* tell you that the proper authorities seem to have a great deal of... *enthusiasm* about this matter. In fact, it sounds to me like they'll pursue it to the end. In other words, Coach, they'll *never* give up. They'll *never* surrender."

I smile, reach into the front pocket of my shorts, and slide a Marlboro out of its pack. Popping it between my lips, I strike a match and begin smoking a cigarette within the hallowed confines of the Blaine Memorial High School football locker room.

And it feels absolutely wonderful.

"You're full of shit!" Horton finally yells. "Men, don't believe anything you just heard." To me: "Get the hell out of my locker room, Ramsey. You're off the team." His face looks as if it might explode. "And put that cancer stick out!"

I blow smoke toward the ceiling. Then I take another drag, a long one, and blow smoke in Horton's direction.

Horton turns toward an assistant coach. "Get this queer out of my locker room."

"That's not necessary," I say, and wade through a sea of kneeling players on my way toward the exit. "I can show myself out. And correct me if I'm wrong, Coach, but I don't think this is *your* locker room. I have a feeling since it's a public school and all, that it really belongs to the taxpayers."

"Nobody likes a smartass, Ramsey!" Horton screams. Some of the coaches cup their hands over their ears. "Get out of here before I hurt you."

At the door, I stop and turn.

"Just one more thing, everybody. Keep a close eye on your moms. Coach has a thing for moms." I raise my eyebrows. "Isn't that right, Hank?"

Hank Horton raises his arm and throws the football at me as hard as he can.

I duck.

The pigskin sails wide right, through the open door of his office next to me, and shatters a framed team photograph hanging on the wall behind his desk.

"Screw you, Ramsey!"

"No, thanks, Coach."

I wave goodbye to him.

Then I walk outside, close the door, and laugh my ass off.

27

So I'm halfway home, walking the uneven sidewalks of Blaine with a big smile on my bruised face, reliving every word I said to Horton, when my dad coasts past in his rusted-out black Ford and pulls into the driveway in front of me, blocking my path.

I stop and put my hands on my hips, staring up at the overcast sky in disgust, totally pissed that my good mood is about to come to an end.

He kills the ignition, gets out, slams the door, and leans his forearms on the roof of the car. He doesn't say anything and it's obvious he's waiting for me to come to him, so I roll my eyes and walk over to the passenger side, where I mock his posture and allow my forearms to drop hard on the roof.

"Look," I say, "before you even ask, I'll tell you. Tank beat me up."

"I know all about that. I spoke with your mom."

"Great," I say. "So what do you want?" I look around the quiet street, which happens to be three blocks away from our house. "How did you even find me over here?"

"I figured I'd watch your practice. But from a distance, you know?" He pauses. "I was parked in the back of the school lot, and when I saw you walk out alone...well, I figured that was it for you."

"That coach is an asshole, Dad. Did you know he touched Mom when Justin played? And that's only *one* of the reasons why Justin quit. There's more, but I'll let the legal system handle that part."

He doesn't say anything, just looks away and slowly shakes his head a few times.

"Look," I say, "is there something you want to tell me? Because if not, I'd like to go home and sleep."

I take a few steps back.

There's a lengthy silence, and it's awkward as hell because now he won't take his eyes off of me.

Finally, he gives me a quick once-over and says, "You're finally growing up."

"What's that supposed to mean?"

"Yeah," he says, ignoring my question. "I never saw it until just now." He opens the car door and gets inside. Looking at me through the rolled-down passenger window, he says, "There. Guess that's all I wanted to say." Then he turns the key. The engine struggles to life. Backing out of the driveway, he adds, "As for what it means, Zach...you'll have to figure that out on your own."

And that's it.

He drives away and I'm left standing there like a total idiot, having no clue what he was talking about.

———

I know something's wrong the moment I set foot on my street.

Approaching the house, I see Sarah speaking with Mom on the porch. It's barely past eight on a Monday morning, a strange time for a visit. Part of me hopes it's as simple as Sarah telling Mom more about what happened yesterday morning.

Sarah has her back to me, so it's Mom who sees me first. And there's this big look of surprise on her face, because she's not expecting to see me until late afternoon. She says something to Sarah. Sarah turns, forces a smile, and holds my gaze.

I quicken my pace and cut across the front lawn. When I reach the porch, they don't say anything.

"What's going on?" I ask.

Sarah looks at her feet.

Mom says, "Maybe you two should talk out here. I'll go inside." She opens the door, steps inside, and disappears toward the kitchen.

"We should sit down," Sarah says. "How's your face feel? It *looks* horrible."

"Looks worse than it feels. It's not so bad." We sit on the porch. "Sarah, what's wrong? Is it Tank? Is he okay?"

"Tank's fine. Well, physically he is. He's just too upset to leave the house right now. He feels awful about what he did to you."

"I don't see what the big deal is. So he beat me up a little. Who cares? It's over." A train whistle sounds in the distance. As we listen, I close my eyes and take her hand. She squeezes hard. I caress her palm with my thumb, savoring the feel of her skin.

Staring at the empty street, she says, "Zach, don't get mad, but my dad's decided to take a transfer to Colorado."

It takes a few moments to register. Then I open my eyes. The street seems to spin. After everything that's happened the past forty-eight hours, her words are so unbelievable that I pray I've misunderstood them. But I know I haven't.

As the train roars past, the porch vibrates beneath us.

"Jesus," I say when the train is gone. I pound the bottom of my fist onto the concrete. "Colorado? Why?"

She kicks at the cement, frustrated. "Everything's so messed up right now." She grabs my other hand. "Zach, look at me." I look. "It shouldn't make a difference where we are. We'll find a way to make it work."

"Yeah, but why Colorado? It might as well be China."

"He told us about the offer back in May, but he said he wasn't interested."

"Tank never said a word about it."

"That's because it wasn't an issue."

"Until now."

"This whole thing with Tank has changed his mind,

especially with Horton involved." She rubs her puffy eyes. "My dad wants out of Michigan because there's nothing left for him here."

"What about your mom?"

She shakes her head. "He's done everything he can. She's never coming back. We've known that for a long time."

"So, when?"

Silence.

"When, Sarah?"

She wipes tears from her eyes. "He wants to leave next week, to get us settled in before school starts. I get to spend my senior year in a school full of strangers."

I lower my head and stare at the porch. Tears stream down my cheeks and make tiny wet circles as they hit the concrete.

"I'm sorry, Zach," she says. "I'm so sorry about all of this."

"It's not your fault. You didn't do anything wrong." I look at her. "But maybe I did."

She doesn't respond.

We sit there for twenty minutes, holding each other close, each of us completely in the moment, making the most of every precious second.

SEPTEMBER

28

There isn't much more to tell.

True to his word, Dale Foster has the house packed up within days and the family flies to Boulder the following Sunday. Sarah comes by to see me twelve times during that seven-day stretch, but each visit grows increasingly bitter-sweet because we both know the end draws nearer every time we lay eyes on each other.

We never have a chance to be alone again, and we don't even kiss during our last visit—not because our feelings have changed, but simply because it's too painful knowing *that* kiss will be our last. We exchange a few half-hearted hugs and make all these promises about daily emails, texts, and IMs and all that, but I think deep down we both real-ize the distance will somehow take its toll.

Which I suppose is exactly what's happening as I write this, because it's been nearly three weeks since we've emailed or spoken to one another. There's this constant, aching pit in my stomach that won't go away, and it intensifies whenever I think about her, which is pretty much all the time. Mom says I'm experiencing my first broken heart and that eventually each day will get a little easier.

Whatever.

As for Tank, I haven't seen or heard from my former best friend since the day he beat me up. True, Sarah said he felt horrible about what he did to me, but the idiot never bothered to say it to me in person. I mean, he had seven days to apologize, but he never did.

So, I say screw Tank Foster.

A confession: Actually, I have no clue how to express my feelings about Tank.

I mean, I can feel my face and ears get all red when I think about him and everything we've been through, and other times I'll just break into these hysterical laughing fits as I relive our various exploits. Sometimes I hate him, but most of the time I really miss him. In fact, I think I miss Tank more than I miss Sarah.

I'm still Huey's stock boy, by the way. Ditching football has allowed me to work every day after school. Huey's still constantly drunk. He hasn't said a word about Helen in weeks, leading me to believe she's either left him or they're in some mega-huge fight or whatever. Who knows, maybe she bought a one-way ticket to Boulder to be with Big Dale. It wouldn't surprise me.

Anyway, I'm working my ass off and using most of the

cash to help Mom pay for gas, groceries, and other stuff around the house. That makes me feel good, knowing that I'm doing my part to help her through this mess. I put a good word in to Huey for Barry Deck, Jr., too. Huey says he might hire him for extra help when the holidays roll around. We'll see.

Dad's out for good, too, which is the best thing that's ever happened to Mom. The divorce isn't official yet or anything, but he's moved out and currently lives with some other laid-off divorced dude he knows from the factory.

Mom was all down in the dumps the first few days after Dad officially packed his bags, but lately she seems much happier. What she doesn't know is that I'm currently in the process of trying to track down Captain Rick North's email address through NASA. I'd like to know his marital status. If he's single, I'm totally hooking him back up with my mom.

I mean, they say first loves never die, right?

And how cool would it be if my mom finally pulled her "Captain Rick" with the *real* Captain Rick? Oh my God. It's too much to think about.

As for school … well, so far senior year is okay. I see Chad Billings and the other wrestlers from that night in Mandy Frack's backyard sometimes. They can't even make eye contact with me. It's like I have this special power over them because I witnessed what almost proved to be their deaths. I'm guessing nobody—not even Mandy's parents—filed a single police report relating to the evening of August 10th. Legally speaking, it's as if the incidents of that night never happened.

I bet Dale Foster had something to do with that.

And then there's Coach Horton.

Well, I'm happy and proud to say that Hank Horton is no longer the head football coach at Blaine Memorial. In fact, the man isn't affiliated in any way with Blaine Memorial athletics. See, a few weeks ago a big story broke in the Detroit papers about an alleged steroid scandal at various local high schools. Hmm. Interesting, huh? Anyway, just as Sarah predicted, it's turned into this huge media circus, and Coach Horton's name keeps popping up as one of the ringleaders. I'm told there's this secret ongoing investigation or whatever and that all sorts of students, current and former, have come forward with damaging information. The heat around Horton became so intense so quickly that the school district forced him to resign as head coach two weeks ago. He's currently banned from setting foot on school district property.

Interestingly enough, the name of Tank Foster hasn't appeared in a single story relating to the scandal.

I bet Big Dale has something to do with that, too.

Revenge. Man, it is *so* sweet sometimes.

So the first glimpses of fall are setting in now. The days are shorter, the evenings cooler, the leaves showing less green and more orange and red with each passing day. Although the Fosters have only been gone a little over a month, it's beginning to feel like years.

Tonight, when it seems the entire city of Blaine is at the high school football game, analyzing the interim head coach and hopefully witnessing a record fourth straight loss for the home team (please, God), I grab a pack of smokes from my bedroom stash and walk over to the vacant and still unsold Foster home.

Standing there on the sidewalk, I light a cigarette and stare at the glass triangle of the white front door for what seems like an hour, reliving a summer's worth of memories, most of them happy, others horribly painful.

After smoking my cigarette to the filter, I flick it onto the concrete and walk up the driveway, stopping at the closed backyard gate. A brisk breeze seems to come out of nowhere, so I pull up the collar of my jean jacket to avoid the chill. Opening the gate, I stroll into the backyard and gaze at the exact spot where Sarah and I first kissed. For some reason, I kneel directly over that memorable location and kiss the pavement as if it were holy ground.

After sitting there for a few depressing minutes, I exit the backyard, cross the front lawn, and travel to the opposite side of the house. Lowering myself into a pushup position, I peer through the rectangular basement window into what used to be Tank's sprawling living space. I don't see anything but a few empty boxes. Even the old blue sofa is gone.

Standing and brushing myself off, I round the corner and walk onto the front lawn again, staring at the patch of lawn where Tank body-slammed me. The September breeze kicks up again, sending shivers through my body. I pop two cigarettes between my lips, light them both, and look up at another starless Blaine sky. The street is silent and I feel very alone. After one long drag I toss both smokes onto the grass. Reliving the moment Tank beat me up, I step hard on the cigarettes and watch the orange embers fade to black.

And then, for some reason I can't explain, I drop to my knees and place my dry palms on the cool grass.

The End

Bill Bowen

About the Author

After earning two degrees in American history, Ryan Potter realized he wanted to write about things he made up rather than analyze things that had already happened. The first short story he ever wrote was published in a well-respected online literary journal in 2003. He's had several stories published both online and in print since.

Exit Strategy is his debut novel. Visit Ryan online at www.exitstrategy17.com.